ADVERSITY

DARK HEART

E.J. ECCLES & R.J. SMITH

Copyright © 2025 E.J.ECCLES & R.J.SMITH

All rights reserved

The characters and events portrayed in this book are fictitious. Any similarity to real persons, living or dead, is coincidental and not intended by the author.

No part of this book may be reproduced, or stored in a retrieval system, or transmitted in any form or by any means, electronic, mechanical, photocopying, recording, or otherwise, without express written permission of the publisher.

Cover design by: Radu Mureson

Printed in the United Kingdom

Dedicated to Bill Russell

CONTENTS

Title Page
Copyright
Dedication
ONE 2
TWO 7
THREE 17
FOUR 23
FIVE 26
SIX 30
SEVEN 35
EIGHT 39
NINE 42
TEN 49
ELEVEN 52
TWELVE 55
THIRTEEN 63
FOURTEEN 68
FIFTEEN 75
SIXTEEN 81
SEVENTEEN 87
EIGHTEEN 92

NINETEEN	100
TWENTY	107
TWENTY-ONE	116
TWENTY-TWO	122
TWENTY-THREE	126
TWENTY-FOUR	129
TWENTY-FIVE	136
TWENTY-SIX	145
TWENTY-SEVEN	150
TWENTY-EIGHT	155
TWENTY-NINE	160
THIRTY	165
THIRTY-ONE	173
THIRTY-TWO	182
THIRTY-THREE	188
THIRTY-FOUR	193
THIRTY-FIVE	201
THIRTY-SIX	206
THIRTY-SEVEN	216
THIRTY-EIGHT	223
THIRTY-NINE	231
FORTY	237
FORTY-ONE	242
FORTY-TWO	247
FORTY-THREE	252
FORTY-FOUR	259
FORTY-FIVE	267
Acknowledgement	278

About The Author 280

E.J. ECCLES

ONE

London, 1965.

"Who do you think tried to murder him?"

This would be the day that would shape the rest of their lives. Eric led the way with a strong, decisive, steely attitude. He was a tall, athletic lad with a mop of jet-black hair and browline glasses that framed his pale, virgin face. John deliberately lagged behind Eric, his shoulders embracing his face and his hands twisting the lining of his pockets. He did not want to be anywhere near this hospital. He'd rather be in school, which he despised, or down by the river, where he'd spend the hot summer months fishing for tadpoles and sticklebacks, climbing trees, and building improvised caves out of whatever he could find. That was where he felt most comfortable and happy. That was where he felt at home—and home was anywhere but here.

They walked down the hospital's long, bleak corridor toward the intensive care unit. Shafts of light poured in through the massive arched windows that flanked the walls and reached into the distance, sending dark, gloomy shadows along the narrow hallway. A musky, stale stench filled every nook and cranny of the place, a ghostly, lingering reminder of everyone who had walked through over the years. They could almost sense spirits lingering in the air as their shoes clicked and clacked across the smooth, polished floor.

The sound of shouting and screaming from neighbouring rooms echoed loudly up the corridor. The excruciating, agonised screech of a woman who sounded like she was being butchered in her bed rang out, passionately pleading for help. Another poor lost soul in some dark, faceless ward. Men with mid-range baritone voices were yelling for attention, while overworked nurses ignored them.

The rattling of trolleys and gurneys clattered over the floor, drowning out the faintest murmur of indecipherable conversation as various medical staff bustled around the packed place. This was an indoor market for the sick and infirm.

The place started to get crowded as they walked through it. A man in a smart two-piece pinstripe suit strolled past them, a lit cigarette dangling from the corner of his lips. He scraped his slicked blonde hair off his face, revealing a large cotton wool eye patch covering his left eye.

A young woman wearing cat-eye glasses and a long grey tartan overcoat escorted a small boy with red eyes. A thick, milky-white plaster wrapped his fractured arm, nestling it in a bandaged sling over his chest, his hand resting on his heart like he was taking an oath. His mother had his other hand tightly in hers, and the boys could hear her promising him a lollipop from the local store as a reward for being such a brave little boy. Despite the throbbing ache in his arm, he managed a half-hearted grin.

With his eyes flicking up and down, left and right, Eric headed further into the hospital, searching for the sign that would lead them to the Intensive Care Unit. John followed a few feet behind, his chin against his chest and eyes fixed on the floor. He whispered some profanities under his breath as his brother yelled for him to hurry up.

Let's just get this over with; then we can go home, he thought as he quickened his step and caught up.

John noticed a small sign on the wall directing them where they needed to go. "It's down here," he remarked with a flick of his head, pointing to two large wooden swing doors. Eric narrowed his eyes through his thick glasses, checking the sign for himself before nodding in agreement. They pushed through the doors and headed down another soulless passageway with rooms on either side. At the end was a large, solid oak table with two nurses seated behind it filling out paperwork. The nurses' station looked out into a vast ward with five beds on either side of each wall, all lined up like soldiers in a barracks. It smelt like bitter antiseptic and wet mops, with a hint of sweat and stale secondhand smoke.

Every bed was full of desperate patients requiring specialised care and attention. A thin, elderly gentleman dressed in blue and red-striped pyjamas huffed and puffed to himself as a nurse began wiping the beige and orange vomit dripping from his brittle jaw. A pale, lifeless hand protruded from beneath a large pile of white sheets in the next bed.

A mummified individual lay prone across from them, wrapped in thick, heavy bandages. Next to the bed, a small, see-through machine hissed and wheezed as the tube inside it expanded and contracted like an accordion, pumping its silent tunes into the lungs of the invisible man.

The nearest nurse greeted the boys as they approached the desk. She had a round face with rosy cheeks and warm eyes that twinkled under the harsh ceiling lights, and her curly brown hair peeked out from beneath her white nurse's cap. "Hello, can I help you?" she enquired in a tired, soft voice.

"We've come to see our father, Joe Maxwell," Eric explained casually, as if he were checking in for a routine appointment. "We're his sons, Eric and John."

The nurse was quite taken aback. She hadn't expected to see two young lads arrive unannounced. She also hadn't expected them to appear so composed and calm. They should be heartbroken, she reasoned, given the circumstances. "Oh, right, I see."

The second nurse looked up from her paperwork and peered at the boys, as if she were a teacher monitoring students during an exam. She arched her brows as she ran her eyes over the pair of them, then gave her colleague a quick glance before burying her head back in the manila-coloured file.

The first nurse took a quick glimpse over their shoulders before returning her attention to them. "Has anyone accompanied you today, or..." She trailed off when she saw Eric's eyes were everywhere.

He seemed preoccupied with surveying the ward, like a security guard, his eyes darting from one side to the other, taking in all that it offered. He appeared agitated, even anxious, but given the circumstances, she didn't give it much thought. While she was pressing for a reply, she couldn't help but notice that John was staring at her breasts as they rested on the desk.

"Excuse me," she said, a little firmer and louder this time. "Have you come here with your mother or...?" She trailed off once more and waited for their response whilst glaring at John, his eyes meeting hers. She had caught him looking down at her chest. His cheeks became a deep shade of red as John bowed his head to the floor.

Eric refocused his attention on her. "What? Sorry, it's just the two of us." After a long, awkward pause, he said, "Uncle Ronnie is outside if you want to see him."

"No, it's fine," she replied sympathetically. "Your father is just through there in room three." She pointed out a few side rooms near the entrance to the ward. "Would you like me to take you through? Sister is currently in the room with him."

Eric quickly responded, "No, we'll be fine, thank you," taking John by the arm and leading him away.

"I hope those poor boys won't be too overwhelmed seeing him like that," the nurse whispered to her colleague.

"They will be fine," the second nurse said without a shred of empathy. "They always are."

TWO

The boys reached the room and stopped outside the door. Eric turned and nodded to John. "Are you ready?"

John stared blankly back at him. He half-heartedly shook his head and looked to the floor. He had made it this far, but now, in this precise moment in time, he realised there was no turning back. His guts twisted like he had a bellyful of snakes, and his heart started thumping through his chest like a bass drum. "I don't wanna see him. I can't do this."

Eric jabbed a sharp finger into his shoulder and barked back. "Well, tough tits, you *are*, so man up, and let's just get this over with, okay?"

John gave a reluctant nod, and they both entered the room. The sister was sitting on a wooden chair next to the metal bed with her back to the boys. From behind, they could see that she was a painfully thin woman with sharp shoulder blades protruding from underneath the blue stripes of her uniform.

The constant beeping of the life support machine and the rhythmic sighing of a ventilator filled the air of the small, dimly lit room.

The sister half-turned in her seat and acknowledged them as they stood in the doorway. "Hello, can I help you?" Her eyes flickered from boy to boy as she twiddled a pen in her hand.

"We've come to see our dad," Eric said.

The sister raised her head slightly, looked down her bony, beak-like nose, and smiled. "So, you're Joe's boys?"

"That's what I said, didn't I?" Eric replied curtly.

"Usually we don't allow visitors to turn up willy-nilly. But, given the circumstances," she nodded towards the bed, "I'll allow it this time."

She smiled, turned her attention to her patient, and gently touched his shoulder. "Joe? Your boys are here to see you." She stood up from her chair. "I'll leave you with your dad. I'll be up the corridor in the nurses station if you need anything."

She nodded as she brushed past them and left the room. The heavy wooden door closed with a loud bang. Eric walked across the room with an assured and determined confidence and sat down next to the bed. John nervously hung back and stood by the door. He struggled to look at his stricken dad. He looked aimlessly around the room and shuffled uncomfortably on his feet. He had never seen him look so vulnerable and fragile.

Joe lay lifeless, far from the monster they had known. The machines that were keeping him alive seemed to have replaced the fight and anger that had once consumed him. John stood at the end of the bed, his face softened with the relief of seeing his dad alive. "I can't believe he's still here," John whispered, his voice thick with emotion. "I thought—I thought he was gone. But look, Eric, he's still breathing. Maybe… maybe he'll wake up soon?"

Eric didn't acknowledge or respond. His eyes fixated on the machine that was keeping him alive. He tilted his head and stared at it in wonder as he watched the lines on the monitor rise and fall. He turned to John. "Pop out and get us a cup of tea, will ya?"

"Did you not hear what I said?" John gasped.

"Yeah, I did, but that's not important now. Go and fetch the teas, will ya?"

"But I don't know where to get tea from. And I don't wanna go out there on my own," John replied nervously.

Eric rolled his eyes and tutted. "Well, I suggest you grow a pair and ask the nurse!" He snapped back. "She said if we need anything, we could ask her, so go and find her and ask her!"

John's shoulders dropped. He sighed. "I don't have any money."

Eric puffed out his cheeks and muttered under his breath, "You've never got any bloody money!" He reached into his pocket, took out a few coins, and handed them to John. As John grabbed the money from him, the coins slipped through his fingers and scattered onto the floor. "Are you incapable of doing anything fucking right?" Eric huffed, shaking his head as John dropped to his knees and nervously fumbled for the coins. He glanced at Joe, then at Eric, confused as to who the monster really was. "Take your time, why don't ya?" Eric continued to bark his orders.

John stood up, a tear rolling down his cheek. "Will you just stop shouting at me? I know you're upset, but he's my dad as well, y'know!" He raised his hand and wiped his cheek with the sleeve of his jumper.

Eric's eyes widened and his jaw dropped open. "I'm sorry, John, you're right. He is our dad. Look, go and get the drinks. Everything's gonna be okay, I promise ya. I just need a few minutes alone with him."

The door closed behind John. Eric took a moment to confirm he was alone. He concentrated on the tubes emanating from Joe's nose and mouth, and then his eyes followed the wires plugged into the wall sockets. He turned to check the door one last time before focusing his attention on Joe. He moved closer to the bed, looming over Joe with a mixture of hatred and disgust. This man, lying there helpless, was the source of all their pain.

Without a flicker of emotion, he reached over and switched the machines off. They let out a sharp, jarring beeping noise before falling silent. The lights on the monitor began to flicker off, one by one, as the life support system powered down, cut down like a brave soldier running into No Man's Land.

Eric stood up and loomed over his father, watching his chest gently rise and fall before Joe immediately started to convulse, his body shaking violently in the bed. He remained calm and composed. He placed one hand on his dad's chest and pushed him into the bed, pinning him down with all his might. With his other hand, he placed it over Joe's nose and mouth, pushing the tubes firmly into his face and pressing his full weight on his convulsing body.

Any noise coming from the room would instantly alert the nurses outside, so Eric gritted his teeth as he grappled with his father. Joe's eyes flickered repeatedly as he tried to gasp for air until his body finally succumbed to Eric's torrid attack and he became limp.

Eric was panting. He released his grip and stood back from the bed, putting his hands on his hips and looking at the ceiling as he caught his breath. He puffed his cheeks out and looked down at his dad's lifeless body before reaching over him to turn the machine back on. The ventilator sprung to life, but the heart monitor showed no signs of it.

"Fuck you! You can't hurt us anymore, so rot in hell, you dirty cunt!" he said with venom. There was a real hatred and resentment in his voice and not an iota of sorrow or remorse in his dark, empty, and soulless eyes.

Eric calmly walked over to the door and composed himself for a moment. He took a deep breath, then started to pound on his chest with his fists like a gorilla, psyching himself up for what was about to ensue. He raised his arms and furiously started slapping his cheeks with the palms of his hands. He felt the blood rushing from his feet to his head, adrenaline coursing through his veins as a euphoria swept over him. He grabbed the door handle and flung it open.

"Nurse! Nurse!" He screamed at the top of his voice, his cheeks flushed from his self-inflicted slaps. He stood aghast. "I need help; there's something wrong!"

The two nurses sitting at their desk in the station heard Eric's plea for help and immediately got up and ran towards him.

"He's... I think he's stopped breathing. There's something wrong with the machine. Please help him!"

Eric wailed as the nurses barged past him and entered the room to see what was happening. One of the nurses leaned out the door and shouted loudly. "Can someone get a doctor? We need some help here." Another nurse appeared and gently placed her hand on Eric's shoulder.

"Please take a seat in the corridor, and I will come back to you as soon as possible. We're going to try our best to help your dad, okay?" As the chaos erupted behind her, she calmly raised her hand and gestured towards the swing doors, saying, "Just go through there, my love."

"Okay."

The nurse disappeared into the room, the door closing behind her. Eric leaned against the clinically cold, whitewashed wall and slid down until his bum hit the floor. He brought his knees up to his chest and waited. Anyone observing him at that moment might assume he was a young boy, grieving the loss of his father, but in reality, he was exhausted from murdering him.

A doctor brushed past him and entered the room. Through the wall he could hear an indecipherable commotion going on inside. Eric just stared into space, his eyes empty as he bit on his bottom lip.

A few minutes passed, but it felt like hours when the doctor appeared. Eric quickly stood up and readied himself for the news. He looked at the stern, stone-faced doctor as a wave of doubt washed over him, his mind swirling with confusion. *What if he is still alive? What if they know that I've killed him? What will I do then?*

Eric's heart started pounding like it was going to burst out of his chest. Beads of sweat appeared on his brow. He rolled his sleeves up and started hyperventilating, panting nervously.

With his hand on the wall for stability, he awaited the doctor's words. The doctor looked Eric straight in the eyes. "Are you Mr. Maxwell's son?"

"Yeah, I am. I'm Eric."

The doctor reached over to Eric and attempted to grab his arm in sympathy. Eric instantly flinched back, as he disliked physical contact.

"I am so sorry to tell you this, son... Unfortunately, we were unable to save your father. He's gone."

Eric softened; he pulled his hand away from the wall and looked hard at the doctor. He kept his eyes wide open until they began to sting, and then he blinked, forcing a single tear to roll down his cheek. He placed his head in his hands and sniffed. On the surface he looked like a broken boy, but inside he felt a tremendous sense of relief, ecstatic that he didn't have to see that bastard ever again.

"We made every effort to save him, but he arrested, and tragically died before we could help him. There was nothing we could do to save him. I'm ever so sorry," the doctor sympathised.

"It's alright," Eric said softly.

"Would you like to go in and sit with him for a while?"

"No, I need to find my brother. I need to tell him what's happened," he replied matter-of-factly.

The doctor replied, "I can get one of the nurses to find him for you if you like."

"No. I need to do this. I need to find him, and I need to tell him myself."

The doctor nodded. "Okay, take your time, and once you've found him, come back to the nurses station, and we'll discuss what happens next."

Eric headed through the swing doors and disappeared up the corridor. He spotted John ascending a sweeping staircase, carrying two teacups in his hands. Before he could say anything else, John noticed Eric approaching and bellowed down the corridor. "I got lost!" He rasped, "I've been wandering around this place for bloody ages, and these are probably cold now!" He raised the cups in the air, and immediately knew something was wrong. "He's gone, hasn't he?"

Eric bowed his head and looked at John's feet on the stairs. Taking a deep breath, he raised his head and looked him straight in the eyes. "Yeah, he has."

John let go of the teacup handles, causing them to smash into pieces and spill tea down his legs. The tea was indeed cold and prevented him from feeling anything. He slumped on the step, chest-high knees, hands over eyes. His throat tightened, but he was unsure of what emotions he should be feeling. Eric sat beside him, draped his arm over John's shoulder, and comforted him. "The doctor said they tried everything they could, but it was too late."

John buried his head into Eric's shoulder. "If you hadn't sent me for the tea, I would've been there as well."

"Well, ya weren't, were ya? He's no longer with us, and he will never harm us again. We're free, kid."

"But what happened?" John asked.

"To be honest with you, I'm unsure. All I've got to do is look after you now. That's what's important."

A cloud of conflicting emotions clouded John's mind as he tried to suppress his confusion. He started crying. Eric's words were cold and distant, like an echo in his mind. Eric pulled John closer and wrapped his arms around his shoulders. They both held each other as John quietly sobbed. "Look, it's going to be okay," Eric whispered, tightening his grip.

John's shoulders shuddered as Eric continued. "Right, listen to me, John. Pull yourself together. Let's go and chat with the nurses. They'll tell us what happens next and what I need to do."

John half-nodded his approval.

"But let's get one thing straight," Eric continued firmly, "He's not coming back, so there's no point in going to see him."

John clung to every word his brother spoke. Eric always had his back; he always fought his corner when faced with adversity, always had been the one to get him out of the shit when backed into a corner or facing a dangerous situation, and always had been the father figure in his life. John relied on Eric. He needed him. He idolised him. And in that moment John realised the world would be totally different from now on. Everything had changed—maybe for the better—but as long as they had each other, the future suddenly looked brighter.

They appeared at the nurses station and loitered nervously nearby. "Sorry about your dad's passing," the nurse remarked in sympathy. "Did you want to go in and see him?"

"Erm, no, not really," Eric responded. "We don't want to see him; we just wanna get out of here."

The nurse continued, "I know this is difficult for you to take in at the moment, and I totally understand this is a very emotional time, but we need to contact your father's next of kin. Now, would that be your mother or…?"

"We don't have a mother," John interrupted. "We don't have anyone now."

Eric dug his elbow into his ribs. "She died. There are only us two now. But we do have Uncle Ronnie; you can contact him."

Eric reached into his back pocket and pulled out the business card Ronnie had given him. "Here," he muttered as he passed it over to the nurse, "you can reach him on this number." The nurse took the card from Eric and fashioned a smile. "I need the card back though," Eric added, "it's the only one I have."

Ronnie stood at the window in his office puffing on a fat Havana cigar. The phone rang. He walked towards his desk and picked up the phone.

"Ronnie Fitzpatrick," he answered, breathing cigar smoke all over the mouthpiece. A woman's voice began speaking to him from the other end. He sat perched on the end of his heavy oak desk and listened intently for a while, confirming who he was and that he'd be down to collect the boys as soon as possible. Putting the receiver down, he took a long drag and smiled. "I knew he'd fucking do it!"

John and Eric pushed their way through the large, heavy front doors of the hospital entrance and walked outside. Their eyes narrowed to a squint as they adjusted to the light of the day. They felt the warmth of the sun on their faces as the cacophony of sound engulfed their senses. Ambulances hurtled by, their sirens wailing their warning as they headed toward another emergency. As people went about their day, the noise of the congested road sent clouds of toxic fumes hurtling into the air.

John sat down against the red brick wall of the Victorian building, closed his eyes, and sighed. Eric casually leaned up against the wall, his right leg bent up behind him. He lit a cigarette and took a big drag. He exhaled, blowing out a grey plume of smoke into the air and looking down at his brother. "Here, have a drag."

"No, I don't want to," John snapped as he continued to stare into space.

"Erm, you are," Eric insisted, "just one puff."

John reluctantly took the cigarette from Eric's hand. He took a drag and immediately started coughing. John handed it back to Eric and spat on the ground in disgust. Eric found the whole thing amusing. "You have a lot of growing up to do, boy!" he laughed.

John scowled back. "You sound just like Dad."

Eric spotted a familiar car in the distance turning off the main road and into the hospital grounds. With its bulbous side panels and quad headlamps, this black Jaguar Mark X stood out among the Austin/Morris 100s and Ford Anglias that populated most of the country. The car exuded a sleek, menacing, hulking, musclebound grandeur. Its chrome nose glinted in the summer sun as it snaked its way slowly towards the entrance, reminiscent of an orca cutting through the ocean, looking for prey. It crawled to a halt and stopped right outside the entrance where the boys were waiting. The driver, a smartly dressed middle-aged gent, got out, walked round to the back of the car, and opened the back door.

"Come on, John, our lift has arrived," Eric remarked as he flicked his fag butt onto the pavement.

He grabbed John's hand and pulled him up onto his feet. Eric led the way with a confident spring in his step, suddenly energised and excitable, like a small puppy. John slowly trailed behind Eric, his reluctance glaringly obvious. He didn't want anything to do with these people, but he had no choice.

The passenger window wound down, and a huge cloud of white smoke gushed into the air. As the smoke disappeared, Ronnie leaned out of the window. The thick gold rings on his hands sparkled in the sunshine. He was delighted to see the boys. "Get in, lads," he bellowed as he gestured to them to do what he said. They climbed in, and the driver closed the door and drove off into the busy streets.

THREE

London, 1964

At every opportunity, the boys escaped the confines of their home and got as far away as possible. Even at their tender ages, they were delighted to explore the world that lay beyond their domesticity. Beyond the back gate and the front door was a world of fun and happiness—a world of play and imagination. They could be free; they could express themselves without ridicule, judgement, or fear.

On hot, sticky summer evenings and most weekends, the boys would ride their shared, rickety Elswick Hopper bicycle and spend their days by the river. They would take their fishing nets, which consisted of a cane stick with mesh at the end and wire holding it all together, along with empty jam jars, and spend hours standing barefoot in the cold river, the water trickling through their toes.

With the exception of the occasional tadpole or stickleback, the likelihood of capturing any species was minimal. Despite the odds, they persevered, trying to fill their nets with any creature they could find, all the while laughing and joking carelessly. This oasis was their blissful place. It may have been only a few miles from the urban, decaying streets they called home, but it may as well have been a million miles away. As the sun began to set on another scorching day, they eventually had something to take home.

Eric remarked, holding the jar up to the light and squinting through his thick glasses for a closer look, "Weird, aren't they?

I mean, they are just black blobs with tails, yet they transform into frogs!"

John replied sharply, "Careful, Eric, don't look at the jar too long; you might burn your eyes out with that bike on ya schnoz!"

Eric gave him a playful shove, saying, "There ain't nothing wrong with these glasses, ya cheeky bugger!"

"You need good eyesight to see through them, don't ya?" As they meandered up the steep bank toward their bikes, John laughed heartily. They put their socks and shoes on and headed triumphantly back home to show their mother the fruits of their labour. There may have been only a few tadpoles and sticklebacks today, but tomorrow…

They took turns wheeling their bike across the bumpy scrubland. This was no straightforward task. This once-proud, sturdy stallion had sadly seen better days. With its huge 23-inch wheels, it was a heavy beast to manoeuvre. Handling this relic on the relatively flat, even surfaces in town was challenging, but on the uneven, dusty terrain here, it was an arduous task. As they trekked through a farmer's field, they noticed some cattle herded together underneath a huge oak tree. Several cows raised their heads, gazed curiously at them, and then resumed their grass-eating duties.

They made their way to a meadow abundant with long grass and wildflowers. The colourful carpet swirled and swayed in the wind, as if it were dancing to nature's tune. John lagged behind as always. Eric ambled onwards with a bit of grass hanging out the corner of his mouth, drinking in the beauty that surrounded him, the warmth of the sun licking his face.

The peace and tranquillity of it all was something to cherish. He closed his eyes and filled his lungs with the clean, countryside air. But John's sneeze behind him rudely interrupted that moment of peace, causing Eric to jolt. Eric turned to John and said, "Bloody hell, John, do you have to do that so loud?"

John snapped back, shrugging his shoulders and waving his arms in frustration. "You know it irritates my nose, and I can't help sneezing. You know I've got allergies."

Eric sighed, "Shut up, catch up, and stop ya whining."

They made their way through the lush green grass, leaving behind the vibrant blue sky as it faded into the dull, grey haze of the city. The drab streets and lifeless buildings ahead replaced the river and the fields they had played in.

Twenty years previously, it was the loud, ominous wailing of the air raid warnings that would make people scuttle back inside their homes, to their air raid shelters in the garden, or head toward the safety of the underground stations. Now, it was an unwritten law that as soon as the street lamps flickered into life, every kid had to head home.

Annie stood at the kitchen sink drying the dishes. If she wasn't out running errands or keeping the home immaculately clean, then this little spot is where she always found herself. This was the spot where she would stand and daydream, gazing out of the window with its net curtains overlooking the small backyard. She was a petite, slim, and elegant-looking woman with a shock of black shoulder-length hair. Most days, she wore a pinafore, a uniform common to most, if not all, women.

Joe was sitting at the table reading the paper. He was a brute of a man with broad shoulders and huge, rough, shovel-like hands. The sallow complexion on his leathery, craggy face made him appear older than his actual age, a result of his addiction to alcohol, the numerous cigarettes he smoked, and the secrets hidden deep within his soul. He definitely was no white-collar worker.

Annie wiped another pot clean and placed it on top of the oven with a clang. Joe grimaced, sighed, and continued to look at his newspaper, clearly irked. Annie began to put the dishes away. She opened the cupboards and began to carefully clear away the crockery to avoid provoking him, but to Joe's considerable annoyance, the plates and saucers rattled and clattered together.

"Will you stop making so much noise? With all your clashing and banging, can you not see that I'm trying to read the fucking paper?" He shouted.

Annie froze on the spot. She could sense his unpredictability, like a storm brewing just beneath the surface, ready to erupt at any time. No matter what she did or didn't do, it was one of those nights where she couldn't win. He was definitely spoiling for a fight, and the tension in the air was almost suffocating.

She tried to placate him: "Why don't you go through to the living room while I'm tidying away, Joe, so you can read your paper in peace?"

Joe turned to her, scowling, "Rather than telling me what to do, why don't you make less fucking noise?" His voice boomed, "'Cause I ain't moving!"

Annie frowned and carried on nervously, "The boys will be back soon," she said softly. Her voice was barely audible because she knew better than to meet his aggression head-on. She'd learnt to keep her head down, avoid eye contact, and stay out of his way.

Joe immediately jumped up from the table, "Fuck the boys!"

Her eyes widened with fear, and her breathing became shallow.

"I don't care if those little bastards are on their way home! How dare you tell me what to do in my house!" He stood up and pushed the chair away with the back of his legs before throwing the newspaper onto the floor. He walked over to Annie with purpose. She cowered and dropped a plate, sending it crashing to the floor and smashing into pieces.

The debris crunched under his feet as he grabbed the back of her hair, turned to face the window, and pushed her face into the bowl of water in the sink. She braced herself for the hit, her body tensing, her mind retreating to that familiar place of numbness.

Annie was soon gasping for air and started flailing her arms, trying with all her might to escape his grip. Panic set in, and she started to struggle, her life flashing before her eyes. She attempted to rise, but his strength proved to be too overwhelming. No matter what she tried to do, it soon became futile.

He held her head under the water longer than necessary as she attempted to lift it out of the bowl to breathe. Bubbles of air started to appear amongst the greasy suds, and a sickening, gurgling sound emanated from the sink. She was in a state of frenzied panic, and on the verge of drowning. She could fight no longer, and her body started to go limp, when he loosened his grip slightly and removed her face from the basin. She drew a deep breath as the water splashed up the walls of the kitchen and puddled on the floor. She tried to wrestle him off her, but he was far too strong.

"Next time you'll be quiet, won't ya?" He growled.

He glared into Annie's bloodshot eyes and forcefully dunked her head under the water one more time. He held it there for a few more seconds before lifting her out. She was absolutely drenched. The water tumbled from her hair onto her face and to the floor.

It was a stark reminder of Joe's volatility. He had continually dominated and controlled her into submission. Annie realised she had no way out and had transformed into a distorted version of herself. This wasn't the man she'd met, married, and fell in love with.

She gasped for air again; her whole body trembled with fear as Joe turned her head and pressed his face against hers. All she could smell was stale alcohol and cigarettes on his breath. Annie turned her head away; her tears cascaded down her cheeks, and her shoulders shuddered as she shook.

Joe released Annie from his clutches and watched her slide down the cupboards and onto the sodden floor. Cold and impassive, he picked up a tea towel from the worktop and threw it at her. "Clean yourself and this bloody mess up, you lazy bitch; the boys will be home soon." He walked towards the table, picked the newspaper up from the floor, and headed to the living room.

I can't—and won't—let him do this anymore. I won't let him win. I must stay strong for the sake of my boys.

FOUR

John and Eric wobbled their way through the main roads in town on their bike. Eric peddled frantically while John sat on the handlebars and skilfully held onto the water-filled jam jars. It was a perilous, comical sight as Eric grimaced and yelped, feeling every bump, every jolt, every rattle, and every shake through the worn saddle. The vibrations ran up his spine, making his teeth chatter.

The pilgrimage home soon became a challenge as they turned into the back lane that ran behind their house. The cobbled maze of decay and desolation resembled a battleground, making it a challenging terrain to navigate. This was no foreign land, though. They were intimately familiar with every aspect of these streets, including every pothole, loose cobble, and every inch, as if they knew them by memory.

They instantly headed into their first test—the cobbled lane. Eric pounded the pedals with enormous effort as every turn of the battered old wheels sent a shockwave of discomfort through their bum cheeks. His feet would often slip off the metal pedals, their jagged teeth digging into his ankles, leaving him with many battle-worn scars.

In a desperate attempt to stabilise himself, John clenched his legs together, gripping the handlebars with one hand and desperately clinging to the jars with the other.

Their bike, an indomitable steely steed, skilfully navigated the boys through the uneven back alley. Despite being thrown about like a rodeo cowboy, they managed to stay upright and swerved through the lines of washing that stretched from one backyard to the other. Several children of all ages played in this suburban jungle.

A small group of boys played football with boisterous enthusiasm, while a group of young girls jumped in unison to the rhythmic beat of their skipping ropes. A couple of housewives stood outside their back gates, engaging in idle gossip. They paid no attention as the boys raced past, nor did they notice a feral dog that offered a pathetic, innocuous bark before pissing against a metal dustbin.

They finally reached the back gate to their house. John hopped off the front, miraculously still holding onto their jar-filled bounty, and Eric squeezed the brakes as hard as he possibly could, planting both feet on the ground and sliding to a rather rough and bumpy stop. Eric caught his breath; it was hard work pedalling a bike that was on its last legs—or wheels—but it was a brave and battle-hardened beast that had never let either of them down.

It was sobering to think of the river so far away and their father at home. At best, their dad would typically respond to any frivolity with a disinterested grunt and a filthy look. At worst, they would face a severe beating similar to the one they had grown accustomed to. John opened the gate and headed into the backyard, followed by Eric, who wheeled his bike to the back door and leaned it up against the wall.

Annie stood at the sink, staring into space, still dripping wet as the boys entered through the back door.

"Mum, look what we caught," John shrieked with excitement as he held the jars aloft, his eyes wide with pride but oblivious to the mess. "We caught some tadpoles. They're gonna grow into frogs! We can watch them change."

For a moment, the weight of everything seemed to lift as she saw the spark of joy in her boys' eyes. It reminded her of the simpler times before things got so complicated. She dabbed her face with a tea towel and mustered a warm, yet disingenuous reply. "Oh wow, that's really lovely. Have you had fun?"

Eric noticed she was soaking wet; there was a smashed plate, and the kitchen floor was sodden underfoot. His eyes darted around the room, noticing clumps of his mother's beautiful hair sitting in pools of water at her feet. He walked over towards her, bent down, and picked up the hair. Grasping it in the palm of his hand, he stood up and held it in front of her face. "Mum, what's happened? Why are you...?"

He trailed off as Annie stopped Eric mid-sentence, as she always did when something like this had happened. She gently raised her hand to his face, placed her finger over his lips, gestured for him to be quiet, and then pointed with her other hand towards the living room.

John stood in shock and fear. He gripped the makeshift rope handles that the jars dangled from. His throat tightened, and the tears started to form in his eyes. He looked at his brother, then his mum, and tried hard not to cry. Eric slowly and silently skulked his way over to the kitchen door and peered into the lounge. He could see the back of his dad's head and cigarette smoke billowing from the chair.

Eric turned and stared at his mum with frustration, anger, and pain etched all over his face. He pushed the chair back under the table and started tidying up and cleaning the mess his dad had caused. John gingerly made his way over to her. She took the jars from his grasp and held them up to the window. She peered through the murky, black water and caught sight of something swimming and wriggling. She smiled at John and gave him a reassuring wink, her eyes filled with so much love and affection despite the unhappiness and sadness she felt. He gently put his hand on his mother's face and wiped away a solitary tear from her eyes. He shook his head disapprovingly, sad that he and Eric couldn't do anything to help and frustrated that his mother wouldn't do anything to change things.

FIVE

It was around midnight, and the boys were lying in their single beds in their cramped, cold bedroom. The faintest light from the street lamp outside illuminated the room. Both of them lay wide awake, wanting to sleep after a long day of fun and an evening of dread and apprehension. Sleep, however, wouldn't come, no matter how hard they tried. John lay on his side facing Eric, who was flat on his back with his arms stretched behind his head. He stared vacantly at the ceiling. "Are you awake?" John whispered softly.

"Yeah," he replied faintly, "what's up?"

John sat upright in bed. "I'm sad and scared."

Eric was taken aback. It was a very rare thing for men to express their feelings at any age, let alone young boys. It was customary to swallow your pride, puff your chest out, and just get on with things. Eric invited his brother to join him in bed, unfolding his bed blankets like a spacious cotton envelope. "Come here, you soppy git," he said. "What are you worried about?" He lay back down on the bed, and John climbed in beside him. He rested his head on his chest, and Eric pulled him in tightly.

"Dad scares me," John whispered. "He's horrible to us and even more horrible to Mum. He's gonna really hurt her one day, you know. Or even kill her."

"No, he won't; don't be fucking stupid! I promise you, I'll fucking kill him first." Eric replied defiantly.

John cuddled into Eric, gave him a tight squeeze, and tightly closed his eyes. "I've seen things."

Eric tutted disapprovingly, "We've both seen things, okay? Look, just go to sleep; he might hear us talking. Please get into your own bed, will ya?"

*

Still lying beside his brother, John started to stir. He opened his heavy eyes and yawned. He got out of Eric's bed and placed his bare feet on the cold floorboards. This attack on the senses—this coldest of chills in the dark of night—ran up his spine like a bolt of iced lightning. He shivered and exhaled as he made his way towards the door and downstairs to the bathroom where nature's call awaited.

It was the dead of night. John shuffled his feet across the upstairs landing, trying his best to silence the floorboards that seemed to creak with every footstep. As John began to descend the stairs, he noticed a white/grey hue of light flickering brightly from the crack in the living room door. Taking a few more tentative steps, he noticed the familiar fuzzy glow of the television emanating from the light source. It was a common sight to see his father, asleep in his armchair in front of the television, with an empty bottle of scotch on the coffee table and a mountain of cigarette butts piled up in the glass ashtray he had permanently borrowed from the local pub.

As John made his way down the stairs, he heard a commotion in the kitchen.

Shit!

Instinctively, he realised that his dad was not only awake—which was already problematic—but also very drunk. He could hear him fumbling and stumbling about, mumbling under his breath, his gruff voice drunkenly cursing and spitting expletives to himself. A small door at the back of the kitchen led to the bathroom, where an increasingly agitated Joe stood in John's way of having a peaceful piss.

John was shaking, desperate for the toilet; his knees buckled together as he walked through the living room to the kitchen door. Desperate not to make any noise, he pinched the end of his penis to stop himself from pissing on his pyjamas. He winced in pain and sucked his saliva through the back of his teeth as the ever-growing need to pee became almost unbearable.

He approached the kitchen with caution and peered round the door. His eyes widened, and he gasped in shock at the sight of his inebriated father waving his arms about, brandishing a handgun. Joe swayed from side to side, unsteady and erratic, aiming the gun at the jars on the kitchen worktop and mimicking the sound of a gunshot. *Paa-chowww!*

He watched on nervously, holding his breath for fear of detection. He gripped his crotch more firmly, just in case he couldn't hold his bladder any longer. He started to shake and couldn't believe what he was seeing: his dad was in possession of a very real-looking gun. Even worse, his *shit-faced* dad was in possession of a very real-looking gun. He always knew his dad was a loose cannon, but he didn't know he was this unhinged. At that moment, John realised he needed to get away from this lunatic and go back to bed.

His mind was racing with fear. *Why does he have a gun? Is he gonna use it? If he does, will it be directed towards me, Eric, or my mother?* He preferred the risk of pissing himself over the threat of a stray bullet. Trying to remain as calm as possible, despite his heart thumping through his chest, he turned to walk away. Joe halted abruptly and angled his head towards the door, convinced he had heard something. He listened with great intensity, trying to fathom out what it was.

A few moments passed. He opened a drawer and produced a grubby tea towel. Wrapping the gun in it, he stood on his tiptoes, reached into the cupboard hanging on the wall, and pulled out an old biscuit tin. He placed the gun carefully inside, put the lid on, and replaced it in the furthest corner of the cupboard. He closed the door and turned his attention to the two jars situated near the sink in front of him. John watched on, too frightened to move. This accidental voyeur remained motionless, a spy in the semi-dark hallway during a dark and twisted surveillance exercise.

Joe lifted the jars up to his nose and took a sniff. The pungent, obnoxious odour filled his nostrils. He thought the pong was coming from the jars, but it was probably coming from his breath. Without any hesitation, he poured the disgusting witches brew straight down the sink and threw the jars in the bin. John gasped in disbelief. His nose tingled as he tried to stifle his emotions. Joe headed out through the kitchen door and into the backyard as John, sensing his opportunity, bounded back up the stairs and back to his bedroom, where he relieved himself in one of his school shoes.

SIX

It was a dark, rainy Saturday morning. John was standing at his bedroom window, his elbows firmly planted on the window sill and his hands pushed into the cheeks on his face, squashing them like a blob of putty. He gazed out over the rooftops that lined the back lane like dominoes in a row, watching the rain plinking over the slate tiles and the puddles forming on the shiny cobbles below. The rain's dance against the windowpane captivated him.

There was something beautiful about a heavy rainstorm. The dark, treacle-black clouds gathered in their masses above the rooftops, forming an ominous army of threatening, natural beauty, strategically positioned to provoke and agitate, reminiscent of the Martians wreaking havoc in H.G. Wells' War of the Worlds. They had sent down their watery bullets for hours, but it was now time to unleash their next attack. A flash of lightning strobed across the sky, accompanied by a loud, thunderous roar.

John's vivid imagination could conjure up any scenario he wished, transport him to anywhere, and allow him to be anyone he wanted to be. This form of creativity was his way of coping. He would lose himself in his own imagination and often daydream the days away.

He was fascinated by this onslaught. Down below, he watched people hurriedly bringing their washing in off the lines, the rain relentlessly beating down on their heads, while a feral dog barked incessantly at a tabby cat perched on top of a back wall. The lane soon started to fill with water. It gushed over the bumpy cobbles as the persistent deluge from the furious sky showed no mercy.

"Boys, breakfast!" Annie shouted from the bottom of the stairs, breaking John's concentration and waking Eric with a jolt.

There was no such thing as a lie-in in this household. Every morning, even on a piss-wet Saturday, the boys had to get out of bed, wash and dress, and head downstairs by eight o'clock. Annie was always the first to rise. Some days in the wintertime, the house was so freezing and damp that there was frost on the inside of the windows. As she made her way downstairs to start her chores, she could see her breath condensing in the chilly air.

Her first job was to start the fire, which was the only heat source in the place. She gathered yesterday's newspaper and some kindling wood and whatever else she could muster and placed them strategically in a pile before adding a few pieces of coal. She lit it from the bottom instead of the top to catch the paper, kindling, and coal. This way would ensure a slow burn that would last all day. She had inherited this skill from generations past, and once the fire was safely burning, she proceeded to make a pot of tea and prepare breakfast.

She always made sure the home was warm and clean for her boys, as this was the only time she ever felt she was in control.

The boys walked into the kitchen and greeted their mum with a token 'Morning!' and a peck on the cheek. Every day this was the norm: start with a friendly, loving greeting before discussing the day ahead over their boiled eggs and soldiers, as they never knew what the day had in store.

Today was just like any other day in the past. There was a distinct sense of tension in the air. The slight bruise on Annie's face served as a stark reminder of the violence from yesterday. The boys looked at each other, not knowing whether to start a conversation or keep quiet. Annie pottered around them. She poured the tea, removed the tops of the eggs, buttered, and cut the toast into soldiers. She was ever the hostess and a loving mother, but they knew her busyness was just a ruse, a way to hide her troubled feelings behind a false smile and a facade of togetherness.

John rolled his eyes at Eric as Annie busied herself. Eric kicked John's shin underneath the table as if to say, '*Not now.*'

"Have you seen the weather, Mum? What a horrible day," John bravely spoke, taking the initiative to lighten the mood by bending down under the table to rub his shin.

Eric snarled at him. "Of course she's seen the weather; we have windows, don't we?" He pointed to the window near the sink. "Look at it; it's so bad I swear I've just seen a boat float past." Annie sniggered, walked over to the table, and ruffled Eric's hair approvingly as John laughed loudly, a piece of soggy toast hanging from the corner of his mouth. Eric chuckled to himself: he was proud of coming up with that joke at the perfect time. He looked over to the sink and noticed the two jars missing. "Mum, what have you done with the tadpoles and fish we caught yesterday?"

"Dunno, I haven't seen them, darlin'."

"Forget the tadpoles; Dad's got a gun in that cupboard." John pointed at the cupboard in the corner of the room. "I saw it with my own eyes last night."

Annie looked at John, her face ashamed. "What? There's no gun in that cupboard! You and your bloody wild imagination! Now eat your breakfast; I don't wanna hear any more of this."

"But, Mum, I did see it!"

Annie opened the cupboard, reached into the top, and tapped the top shelf. "See, there's nothing there. Now, eat your breakfast."

John looked at Eric and silently mouthed, 'I did see it.'

Eric winked across the table. He put his finger to his mouth and shushed him. He mouthed back at him. 'I know!'

Joe walked into the room, and the mood changed immediately;

the air became vacuous, like it always did when he was around. The boys stared into their cups, trying hard not to make eye contact. Annie put on a brave face, the one that she always wore when he walked in the room. She smiled and composed herself, much like a nervous actor waiting in the wings, trying to remain calm and unperturbed before the show.

"Morning, dear!" she exclaimed confidently, her anxious heart nearly collapsing. "Cuppa tea?" She lifted the teapot from the table and started to pour a cup. Joe arrogantly swaggered towards the back door, opened it, and left without saying a word, the door slamming behind him.

Through the window, Annie watched him walk towards the back gate, again, slamming it behind him. As usual, her smile melted instantly, and her heart fell to the ground. The boys watched on in silence. She knew where he was going and what he was up to. She sat down at the table, knowing she'd lied about the gun and was always covering for him—her husband, their dad—but they could see the emptiness in her eyes, knowing they couldn't change anything unless she did.

But she never would, and they had a feeling that one day this could all end badly.

Annie tried to remain apathetic to her husband's behaviour, but her long suffering ate away at her like a cancer that she'd never get remission from. She had to remain strong and resolute for her own sake and for the sake of her boys, who were the shiny red apples in her dull emerald eyes. Every day she died a little more, another piece of her once-loving, playful, and endearing heart broken away and crushed to dust.

Annie clapped her hands playfully. "Come on, you two, you're making the place look untidy, and I've got things to do."

Eric chirped up. "What? Mum, what about *him*? What about your bruises? What about us?"

"And what about the tadpoles?" John interrupted.

Eric gave John a gentle clip round the ear. "Fuck the tadpoles!"

Annie fixed her gaze on Eric and scolded him. "Eric, language! I don't want you cursing around this house and talking ill of your father."

Eric was dumbfounded—almost aghast. *This bastard can get away with everything, and here I am getting told off for saying fuck! He's horrible to us, and he makes our life—and your life—absolutely miserable,* he thought.

Annie angrily slammed her hands on the table. "Your father works hard. He gives us everything; look around you! Some people in the street don't even have half what we've got, so think yourself lucky. I won't hear any more of this."

An awkward silence hung in the air. Despite the frayed nerves, crossed lines, and revealed truths, Annie remained resolute. She refused to play the victim, especially in front of her boys, and would continue to act like everything was—and is—absolutely fine.

At that moment, he realised he had gone too far. He stood up from the table, head bowed, and walked off into the lounge. John followed suit, forever in his brother's shadow. Annie sipped her tea and gathered her thoughts as she looked out the window. She sighed, her shoulders sagging as she agreed with everything Eric had said but refused to show it.

SEVEN

In the days that followed, the image of the gun haunted John. Every time he saw Joe, he wondered if today was the day his father would use it. Every time he heard a raised voice or the sound of something breaking, his heart leapt into his throat, terrified that the next sound would be a gunshot. The knowledge of the gun weighed heavily on him, and the fear it brought was suffocating.

The gun was a symbol of his father's control over them, and no matter what John did, he felt there was no way to escape. He was in a house where violence always simmered just beneath the surface, and now, with the gun hidden in the kitchen, that violence had the potential to become deadly.

The letterbox on the front door rattled as it slammed shut. Joe had left the house as he usually did. Whether he had used the front door or the back door, it didn't matter; it always slammed regardless. The boys stood at the front window in the lounge, peering through the net curtains.

They watched Joe turn his coat collar to the relentless rain as he hurriedly made his way towards an awaiting, flashy car. Joe climbed into the back, revealing two silhouetted figures in the front seat. The car set off down the road and disappeared.

"Whoa, see that car, Eric?" John innocently said, "I bet that cost a few bob."

Eric, still looking out the window, answered inquisitively. "Yeah, you don't see them often, especially around here."

John replied naively. "He must be important if he's riding around in a car like that."

"Just because he got into a posh car doesn't mean he's important." Eric replied scornfully. "And anyway, it's not even his car, is it? It's probably Ronnie's."

Eric moved away from the window and slumped down onto the sofa. "Tell ya what, when she goes out we're gonna get it from the cupboard."

"Get what?"

"You know full well what."

"No, Eric, we can't. He might have taken it with him."

"Oh yeah?" Eric scoffed, "Well, we'll soon find out, won't we?"

Annie popped her head round the door. She wore a chiffon dress with a headscarf at the front and a stylish yet well-worn beige trench coat. "Alright boys, I'm just going to pop over to Aunt Peggy's, okay? I won't be long. I expect this place to be as tidy as it is when I get home, understand?"

Channeling the style of Monroe or Hepburn, she looked effortlessly glamorous, albeit slightly overdressed for a gossip session with her neighbour and best friend who lived directly opposite. But this was Annie, always making the effort, always looking her best no matter where she was going. She always maintained that if she looked good, she felt good, even when she was crumbling inside, which these days was often.

Both of them nodded, and Annie vanished behind the door. They waited until they heard the front door close, at which point Eric stood up. "Right, come on, then." He headed into the kitchen with John reluctantly following behind.

"This isn't a good idea, Eric. It's dangerous."

"Just grab that chair and give me a hand, will ya? Stop being a baby. I'm going to get it out with or without your help, so do as ya told and grab the fucking chair."

"Alright, alright!" John dragged the chair across the floor to where Eric was standing. Eric stood on it with John holding the back to keep it steady. After fumbling about, he found the tin in the back of the cupboard. He stepped down from the chair, walked over to the kitchen table, placed the tin on top, and removed the lid. In front of him lay a dirty tea towel and a blue/grey wad of rolled-up five-pound notes. The boys stared at the cash open-mouthed. They'd never seen so much money in their life. Unfolding the tea towel, Eric smiled in astonishment as the gun slowly revealed itself.

John said anxiously, "See, I told you, now put it back, will ya?"

Eric picked the gun up and stared at it in awe. His eyes lit up as he ran his fingers over the handle and looked down the scuffed metal barrel. He noticed a few words etched onto it. It read: MODELE 1950 CAL 9mm.

"Here, they've spelt the word 'model' wrong!" Eric said.

"Okay, you've had a look; now put it back, will ya?" John pleaded.

Eric caressed the gun in his hands. He felt its weight and realised what power it held. Closing his eyes and tilting his head, he allowed his imagination to soar, as if he was in a movie. John, on the other hand, was too busy shitting himself; his imagination threatening to fall out the bottom of his arse.

A few nights ago, John was gripping his penis tightly to prevent himself from pissing himself while his father was frantically waving the gun around. Now, he was clenching his arse cheeks in desperation as Eric continued to wave the gun around.

"It's a beauty, innit?" He exclaimed with enthusiasm, his eyes wide and his mouth wide open, resembling a pale-faced frog.

"Eric, put it away now, will ya?" replied John. He was growing increasingly nervous. "It's not a toy; it's real, and it could kill you."

Eric ignored him and pointed it at the back door. "Stop being a pussy." He held it at arm's length, closed one eye, and looked down the barrel one more time, his finger gently resting on the trigger, desperate to pull it.

This was a moment he needed to savour. This piece of metal he had in his grasp held his attention like nothing before. He felt connected and at one with this deadly machine. The danger, and the damage it could do possessed Eric with its intoxicating power. The subconsciousness of his brain triggered a switch, causing him to suddenly feel excited and alive.

"Right, put it back now." John spoke nervously, feeling scared and overwhelmed at the sight of his brother holding the gun. "Dad's going to lose his mind if he finds out what we're doing. Can you put it back now?"

"Oh, shut up, will ya?" Eric growled and waved the gun in front of John's face. "Where's ya sense of fun? Nobody's gonna find out, are they?"

John stumbled, unsure what to say or do to stop him from being so stupid. "Mum'll be back any minute now. She's only popped out for five minutes; she'll hit the roof if she sees what you're up to. "

"Five minutes?" he smirked. "She'll be hours; you know what they're like when they get together. She's gotta get through a tonne of cake, fifty cups of tea, and a hundred fags—and that's just moaning about Dad and poor old Uncle Albert." Eric tucked the gun into the waistband of his pants and turned to face John. "Put ya shoes on, we're going."

"What, are you mad? I'm not going to go out with you in the pissing rain, on a bike, with a gun. Do you want to get caught? Is that your plan? Do you want him to find out so he can leather the shit out of both of us? No way, I'm going nowhere."

Eric glared at him. "You are, so hop to it and fetch the fucking bike!"

John tutted and rolled his eyes. He knew where he stood in the pecking order of the family—and that was definitely at the bottom—and Eric had just pulled rank.

EIGHT

It only required a cup of sugar, a little box of tea leaves, and a pint of milk to resume their friendship.

Moving house was always a stressful occasion, a physically demanding day of travelling to the new place, lifting and lugging every single possession from a van or a cart, and placing and replacing furniture items with a nervous anticipation that everything would fit.

It was exhausting work, as she and Albert were the only ones left. Her twin boys had joined the Army the previous year. However, when the chance presented itself to relocate to a smaller, more affordable council house, they couldn't resist it.

Albert and Peggy had made the journey from a substandard, dilapidated suburb to this two-up, two-down. They had no intention of moving; they were neither happy nor unhappy, and that summed their relationship up. They were like a pair of old slippers.

The government's introduction of mass social housing and the massive undertaking of demolishing the old, decrepit Victorian slums and condemned buildings, which had fallen victim to the Luftwaffe during the war, presented them with a new opportunity.

The fact that the previous tenant, a white-haired and seldom-seen widower, had died in her sleep and remained undiscovered until the police broke down the door to discover a sludgy mess in her bed also played a significant role. And who were they to turn it down?

Annie was sitting in the living room reading her book when

there was a knock at the front door. She put her book on the coffee table and went to answer it. As she opened the door, she was filled with surprise.

"Bloody hell... Peggy!" She was shocked to see her best friend, whom she hadn't seen in years, standing on the uneven pavement. Shaking, she brought her hands up to her chest and gasped, then flung her arms around Peggy's shoulders and gripped her tightly.

Peggy dropped the small mug she was holding in her hand. It fell onto the concrete pavement and smashed into pieces. "Oh my god, Annie!" She screamed with excitement, "I... I can't believe it. What the bleedin' hell are you doing here?"

"I was just about to ask you the same thing."

They stood in a tight embrace, excitedly screaming and jumping on the spot just as they had done as little girls all those years ago. Several neighbours glanced over at the noise emanating from the Maxwells' house, their faces contorted due to the frequent shouting, screaming, and drama occurring there. Annie finally let go and placed her hands on Peggy's shoulders to take a closer look. "I can't believe it. How come you knew where to find me?"

Peggy looked confused as she had not expected Annie to open the door. "I came over to get some sugar."

Annie looked perplexed. "Sugar? Why do you want sugar?"

Peggy peeked over her shoulder and pointed to the house across the road. "We've just moved in."

"What? You must be joking... seriously? I don't believe it!" Annie exclaimed, "Out of all the places in town, not only did you move into my street, but you also ended up across the road! Bloody hell, we have so much to catch up on!"

Annie fetched her best china teacups from the dresser. She only produced these for special occasions, and this one was no exception. As the tea flowed, so did their conversation, with neither of them pausing to catch their breath or truly listening to each other.

This was the most alive and animated Annie had been in months—even years—discussing their childhood memories, laughing, giggling, and reminiscing about the wonderful old days. Here they were, two women engaging in conversation over real cups of tea and genuine cigarettes, a stark contrast to their earlier pretending to do the same in Peggy's backyard with their dolls, teddies, and tea set.

The back door flew open, and the heavy, smog-like smoke from the cigarettes Annie and Peggy had consumed whooshed out into the backyard. The boys bundled into the kitchen, only to halt when they noticed a stranger seated at the table. "Who are these two handsome chaps then?" Peggy asked.

Annie got up from her chair and walked over to her boys. She put her arms around each of their shoulders and grinned. "This is Eric, and this is John," she announced proudly. "Say hello to your aunt Peggy, boys." The boys waved and gave a cheery hello.

Peggy straightened her posture in her chair and took a slow breath. Her throat tightened, and her lips started to quiver as her emotions kicked in. She usually wasn't the type to get emotional, but the fact that Annie had called her auntie really resonated with her. The boys looked at their mother and smiled as they hadn't seen her this happy in a long, long time.

NINE

1946

The dance hall was alive with music, laughter, and the swirling skirts of women dancing with their partners. In this post-war era, people were eager to forget the hardships of the past and embrace life again. The room was packed and filled with the sounds of jazz, swing, and the chatter of couples dancing the night away.

Annie, Peggy, and Albert arrived together, all dressed in their finest. Annie's excitement was palpable; she was young, vibrant, and eager to enjoy a night of dancing and fun. Peggy, her closest friend, was always the life and soul of the party, and Albert—Peggy's steady boyfriend—was a kind and reliable presence. For Annie, this was just another fun night out. But she had no idea that this would be the night she would meet Joe—the man that would change her life forever.

The sexy, sassy blonde singer wiggled her hips and snapped her fingers as she effortlessly sang her way through a Glenn Miller number. The band accompanying her swayed about the stage with outstanding energy and gusto as the dance floor throbbed with couples jiving and swinging to the music.

'Club CasaNova' was a former dingy and decrepit cinema that had been remodelled at a significant cost with no expense spared and was now renowned for its palatial décor and Las Vegas-style glitz. It boasted a large, expansive seating area that surrounded a deep stage, placing the entertainers among the audience. With lamps on the tables and waitress service, it had become the talk of the town.

Annie leaned over the balustrade and looked down at the dance floor below. She felt a thrill of anticipation as she looked around at the crowd, taking in the lively energy and the wonderful atmosphere.

"Cor, he's a bit of alright," she said, pointing towards the bar situated at the far side of the room next to the stage. Peggy puffed on her cigarette and blew the smoke out the corner of her mouth.

"Who?"

"That one there, the one with the round glasses and grey suit."

Peggy's eyes darted around until they settled on Annie's target. She scoffed, saying, "He looks old enough to be your dad. He's a wrong 'un, I'm tellin' ya."

Annie raised her eyebrows and smiled. "Ooh, I don't mind having a sugar daddy to wine and dine me. And a wrong 'un might add a bit of excitement to my life."

"Bloody hell, girl, what's the matter with ya? You're like a dog in heat tonight. I never thought you wanted to be a kept woman; I thought you were the independent type."

A man approached the girls and placed one hand on Peggy's small, round belly. "Here, you shouldn't be doing that in your condition," he said as he grabbed the cigarette from Peggy's mouth.

"You drain the fun out of everything, you do!" Peggy huffed and glanced over towards the booth down below.

"Drain the fun out of everything? You're carrying my babies, don't forget. Anyway, what have you two been gossiping about, or need I ask?"

Peggy placed a hand on her belly. "Actually, we were talking about Annie, about her meeting a man. And do you know what,

Albert? I think tonight's her night. She's gonna get whisked off her feet, ain't that right, Annie?"

Annie rolled her eyes. "I don't know about that. Sometimes it's more hassle than it's worth."

Albert chirped up, "Hold on a minute; have you looked at yourself? You're bloody gorgeous; you've got everything."

Time stood still as Albert realised that he'd said it aloud rather than thought it. Peggy glared at him, and Albert knew he was in deep trouble at that moment. "I meant you're a real Bobby Dazzler," he said, stuttering nervously, trying to redeem himself. "There's bound to be some fella in this gaff for ya, ain't there, Peggy?"

Peggy's eyes widened as she tilted her head to the side, signalling to him that he was about to face her wrath for going too far. She gave Albert a filthy look and grabbed Annie's wrist. "Come with me. I ain't listening to his waffle anymore."

Peggy pulled Annie through the crowd, Albert's words ringing in her ears. She had always known in her heart how he felt about her, but the reality of hearing it upset her. They made their way towards the top of the staircase. "Wait here a minute; I'll be back," she said to Annie.

She strode over to Albert with purpose. He watched her approach him and gulped. "Alright, love?"

"Don't you fucking 'alright, love' me! You've always had a thing for her, and I've always known it," she said, her teeth clenched.

Albert shuffled nervously. "What ya on about?"

Ignoring him, Peggy leaned in closer; he could feel her warm breath on his ear. "You know *exactly* what I'm on about. I suggest you get yourself a fucking shovel, because you're digging yourself into a deep hole, and I might just push you in."

Peggy stepped back, smirked at him, and whispered, "Enjoy your drink; don't choke on it." Turning on her heels, she headed towards Annie, who was waiting for her at the top of the stairs.

Albert wiped her spittle from his face and muttered to himself. "Fucking hell!"

Grabbing Annie by the arm, she looked deep into her eyes. "Right, me and you are gonna go downstairs, and we're gonna find you a fella to dance with, so chin up, tits out, and smile, okay?"

Annie closed her eyes and took a deep breath. "Okay." Grabbing the wrought iron rail, she made her way down the sweeping staircase.

In a private booth at the back of the room, two well-dressed gentlemen were chatting over drinks. Ronnie and Joe always occupied this booth, with no one else permitted to join them unless they received an invitation.

Ronnie Fitzpatrick was the owner of this establishment. He was a man of influence, well-dressed, and well-known for what and who he was. He wore the finest suits from Savile Row. His dark brown hair was slicked back from his face, revealing his piercing eyes and a crooked nose that had been on the end of a few fists in his younger days. He puffed on a fat Cuban cigar as a tall, curvaceous blonde appeared, dripping in diamonds—and exuding a bit of class.

Both gentlemen stood as she took her seat. Ronnie leaned over, kissing her on the cheek. "You look beautiful, my darling, as always." He placed his hand on top of hers and ran his fingers over the diamond rings he had bought her.

Joe acknowledged her with a half-grin, "Evening, Virginia, you're looking lovely tonight, girl." Virginia chuckled and gazed at him.

"Thank you, Joe. Ronnie bought me this today," she said, looking down at her dress. "I feel a million dollars."

"You look it 'n' all, darling," Ronnie said. He raised his hand in the air, clicking his fingers. A waiter appeared from nowhere within seconds. "Bottle of my finest Champagne, Dick."

Dick nodded, "No problem, Mr. Fitzpatrick." He turned and headed off towards the bar.

Joe was Ronnie's right-hand man. Despite being younger and quieter, he exuded a dangerous energy, his predatory gaze scanning the room as he assessed everything and everyone. His broad shoulders filled half the booth, and his enormous, shovel-like hands rested on the table. His shock of wavy black hair was short and parted to one side, and his pale skin showed off his chiselled jaw. He was a very handsome and distinguished-looking man, but his eyes were dark, vacant, and empty.

Like his soul.

Dick appeared with the champagne, opened the bottle, and filled their flutes before placing the bottle into the ice bucket beside Virginia. Ronnie thanked Dick, raising his glass toward hers. *Cheers!*

Joe sipped on his drink and sat back in his seat. While Ronnie chatted with Virginia, it was Joe's sharp eyes that first landed on Annie. Something about her caught his attention. Maybe it was her bright smile or the way she stood out from the usual crowd. Whatever it was, he wanted to get to know her.

He watched her every move intently as they walked down the stairs. "That woman with Peggy, the one coming down the staircase," he nodded in their direction, "Do you know her? I haven't seen her here before."

Ronnie replied. "I don't know who she is, but if you'd like her to join us, I'll have Franco arrange it."

Ronnie raised his arm, and Franco made his way over to their table. "See that young lady coming down the stairs with Peggy? Bring her over here for drinks. Only her."

As Annie and Peggy reached the edge of the dance floor, Franco approached them and tapped Annie on the shoulder. Annie turned, and there in front of her stood a tall gentleman. "Sorry, am I in your way?" Annie said, stepping to one side.

"You're not getting in his way; it's just Franco." Peggy said abruptly, "Can we help you?"

"Actually, you can. Mr. Fitzpatrick would like your friend to join him for drinks at his table."

Peggy didn't care for the intrusion. "Does he now? Um, I don't think so. I don't think it's a good idea."

Franco pointed at Annie. "Well, actually, I wasn't talking to you. I was talking to your friend here."

Peggy wasn't impressed. "Franco, can I have a word, please?" She walked off, Franco following her.

Annie stood there, perplexed. *How does Peggy know him, and most of all Mr. Fitzpatrick?* She looked over in Peggy's direction, who was leaning into Franco's ear.

"I don't think so, Franco. You can tell him from me that I said no, and she's not going over there!"

Franco glared at her. "Move out of my way because she *is* going over there, and you don't have a lot of choice over the matter." He prodded her shoulder and firmly whispered in her ear, "Now, you don't want to be making a scene, do you? 'Cause if you do, I'll get you slung out. And you don't want that, do you?"

Peggy sighed. "Hold on a minute; I just want a quick word with her."

Peggy approached Annie. She opened her mouth to speak but was beaten to it. "How do you know him *and* Mr. Fitzpatrick?" But before Peggy could even reply, she added excitedly, "Well, are we going over for drinks, or not?"

Peggy put her hands up, palms out, to slow Annie down. "Look, hold on, will ya? We aren't… but you are."

Annie gasped, "Really, on my own? But I don't know him."

Franco interrupted, having heard everything that had been said. "I'm sorry to interrupt," he turned his back on Peggy and addressed only Annie, "are you ready, as Mr. Fitzpatrick doesn't take kindly to being kept waiting?"

Peggy peered over Franco's shoulder, clearly perturbed and annoyed at being ignored and pushed out. She had always stood in Annie's shadow. People seemed to migrate to her. She was pretty, always happy and carefree. Despite being Peggy's best friend, Peggy couldn't help but feel jealous of her. Even more so now. She always knew her husband Albert had feelings for her, and this had been confirmed tonight—the way he had drooled over her upstairs, telling her how beautiful she was—and now, to top this shit night off, she was also going over to sit at Ronnie's table.

The place where Peggy had spent many nights in the past.

TEN

Franco grabbed Annie's arm and led her toward the booth. She accompanied him across the dance floor without resistance. Peggy followed behind before heading towards the staircase, her eyes fixed on Ronnie.

She reached the top of the stairs and locked eyes with Albert, who was leaning over the balcony. She assumed he was watching Annie's every move. Whether he was or not didn't matter; he was going to get it in the neck anyway. Peggy strode towards him, barging into his shoulder with force. He grabbed the railing to stop himself from falling. "Like what you see, do ya?"

"What are you on about?"

"I ain't stupid; you know *exactly* what I'm on about. I've seen you watching her. I always knew you'd had a thing for her, and you've certainly confirmed that tonight, haven't ya? Come on, we're going!"

Albert's hand reached out and was just about to touch her belly when she turned and stormed off, making him and everyone else aware that she was totally and utterly pissed off.

Annie sat next to Joe. The company she was keeping made her feel important, something she'd never felt before. She genuinely enjoyed the way he made her feel. Nobody had treated her like this before.

On the other hand, Joe was already making his calculations. He was accustomed to getting what he wanted, and he wanted Annie. In fact, he needed her because of the secrets and lies he harboured. She was not only beautiful, but her eyes held a vulnerability that he perceived as a weakness. He sensed that she was susceptible to manipulation, moulding, and control, even though she wasn't aware of it yet.

She was perfect.

Joe lavished her with compliments and regularly topped up her glass, demonstrating his attentiveness as a host. She relished the attention she received, as she had never encountered anyone quite like him previously. He made her feel safe and special, and he was everything she'd ever wanted in a man.

Over several drinks, Virginia and Annie bonded and grew closer as the night wore on. The conversation flowed, as did the champagne, and as the cabaret came to an end, so did Joe and Annie's evening.

Joe excused himself and headed over to the bar where Franco was chatting to a group of regulars. Joe placed his hand on Franco's shoulder. "Excuse me, gentlemen, sorry to interrupt, but can I have a word?"

Joe stepped to one side, and Franco turned to face him. "She's ready to go home now, so can you fetch the car, and we'll meet you out the front?"

Franco smiled, "Of course I will; I'll see you out there in five minutes."

Back at the table, Joe placed his hand on Annie's arm. "C'mon, let's get you home."

"But I'm not ready," Annie said rather naively, "I don't want the night to end."

"Look, I know you don't want to, but I've got some work to do. We'll have plenty of evenings like this, I promise ya."

Annie smiled and relaxed back into her seat. She picked up her glass and took a sip, the fizz going straight to her head. At that point she knew she was going to see him again. Joe leaned in close and kissed her on her cheek. She closed her eyes and melted a little, knowing that he liked her as much as she liked him.

Joe handed Annie's ticket to the cloakroom attendant and helped her put her coat on before making their way to the front door, where Franco was waiting in a beautiful black and grey Jaguar Mark IV. One of the club's doormen approached the car and opened the back door for them.

"After you," Joe said, holding her hand and helping her into the car. She sat down and shuffled along the back seat. Her eyes widened, and she gasped, as she'd never been in anything as beautiful and plush as this. He got in beside her, the door closed behind them, and they drove off.

They chatted all the way back to Peggy's, Franco's eyes glaring back at him through the rearview mirror the whole journey. Moments later, they turned into the street and pulled up outside Peggy's house.

Peggy was already waiting at her bedroom window, peeking down to the street below from behind her curtains, watching their every move. She looked over to the bed where Albert was fast asleep and snoring like a freight train. She curled her top lip in disgust, frustrated that this was her life—the life she had chosen—and turned her gaze back to the street as she muttered to herself. "You always seem to land on ya feet, don't ya Annie? And now you've gone and bagged yourself a rich one. Alright for some, innit?"

Annie turned the key in the lock, letting herself in. Joe took her hand in his and kissed it before saying his goodbyes. "I'll be in touch. Now go in before you catch your death." Annie closed the door and heard the throaty grunt of the car speed off down the road. She leaned up against the wall, her head spinning with thoughts of Joe, her body tingling for wanting him.

ELEVEN

As the rain pelted down, Annie hurriedly crossed the road, trying hard not to get wet. She opened the front door to Peggy's house, as she always did, and closed it behind her. She removed her coat and hung it on a hook on the wall near the front door. "Only me!" she shouted out, her voice echoing through the sparse hallway.

"Hiya, I'm in the kitchen," came a booming voice from the back of the house. "Come through."

Annie spent most morning's at Peggy's place, chewing the fat and putting the world to right over a few cups of tea, cigarettes, and the occasional homemade Victoria sponge cake.

Peggy was now a small, curvaceous woman with a brusque, uncompromising nature and an acid tongue. Fearless and strong-minded, she was as sharp as she was blunt. She would be your best friend or your worst enemy.

She was the same age as Annie but looked older than her years with her dour, craggy complexion, dark swollen bags under her eyes, and furrowed brow. Her face was almost lived-in and told a story of hardship and struggle, but there was an endearing, honest beauty underneath it all.

Annie made her way through the lounge and towards the kitchen. The layout was exactly the same as her own, but with all the clutter that Peggy had accumulated over the years, it felt much, much smaller. She breezed into the kitchen with a cheery demeanour. "Alright?" she enquired casually.

"Morning, love," Peggy chirped, a cigarette dangling from the corner of her mouth. The ash was as long as the cigarette, defying gravity as it arched perilously in midair.

Peggy stood making a pot of tea with her back to Annie. She had already set the small kitchen table for her regular visitor. There were two cups, a small round ashtray, a pack of cigarettes, and a lighter. It was hardly worth the effort, but the intention far outweighed the execution.

Annie pulled a chair out and sat down. Peggy turned around, carried the pot over to the table, and placed it down. She glanced at Annie and noticed some bruising on her neck.

"I see he's been up to his old tricks again," she snorted as Annie looked shamefully to the floor, ready for her interrogation. "I'll tell ya somethin' for nothin': my Albert wouldn't dare do anything like that, 'cause if he laid so much as a finger on me, I'd wallop the bastard over the head with my bloody frying pan! And he knows it 'n' all. I don't know why you put up with it; I told you the day you met him he was no good for ya."

"Alright, alright, I don't need ya, 'I told ya so's,'" Annie replied, grasping her neck. "You know why I put up with it. I can't leave him, can I? And I haven't come here for a lecture."

She let out a sigh, closed her eyes, shook her head slightly, and made an effort to suppress the tears. As always, Peggy was right. "And in any case, I have nowhere to go, and he wouldn't let me if I tried. There's no escaping him, Peg."

Peggy stood beside Annie, folding her arms like a strict school teacher about to reprimand a misbehaving student. "Well, you can always come here; you know Albert wouldn't mind."

"Yeah right, that'd be fun, wouldn't it, me living across the road from him!"

"I've told you before, love, he needs to be taught a lesson and given a taste of his own bloody medicine. And he'll get one, one day; mark my words."

"Well, let's hope so. Anyway, are you gonna pour the tea or

what? I've come over here to get away from it, not to get nagged at by you!"

Peggy stood open-mouthed. "Oh right, I'm a nag now, am I?"

"No, I didn't mean it like that!" Annie said in a placating voice, "Now come on, let's have some tea and change the subject."

TWELVE

The rain had now stopped, and the dark, threatening clouds began to dissipate, revealing a whitish blue sky underneath. John wheeled the bike through the puddles across the backyard and pushed it out of the gate and into the lane. Eric closed the back door to the house and followed John. He closed the gate and they both headed off.

The place was suddenly alive with activity. The children in the area crawled out from beyond their brick prisons to play in the fresh air and escape from what they needed to escape from.

Eric rode the bike unsteadily through the streets with John walking by his side. They passed through one particular area that had remained untouched since the war. This desolate wasteland, where once stood rows of terraced houses just like the one they lived in, was now a huge urban playground. Bricks and rubble were scattered across this vast area like chunks of stone confetti.

Several boys, some looking no older than five or six years old, were playing amongst the discarded treasures left behind. A pile of dirty, stained mattresses stacked on top of one another was a perfect spot to land on when jumping from a half-demolished wall. Other children were in the process of making a den out of splintered planks of wood and corrugated iron, while a couple of girls kneeled down and prodded a dead cat with a spindle from an old bannister.

This bombed-out, barren land may have been another deep and festering wound in this frail and fractured world, yet it was an oasis of imagination, creativity, and adventure for these streetwise kids.

The grubby, squalid streets and buildings faded into the distance, giving way to the rural landscapes on the outskirts of town. The boys eventually reached their intended destination, a huge wheat field that stretched as far as the eye could see. In the middle distance stood a tall and rather forlorn-looking scarecrow.

He wore a tattered old jumper, ragged trousers, and a battered old sun hat, which adorned a head-shaped hessian sack filled with hay. It stood with its arms stretched out wide, purposely posed to provide a deterring threat to the pesky birds that circled above. Unfortunately, this sad-looking, pathetic excuse for a scarecrow was neither threatening or intimidating, as the crows perched along its branched arms and took turns to shit all over its sleeves.

A ramshackle timber fence stood between Eric, John, and the field. It was a gnarled, crooked structure, six feet tall with sharp spikes at the top. Eric helped John over the fence, then he scaled it himself. He dropped down over the other side and headed off into the field with a spring in his step and carrying a sting in his tail.

John followed unenthusiastically, but this time he had a reason. It wasn't because of his bloody allergies; it was because Eric had a gun, their dad's gun. He was reluctant to take part in whatever Eric had in store, and his gut feeling told him this was not going to end well.

"Come on, John, will you hurry up for God's sake?" Eric shouted.

"I just want to go home," John yelled back. "If Dad catches us, he'll batter us."

Eric plodded through the endless golden sea of wheat, leaving a flattened pathway in his wake as a guide for John. "Just shut up, will ya? I only want to fire it once."

John quickened his pace. "What? No, you can't do that!"

"I *can*, and I *will*. I just want to know what it feels like, so stop being a pussy and shut ya face."

John caught up with Eric and marched side by side through the prickly crop until they reached the sorry-looking scarecrow.

Eric delved into his trousers, pulled out the handgun, and looked at it. It glistened in the sunshine and looked even more beautiful and more beguiling than it did indoors. He felt its weight, and it felt nothing like he had imagined. It was heavier than he expected, cold and solid.

John let out an almighty sneeze. Eric gave him a filthy look. "Will you shut up? You're ruining my moment!"

John held his nose and stifled another sneeze. He mumbled through his fingers, "You know I've got allergies." John felt nothing but dread watching Eric hold the gun. The thought of him firing it terrified him, not because of the scarecrow, but because of what the gun represented. It was a tool of death, something that could end a life in an instant. In their dad's hands it was a weapon of terror. But in Eric's hands, it felt like he was playing with something far too dangerous to handle.

Eric gripped the gun firmly and aimed it at the scarecrow. He'd never fired a gun before, but he'd seen it done in movies. His finger hovered over the trigger, his jaw clenched. For a moment, the world seems to go silent around him—the wind died down, the birds stopped singing, and all that existed was Eric, the gun, and the scarecrow in the distance.

He squeezed the trigger.

The sound was deafening in the open field. The recoil surprised Eric, nearly knocking him back, but he held his ground. The scarecrow jerked as the bullet tore through its chest, straw bursting out into the air.

John spotted two startled horses in the near distance. They stood upright on their hind legs and let out a fearful, deafening whinny before galloping away from the terrifying and threatening noise.

"Whoa, did you see that?" Eric shouted, punching the air with excitement. "I blew it to smithereens!"

John didn't feel the same enthusiasm as Eric did. The sound of the gunshot lingered in his ears, a sharp reminder of the danger they were playing with. Watching the scarecrow fall apart under the force of the bullet sent a cold shiver down his spine. It was too close to real violence—too close to the world their father inhabited. John realised then that Eric wasn't just learning how to use the gun; he was flirting with the same power their dad had wielded for years.

For Eric, firing the gun felt like a turning point. He'd been powerless for so long, always at the mercy of his father's abuse. But now, with the gun in his hand, he finally felt like he'd taken back some of that control. The scarecrow might have been a target, but in Eric's mind it was more than that. It was a stand-in for everything they'd suffered over the years.

John heard someone shouting in the distance, followed by the sight of a very agitated man running towards them, waving his arms in the air.

"Oi, you two, what are you doing, you little bastards?"

Eric started to run, his hand still gripping the weapon. The pursuit heightened his excitement. He dashed a few more yards before stopping, sensing that John was no longer behind him. He was right; he was still standing in the same place. "Move! Run, you stupid twat! It's the farmer. Run! Run!" Eric shouted at the top of his voice.

John emerged from his trance-like state, and with his brother's imploring words echoing loudly in his ears, he began to run. Eric swiftly navigated through the maze of wheat with determination, and soon, the unwavering sight of the fence came into view. He turned to see John running towards him, his cheeks a deep, vibrant red, his eyes streaming, and his brow soaked with sweat.

The farmer wasn't far behind. He continued to make steady progress despite being a fat, old man, still waving his fists and shouting expletives in his gruff, throaty voice. "Wait 'til I get my hands on you, ya little shits! I'll fucking kill you!"

Eric eventually reached the fence and immediately clasped his hands together to form a saddle-type platform. He crouched down and bent his legs as John appeared from the yellow curtain of wheat. He planted one foot in Eric's hands and launched himself up the fence. It was a moment of true faith, a demonstration of solidarity and trust between the two of them.

As John extended his leg over the top of the fence, the sharp spears caught the bottom of his trousers. He was already exhausted from sprinting through a huge crop of wheat, and despite his best efforts, he was unable to muster the extra strength he needed to untangle himself. Fatigue kicked in, and he conceded defeat. He dangled there for a moment to catch his breath with his eyes still streaming and his nose still dripping.

The farmer was almost upon them, having impressively made up the ground. Eric clambered up the fence and reached the top. He threw the gun to the ground beyond the perimeter and frantically attempted to unhook his brother. John, dangling upside down, said, "Just get the bike and scarper. Just leave me here."

Eric continued desperately to free him, tugging away. "There's no way I'm leaving ya. This is all my fault."

"Just go, will ya?" John pleaded. "There's no point in us both getting caught."

"I'm going nowhere, kid," Eric insisted, his mind flicking to something he'd once read in a magazine.

Every soldier has sworn an oath to never leave a fallen comrade behind. It's a promise that even if they die, a brother in arms will do everything possible to bring them home.

ADVERSITY

The farmer arrived at the fence. He hadn't run this far in years. In fact, he hadn't run since he was a child, as evidenced by his panting and puffing. He took the flat cap off his big, bulbous head, put his hands on his knees, and gasped heavily while John desperately tried to break free. He was the proverbial fly entangled in the web, unable to move as he awaited his fate.

"What the hell do you two think you are playing at, coming on to my farm and scaring my animals half to death?" He snorted, still gulping for air as the sweat dripped off the end of his nose.

"Never mind that, mister; are you going to help me get my brother down or what?" Eric snapped, still wrestling with John's trouser leg.

"You what? You cheeky little bastards, I should throttle the pair of you!"

Standing on his tiptoes, the farmer attempted to grab John's ankle when he suddenly heard a loud ripping sound, followed by a thud as he fell to the ground in a heap. Once Eric knew his brother was safe, he dropped to the ground on the other side. Both boys rose to their feet and faced their nemesis through the mangled fence. The man gave them a dirty look and spat on the ground.

"I want to know where you live," he raged, "Bloody idiots running around with a gun, you could have killed one of my animals or each other."

Eric bent down and picked the pistol up from the ground. He waved it in front of his face; only the fence stood between them. He snarled, "Here, mister, if you don't piss off and leave us alone, I'm gonna blow your head off, and you'll end up just like ya scarecrow."

The farmer stared into the abyss that was Eric's eyes. His mind was now a whirr. *This kid may be bluffing. Maybe the gun isn't real? It looks real; perhaps it's a toy gun? But, what if it turns out to be genuine? What if he is telling the truth and will follow through on his promise?*

Regardless of the circumstances, he was certain that this young individual held all the cards.

John was both alarmed and disturbed by Eric's threatening behaviour. He had never seen his brother so cold, so assertive, and so in control. He was almost deranged, just like their old man. Eric stood with his arm extended, the sweat pouring down his face, his eyes fixed on the farmer with an unblinking stare.

"Eric, what are you doing? Put it away, will ya?" shouted John, his voice distressed.

"Now listen here, you. You think waving that thing in front of me is gonna scare me?" The farmer extended his hands in front of him. "You're in big trouble now, boy."

"Oh, am I now?" Eric fired another bullet into the air. The sound rippled across the fields, sending the birds scattering. "Now, if you don't do as I say and just piss off and leave us the fuck alone, the next one will be for you, ya old cunt."

The farmer's shoulders lowered, acknowledging his defeat. He took a few steps backward, tentatively at first, his hands up in front of him. "Look, how about you just leave and don't come back? I don't want you scaring my animals, that's all."

Eric stared at him menacingly, the gun dangling by his side. "I tell you what; you go your way, and we'll do the same."

The farmer nodded, turned around, and swiftly disappeared through the wall of wheat. Eric, revelling in his newfound confidence, turned and looked at John. "You see that? He shit himself, didn't he?"

John didn't reply.

"Right, shall we head back home?" Eric said, "Grab the bike, will ya?"

Eric walked off without a care in the world, nonchalant in fact, with no remorse and as if nothing had happened. Cocky and confident, he caressed the gun that was in his trouser pocket. John, on the other hand, wasn't so carefree. He strolled slowly behind, rubbing his itchy, irritated eyes, bewildered as to what had just happened. He had a million thoughts on his mind. Eric's behaviour was a stark reminder of how his dad was on the night he desperately needed the loo—waving the gun around and acting like a lunatic.

He began to sneeze uncontrollably, and Eric turned and shouted, "There is always something wrong with you; you are always sneezing or blubbering like a fucking baby! It's so bloody irritating."

"Shut up! You know why I'm like this. I told you to leave me behind on the fence, and now you're fucking moaning 'cause once again, you've trekked me through a field full of fucking pollen, shot a scarecrow, and threatened to kill somebody, ya nutter!"

Eric wasn't listening to a word he was saying. In fact, he didn't give a shit about anything. He was engrossed in his own world, chuckling to himself while mockingly impersonating the farmer. "Now listen here, you!" he shouted in an over-the-top voice. John resisted the urge to laugh as he found this whole sorry saga a non-laughing matter.

THIRTEEN

Two hours had passed by, and both Peggy and Annie were still gassing. They discussed a wide range of topics, including the Great Train Robbery, Beatlemania, and Betty Thomas's 'bastard of a husband,' who ran off with some 'strumpet' from the local Working Men's Club, who lived just five doors down.

A haze of cigarette smoke filled the kitchen, swirling around the room like a toxic fog rolling in from the hills. Crumpled on the table lay an empty packet of cigarettes, all twenty having been chain-smoked to the tips and stubbed out in the ashtray. They had consumed half a large sponge cake, finished two pots of tea, and were currently enjoying their third when they heard a knock at the door.

Peggy rose from her chair and gently touched Annie's shoulder. "I won't be a minute," she muttered as she shuffled towards the front door. Opening the front door, she saw a tall, geeky-looking man standing in front of her, dressed in a grey wool suit. He held a briefcase in his right hand and a wooden clipboard and pen in his other hand.

"Good morning, Mrs. Thompson," he said cheerily, his beady eyes peeking out from under his round wire-framed spectacles. "How are we today?"

Peggy pulled the door open, leaned against the door frame, and crossed her arms. "Oh, it's you," she curtly replied, looking him up and down.

"May I come in?" he asked politely.

"No, you may not, Mr. Russell!" Peggy growled, "I have got company; it ain't a convenient time."

Annie could hear quiet voices. She made her way through the living room and loitered near the doorway to listen to the conversation, positioning herself far enough out of the way to avoid detection, yet close enough to hear every word.

Mr. Russell scoffed. "Mrs. Thompson, this is the second week I have come around to collect your payments, and you said you'd have the money last week, but you didn't, so I take it you have got it this week?"

Peggy stood firm and shook her head. "Nope. Now, if you please…" She waved her hand and gestured for him to go away, but he didn't move an inch.

"Please, Mrs. Thompson," he exclaimed, "I'm afraid this won't do. Under your agreement, you must pay what you owe. I understand times are tough, but you're two weeks in arrears already, and quite frankly, we would like some payment. The longer you leave it, the more interest you're accruing."

"Make that four weeks, because I won't have anything for you next week either." Peggy snapped back, "I ain't got fuck all. I wish I did, but I ain't. And as for the interest, I'm not interested."

Annie headed back to the kitchen, picked her bag up off the floor, and opened it. She grabbed her purse and made her way to the front door. She pulled the door back to reveal these two adversaries facing each other like a Mexican standoff, each as tenacious and uncompromising as the other. Annie's sudden appearance startled Peggy; she let out a scream, clutching her chest in shock. "Bleedin' hell, you made me jump!"

Annie addressed the gentleman. "Hello, I'm Annie, Peggy's friend. I'm the company she's been telling you about. And who might you be?"

Peggy interrupted, "It's just the man from the Pru, love. He's come for his money, but I've told him I ain't got it, and I ain't likely to have it either." Her face contorted as if she had been swallowing a lemon. "Not that it's any of your business."

Annie fixed her gaze on the gentleman and smiled warmly. "She ain't got it for ya darlin'."

Mr. Russell straightened up a bit, inhaled deeply, and let out a frustrated breath. "We're going back and forth here, and I can't leave without something, anything."

Annie gave him an understanding nod of the head. She reached into her purse and produced a crisp, blue five-pound note. She extended her arm and waved it in front of his face. "Will this do ya?" His eyes immediately lit up, raising his eyebrows in shock more than surprise. It was an enormous sum of money, a treasure rarely found in this area.

Peggy was mortified. "What the hell are you doing, Annie? Put ya bloody money away; this is nothing to do with you. I can't let you do this; this isn't your debt."

"It's okay, Peg. I know I don't have to, but I want to," Annie replied firmly as she rubbed Peggy's arm reassuringly.

Mr. Russell gleefully accepted this token gesture and quickly wrote out a receipt with his fountain pen. He handed the receipt over to Peggy, who gently took it and stared intently at the writing on it. In her eyes, the small and insignificant piece of paper embodied the Domesday Book, the Declaration of Independence, and the Magna Carta.

"Right, are we done here?" Annie asked confidently, "Is there anything else you need from us?"

Mr. Russell gazed at his clipboard as he put his pen inside his suit jacket pocket. "No, Ma'am, I shall—"

"Okay, now bugger off!" Annie interrupted, slamming the door firmly in his face.

At that point she felt elated to have been able to help her out. She asked, "Why didn't you tell me you were short? I could have helped you earlier."

"Why didn't I tell you? Because it's none of your business, that's why! How dare you think I'd come running to you for help? Before you come over to fix my issues, love, ya need to look closer to home. I've wanted to go over to yours many times to sort that bastard out, but no, you wouldn't have it, would you? You didn't want my help then as much as I don't want your charity now, so I'd appreciate it if you stopped poking your nose into my business and interfering with my financial commitments, 'cause it's got fuck all to do with you. There, I've said what needs to be said, and this'll be the last we speak of it, okay?"

Peggy wrapped her arms around Annie's shoulders and hugged her tightly. She closed her eyes as they held each other in a warm embrace. It was a moment Peggy wanted to treasure; her saviour had come to her rescue in her hour of need. She whispered into Annie's ear, "I'll pay you back, every penny, I promise."

"No, I don't want you to pay me back; it's Joe's money, which he has plenty of, and I don't care. I wanted to help my friend, so that's what I have done."

Peggy tightened her grip on Annie. "I dunno what to say, love," she said softly.

"You don't need to say anything."

Peggy squeezed her tighter before breaking their hold. She looked at the floor. She was a proud woman, and she struggled to accept any kind of handout or acts of kindness. She didn't have much, but she managed to make do with what she had. This was something she'd been doing for years. Peggy found it difficult to accept Annie's generosity— her innocent and sincere gestures. She was so grateful that her best friend, her only friend, had helped her out, but she struggled to accept the notion that someone had to bail her out.

"Now… more cake?"

Peggy swanned off, leaving Annie in the hallway. She began to giggle, then burst into fits of laughter, knowing it was Peggy's way of saying thank you.

FOURTEEN

The anticipation of coming back home to their loved ones made this last trip the most important of all. The carriage was filled with a thick blanket of cigarette smoke as they discussed what they were going to do when they got back to Civvy Street. The mood amongst the men was buoyant, full of fun and laughter, rip-roaring over the chugging sound of the train as it hurtled onward. Everyone, to a man, tingled with excitement.

Apart from one.

With his face pressed up against the glass, staring vacantly out the window as the world whooshed by, Joe showed no emotion. He remained cold and unapproachable even with all this chaos going on around him. No one dared to ask him to get involved. They knew he was an awkward bastard, an outsider, a loner whom they had gotten to know up close and personal under the most challenging of circumstances. Usually, he would dismiss any attempt at conversation. It was best to avoid him, and they did.

Every single person on the train had done their duty and witnessed incomprehensible things, grateful to be making their journey back as some of their comrades didn't get the chance to do so. This group of brothers shared an unbreakable bond. And Joe wasn't a part of that.

The small crowd waiting on the platform could hear it approaching before they could see it. The rhythmic noise rumbled in the distance, softly at first, before growing increasingly louder and louder as it snaked its way along the tracks. It was one of the ladies from the Military Dispersal Unit who first spotted a hazy cloud of white smoke just visible on the horizon, and she smoothed the creases from her already immaculate uniform with the palm of her hand and readied herself for the task ahead.

The smoke began to change shape, growing larger and larger, gathering pace, and engulfing the train like an avalanche charging down a mountain.

As it approached the station, the train started to slow down. A high-pitched whistle signalled its arrival as it huffed and hissed, covering the platform in billowing clouds of smoke and steam before crawling to a halt. Soldiers, eager to set foot on English soil for the first time in so long and excited to finally be home, began spilling out onto the platform before the wheels had stopped turning.

The Demob administrators greeted the men and started to organise the hordes of Tommys that were squashed together like pickles in a jar, ushering them along the platform and pointing to where they needed to go while offering each of them a cigarette to help them on their way. The men were in high spirits, with smiles on their faces as wide as the English Channel. They were grateful for the warm welcome they had received and eager to go through the demobilisation process before returning to Civvy Street.

Joe was one of the last to step off the train. He took a deep breath and filled his lungs with the cold evening air as his eyes adjusted to the bright station lights before dragging his heavy canvas bag toward one of the admin girls. He took a cigarette from her without offering any gratitude and popped it behind his right ear for later. Lugging his heavy cotton bag back over his shoulders, he slowly headed towards the station exit where the coaches awaited to take them to the Disembarkation Unit.

*

Joe stood across the road from The Crown, a small, dimly lit public house tucked away on a quiet street. He stared at the sign in the window that read 'Rooms for Rent' and realised this was perfect, as he certainly loved a drink. He took a long drag on his cigarette and threw it to the ground before crossing the road. He pushed the door open and entered. The smell of old wood, smoke, and alcohol permeated the air. The place was smaller than he anticipated, but this didn't matter to him. All he needed was a place to stay until he got himself sorted.

A scattering of patrons dotted the place, sipping their stout, puffing on their cigarettes, perusing their papers, and completing their betting slips. Joe walked towards the bar where a petite, flame-haired lady stood drying a few glasses with a tea towel.

Doris, the woman who owned the place, had seen her fair share of soldiers pass through the place—some broken, some trying to drink away the horrors they'd witnessed.

"Alright, love, what can I get ya?"

"Sign in the window says, 'Room for Rent'?"

"Nothing wrong with your eyesight," Doris replied, a twinkle in her eye.

Joe remained impassive. "Well, have ya?"

"Yeah, I have. As luck would have it, I've got one left."

"I'll take it."

"But you ain't seen it yet."

"I'll take it."

A man from across the bar looked up from his newspaper and noticed Joe was kitted out in the same demob suit that he was wearing. Doris popped to the back office behind the bar and grabbed the key to the room. She returned, lifted the bar flap, and asked Joe to follow her up the stairs. The guy watched as they both disappeared from view.

Doris' high heels clacked up the creaky wooden stairs as Joe followed behind. Reaching the top, she led him along a dingy corridor, past several brown-panelled doors, until they reached the room at the end. She unlocked the door, but it didn't open fully as there was a single wardrobe partially blocking it. They both squeezed their bodies through the gap and stepped inside the room.

Against the far wall was a single bed situated underneath a small window that looked out onto the street below. The sounds of the city filtered in from the main high street nearby; street vendors calling, people laughing and talking. A small sink was attached to the wall at the foot of the bed. Opposite was a tiny table covered by a lace tablecloth and two wooden chairs that looked like they belonged in a primary school. Doris extended her arms out wide. "Well, what do you think?"

"I said I'd take it."

There was a stale smell that lingered in the air, and he soon discovered the source of it: a damp patch of mould that ran underneath the window sill and up the wall to the ceiling. The place was cramped, tiny in fact, with hardly any space to stretch out in, but he didn't care. He'd been hunkering down on a beach in Normandy as the bullets flew overhead. This was a palace in comparison.

"By the way," Doris added, "the communal toilet and bathroom are down the other end of the corridor. You'll have to share them with the others."

"Yeah, I know what communal means."

Doris remained unfazed. "The rent's 16 shillings a week, paid every Friday without fail, okay?" Doris gave Joe a look that indicated she wouldn't tolerate any excuses.

"Yep, that's fine."

"How long are you thinking of staying?"

"Indefinitely."

"Okay, well, that's that then. I'll leave you to get yourself sorted." She handed him the key, stepped out onto the landing, and turned to face him. "Oh, and another thing—"

Before she could finish what she was saying, Joe closed the door in her face. She didn't suffer fools, but she gave Joe the benefit of the doubt. She had an uncomfortable feeling about him; she couldn't quite put her finger on it, but at the end of the day, all that mattered was he was renting the room for the foreseeable future, and as long as the money rolled in and he didn't cause any trouble, she was alright with that.

It was approaching 9.30 in the evening. Perched on a stool at the far end of the bar, Joe smoked cigarette after cigarette, with five empty whisky glasses in front of him and another nearly empty. He kept to himself, watching the world from the shadows, his mind a million miles away. He drank to forget, but the memories—flashes of gunfire, the screams of men, the ghostly silence after death—still remained.

The war was over, but it was still inside him.

He gestured over to Doris to fetch him another drink, which she duly obliged. Doris had been keeping an eye on him from behind the bar, sensing the darkness in him but not prying. She knew better than to ask questions.

Handing over the money, he grabbed his jacket and his drink and moved to a table over in the corner of the room. The man who was watching his every move earlier that evening was still sitting in the same spot with yet another pint in his hand. He had read his newspaper from cover to cover, peeking over the top from time to time to make sure Joe was still there.

His eyes followed Joe from the bar to the far corner of the room. As Joe settled down, the man placed the newspaper on the table, grabbed his drink, and approached him. Joe closed his eyes and blew the smoke out of his nose. As the smoke dissipated, he could see a man standing before him.

"Is this seat taken?" He asked.

Joe looked him up and down. He picked his drink up, and bringing the glass up to his lips, he pushed the chair out in front of him with his foot and muttered, "Be my guest."

*

It was early. The room was in semi-darkness, just a shard of sunlight starting to break through the crack in the curtains. The clanging of empty beer barrels from the cellar below and the loud voices of men bellowing instructions to each other on the street abruptly woke Joe. He sat bolt upright in bed, his heart racing, shocked by the noise. His body was covered in a cold sweat; his eyes darted around the room before realising he was in bed and not in the field of combat.

His breathing became less erratic. He pulled his knees up towards his chest and placed his head between them. From behind, a hand gently touched Joe's shoulder. "You okay? Lie back down."

Joe shrugged the hand off his shoulder and jumped out of bed. The man who had joined him at his table last night was lying there. "Grab your clothes and get out," he growled through gritted teeth. The man sat up in bed with just a sheet covering his modesty. "What do you mean?"

Joe snorted through his nose, "I'm going for a piss, and you better be gone by the time I return."

The man was confused. "But I thought—"

"Well, you thought wrong, didn't ya?" Joe snapped. "You've got two choices. You either go out the door and down the stairs, or I'll chuck you out that fucking window! Like I said, I'm going for a piss, and when I get back, I want you gone."

Joe headed downstairs and into the bar. Doris was wiping the tables and getting ready to open up. "Morning!" she said cheerily. He looked at her but didn't even acknowledge her, almost looking straight through her like she wasn't there. He opened the door and stepped out onto the street. Doris was unsurprised; she had encountered similar wankers in the past and was familiar with the characteristics of these military types.

Most of them were okay, but a lot of them were a little fucked up, as nobody really knew what they had been through mentally or physically. His attitude didn't bother her one bit. She enjoyed the challenge and was well-equipped to manage and discipline them as needed. She liked the money coming in and the lifestyle it provided for her. Everything was on her terms, and that's exactly the way she liked it.

FIFTEEN

Joe had one goal in mind: to get work and earn money. The money he received at the demob centre would not last long if he continued to spend it on rent, alcohol, and cigarettes while he was unemployed. He spent the day trekking all over the city looking for a job, but there was none. Any labouring jobs had already been filled, as had any manufacturing work, and the enquiries into driving opportunities were met with a quick 'Come back in a month or two.'

Soft excuses for a hard man to take.

Frustrated, he returned to his digs as the sun began to set. After a few glasses, the bitterness began to grow in him. He had done his job 'For King and Country,' and now here he was, spat out onto the streets to fend for himself, much like the veterans of The Great War nearly thirty years previously.

Some had lost limbs, blown apart on some godforsaken battlefield. The Huns' flamethrowers had scorched and disfigured others beyond recognition. Most had endured severe and painful mental anguish. They'd only received a few shiny medals as compensation for their service. Some people believed that the dead were the lucky ones.

As the weeks passed, he became increasingly frustrated with the lack of opportunities. Employers simply shied away from taking a chance on him, with the only explanations hidden deep within a whisky bottle. Day after day, he explored the city for work, but nothing came of it. Night after night, he propped up the bar while Doris occupied herself behind the bar.

Despite his increasing desperation, he had consistently paid his rent on time, and despite consuming excessive amounts of alcohol each night, he posed no threat to others. He kept to himself and only spoke to Doris to order another drink. He'd always stay until the last orders were placed before assisting her in collecting the empties and stacking them on the bar before retiring to bed. Most nights, he'd lie awake with a million things racing through his mind, scared to close his eyes after all he'd seen and heard at war.

The sight of young men in their prime being killed by a hail of bullets—the blood-curdling screams as they were blasted to pieces—the acrid stench of death that soaked into every pore and lingered with him to this day—were etched into his memory forever.

*

Joe had washed, dressed, and was ready to start another day of job searching. He looked in the mirror over the small sink and combed his thick mane. He looked tired, and felt exhausted. He'd spent another restless night, tossing and turning, reliving everything. The creases on his face, slightly craggier and more weathered than before, set his eyes back in his head.

He picked his suit jacket up and paused. He could hear muted voices downstairs. He opened his door and could hear the inaudible talk swing back and forth before the voices became louder and a disturbance erupted. It wasn't the typical cacophony of beer barrels sliding down the ramp into the cellar. It wasn't the guys from the brewery, with their noisy chatter as they went about their job. It wasn't the window cleaner, as he'd been earlier this week.

He knew something was wrong.

He moved along the passage to the top of the stairs, listening closely. The voices seemed clearer now. He could hear a male voice becoming more forceful, and Doris pleading with him to take what he wanted. Doris was normally a strong, feisty lady who could hold her own, but today she sounded vulnerable and afraid.

Joe quietly descended the stairs. Reaching the bottom, he peered through the door. Doris stood in the dim light of the pub, plainly distressed and backed into a corner by a man wielding a knife.

Desperation twisted the man's expression, and his hand trembled as he waved the blade in front of her. She attempted to speak with him, but the situation was clearly escalating. "Look, I've told you to take what you want. Booze, money... it's yours. Just don't hurt me; don't hurt us. I'm pregnant." She cradled her belly, her voice quivering with fear. She had encountered such a situation before, but this time was different. She needed to protect not just herself, but also her unborn child.

She closed her eyes and looked away from her attacker. She flinched as the cold steel blade dug into her skin, bracing herself for what was to come.

Opening her eyes, she noticed a shadow in the doorway. She took a deep breath and attempted to remain calm and composed, not letting him know that someone was behind him.

The attacker pressed the blade deeper into her neck, threatening her. "Don't move, you hear me!" he said menacingly. He let go of her neck and turned towards the bar, where he saw a gigantic figure heading slowly towards him. He sprang back in alarm, recognising that he wasn't alone. "Stay back! Do you hear me? Don't come any closer," he shouted as he jabbed the blade at Joe. "Stay back; otherwise, I'll cut you."

Joe did not hesitate. With his combat training from the war resurfacing, he charged toward him, his hefty boots pounding on the wooden floors. The man barely had time to react when Joe slammed into him, throwing him off balance and knocking the knife to the ground.

The two men began to grapple, the man writhing in terror as

Joe's raw strength quickly overtook him. Joe's face was a mask of frigid rage, his movements were precise and vicious, and the fight ended nearly as quickly as it began. Joe wrestled the man to the ground and stunned him with a powerful punch to the face.

The man looked up and saw Joe's evil eyes staring back at him. Joe picked up the knife from the floor and pushed the blade into his cheekbone. He issued a warning while towering over him. "I eat people like you for breakfast. Scaring a woman, you low-life piss head." Joe grabbed him by the collar and forced him to his feet, his eyes widening. He leaned in closer. "If I see you around here again, I'll slit your throat, ya hear?"

Doris, still terrified but unharmed, slumped back against the wall and placed her palm over her mouth, thankful that Joe had walked in at that precise moment to protect her and her unborn child.

Joe dragged the man over the hard, wooden floor toward the entrance and dumped him on the pavement. Theman grumbled as he lay face down in the gutter, where he belonged, before getting up and running away. Joe returned inside and slammed the door shut.

He approached Doris. "You okay?" Doris' face was ashen with fright. She could feel the darkness and misery inside him. "Here, take a seat," he added, moving a chair over to where she stood. She sat down, bewildered at the reality of what could have happened but did not. How could she ever repay him?

Joe moved behind the bar, picked up a glass, and shoved it into the optic. With his back to her, he whispered quietly, "I didn't know you were pregnant."

"I didn't realise it was any of your business," she said curtly. "And make that two, will ya?"
He poured another whisky, walked through the hatch, and handed it to her; her fingers shook as she received it. "That'll settle your nerves."

"Look, I could never thank you enough for what you've done for me, but I know there's one way I can repay you."

"I'm very flattered," Joe said. "But I'm not that kind of bloke."

"No, I know you're not, and that's not what I meant." She reached across the table and placed her hand on top of his. "I know what goes on around here, and I know more than you think, so we'll keep this one between us, okay?" She tapped his hand lightly.

Joe gave a half-smile and nodded as he took a sip of whisky.

"I know you've been looking for work, and I know just the man who can sort something out for you." Doris said, cradling her tummy, "There's a bloke named Ronnie. He runs things around here, some of which aren't entirely legal, if you get my point. You have the skills that someone like him could use."

Joe's eyes narrowed upon hearing the name. He'd heard his name before: whispers at the pub, rumours of a man running a criminal organisation—someone with connections and power. He remained silent, but the seed had taken root. He recognised that the world he once knew no longer had room for him. But this new world, the one Doris hinted about—this world of crime, violence, and power—could be exactly where he belonged and wanted to be.

Joe stood across the street, taking in his surroundings. The building was massive and imposing, with a gigantic flashing neon sign illuminating the sidewalk. Music and laughing filled the night air, blending with the smell of cigarettes and perfume. Two burly, well-dressed males hailed him as he approached the entryway, unconcerned. "Good evening, sir; how can we help?" The taller of the two enquired.

"I've come to see Franco."

"Is he aware of your visit this evening?"

"He should be. My name is Joe Maxwell."

"Wait here with Ray a minute; I'll go and have a word with him."

Inside, the club was hazy with smoke and gloomy lighting. A jazz band performed on stage, their brassy notes barely breaking through the murmur of voices and the clinking of glasses. Franco was sitting on a stool at the bar as Joe approached him, his eyes narrowing as he assessed him. Before Franco could introduce himself, he initiated the discussion. "Are you Joe?"

Joe nodded.

"Take a seat." Franco pointed to the barman. "Errol, two whiskies."

Joe sat on the stool next to him. He added, "Doris told me what happened and what you did, and she mentioned that you're looking for a job. I spoke with Mr. Fitzpatrick, and we're pleased to give you a trial."

"Doing what?" Joe asked.

"I've heard you have a decent pair of hands on you and know how to deal with problems when they arise. Put it this way: the problem won't be behind the bar. We need somebody on the door. It's not just about opening the door; anyone can do that, but it's about making sure the right people come in and the wrong ones stay outside. Also, there'd be a bit of driving during the day and making sure our girls are looked after, that sort of thing. So, do you want it then?"

Joe swigged his drink. "When can I start?"

SIXTEEN

John carefully placed another floorboard on his bike. He rested one end on top of the handlebars and inserted the other end through the gap in the rope that kept everything else together on top of the seat. He tightened the rope and made sure his load was secure enough to transport it to the allotment. He'd spent the last hour or so scrabbling about the abandoned, half-demolished houses that were decaying among the sprawling wasteland, gathering anything he could find that he thought was useful.

His friends were playing in the ruins. What was once a terraced row had become a castle; Phil and Carl stood on top of a crumbling brick wall, swishing the sticks in their hands back and forth, attempting to repel the roving hordes of soldiers attacking them. Little Dave, Roger, and Harvey were a fearsome force, armed with dustbin lid shields and swords constructed from a broken dado rail.

John parked his bike against a wall and proceeded to another building, where Eric was waiting. "Oi, come and look at this!" Eric exclaimed before disappearing from view. John strolled across a group of girls who'd made a den out of disused household furnishings.

An old sofa, several tables of various shapes and sizes, broken TV sets, and prams created a makeshift living room among the rubble and ruins of this dumping ground. After navigating the bricks and boulders, John entered the house cautiously. As he approached the remnants of a small kitchen, he noticed Eric and his friends, Norman and Spencer, passing a bottle around and smoking a cigarette.

"What are you doing, Eric?" he enquired.

"What does it bloody look like I'm doing?" he said, taking another gulp. He closed his eyes; the liquid burning his throat as it slipped down. He didn't enjoy the taste, but he was in the company of his friends and wanted to appear confident. And the last thing he needed was his younger brother annoying him; he had enough of that at home from his arsehole of a father.

John hated drinking. He was actually repulsed by it. He'd seen firsthand how it could captivate, seduce, and eventually destroy you, just as it had his father. It would chew you up and then spit you out. He'd seen the fights, beatings, cuts and bruises, and bloodied lips his mother had endured from his father over time.

The boys found broken crockery, piles of newspapers, and bottles of spirits—some empty, others half-full—on the kitchen counter, and a large pile of thick, woollen blankets strewn across the floor in the corner near a door. Someone appeared to have been squatting here but was no longer present.

John became nervous and jittery. "Look, Eric, we had better go; Dad will be at the allotment waiting for us."

"Fuck him," Eric muttered as he took another sip. His friends found that humorous. Norman slammed his hand into Eric's shoulder, giggling at his reaction to his brother and sniggering at his disgust toward his father. Spencer stared at John and began massaging his eyes, attempting to scream like a baby.

"C'mon now, run along to Daddy's allotment."

John didn't bite back. He grumbled under his breath. "They'd laugh at anything you said, stupid idiots, but he won't be acting like this in front of him when we are late."

Eric yelled to John. "Did you say summing, John?"

"I am going to get the wood and start heading up there." John stepped out of the room, turning on his heel.

Eric addressed the lads, "Look, I'd better go after that whining twat, so I'll catch up with you later."

The boys responded in unison, "Yeah, see ya later."

Eric stepped out of the building and into the sunlight. He glanced over at the girls, nestled together in their den, basking in the sun while engaging in lively chatter and laughter.

As he swaggered out, he added, "I'll see you later, girls; don't miss me too much." The girls tutted and watched him closely. They disliked him because they saw him as cocky and arrogant. He watched their expressions become sour as he breezed past them and chuckled to himself before approaching John.

Norman faced Spencer and held a box of matches up to the bottle he was holding. "Did you know this stuff is flammable?"

Eric called to John as he rode his bike across the wasteland, "Wait up, will ya?" John turned back and noticed plumes of black smoke and yellow flames pouring from the house in the distance. The girls felt the heat of the fire on their backs, ignorant of the imminent danger they were in. However, the fire quickly took hold and began to rage, causing the heat to become intense and unbearable. The girls began running away, screaming hysterically.

When Eric turned to check what was going on, he noticed Norman and Spencer standing outside the front door, laughing together. He stood there in shock, wondering what the bloody hell had occurred, but he didn't have time to investigate further. However, he was certain that John was right. If they arrived late, their father would go ballistic.

They arrived at the allotment after carefully transporting the wood by bicycle. It was overgrown and untidy, a far cry from the well-kept patches of the other gardeners. Joe's shed stood crooked in one corner, its wooden walls battered and in desperate need of repair. It was a rickety, pitiful-looking object that, like their father, had plainly seen better days. Constructed from corrugated sections of an old Anderson air-raid shelter, abandoned floorboards, and any old bits of wood, it was a miracle it didn't collapse in the middle of a gust of wind.

The boys knew their dad would be inside, holding a drink in one hand and a dirty magazine in the other. They weren't disappointed. There he was, sitting on a sad, saggy old armchair in the corner, its shredded upholstery revealing the underbelly of foam and springs like a furniture autopsy. Plant pots, half-empty bags of soil, and discarded whisky bottles surrounded a huge pile of magazines, stacked like paper tower blocks. The place was a pigsty, and it smelt like the pigs were still there.

They had placed the bike against the side of the shed and were about to unload the wood when the door burst wide, nearly coming off its hinges. Joe looked down at his wristwatch. "You're late!" As he spewed his remarks, his breath smelt of alcohol and halitosis. Eric stood in front of John, the ever-protective brother, and wiped Joe's spittle off his face. "We struggled to carry the stuff you wanted. It kept falling off," Eric complained. Joe swung his arm in the air and swiped him across the face, knocking him backwards onto the ground.

"Don't you fucking dare backchat me, boy." Eric sat up, holding his face. It stung like crazy and began to turn red. Despite the pain, he hoped John wouldn't also receive a slap, as he was solely responsible for this. John stood there, holding his breath. He couldn't believe how hard his father had smacked his brother. This wasn't the first time he had hit him, but it was clearly the most severe. John knew his father despised, if not detested, Eric. He lowered his head and concentrated on the ground, attempting to avoid any unexpected surprises.

"Lift your fucking head up and get on with your repairs," Joe told John, gesturing to the shed.

"Aren't you going to help me, Dad?"

He smiled and turned his attention to Eric. "And you? I suggest you get off your arse and start working on that patch. And I want it done properly. Do you hear me?"

The boys nodded, but they were both thinking the same thing: *Why don't you do it yourself, you lazy old bastard? I hope you'd just die and do us all a favour.*

They spent the afternoon in the scorching summer sun hammering the scrap metal onto the walls of the shed and reinforcing the wood. Joe continued to come out of the shed to criticise Eric and the work he had completed. Like an army sergeant, Joe would frequently start yelling instructions, telling him to hurry up, to hold the shovel this way instead of that, and to ensure the work was to his satisfaction. He belittled and berated him all day long, yet he left John alone. Eric preferred it this way; as long as he bore the brunt of his father's displeasure, John would be safe.

By late afternoon, the temperature was now unbearably hot. The boys, stripped to the waist, felt their skin burn in the intense heat; the metal burnt to the touch under the sun. John hadn't stopped for hours. He was hot, irritated, and weary, yet he still had one more step to go. Eric stood on the top step, holding the ladder with one hand and a hammer in the other. He yelled out to his father, who was sitting in his armchair in the cool shed underneath, drinking beer and listening to the radio. "Can we have a drink, Dad? It's boiling over here."

"What are you saying? You want to drink? Have you finished?"

"Almost," came the response from above, "just gotta nail this last board down and we are done."

Joe took a long gulp, rose from his chair, and headed outdoors. He noticed his boys on top of the shed, looking hot and bothered, with skin as red as a post box. He moved around to the other side, where there was a large water pipe protruding from the ground with a hose attached. He gave it a few turns before returning to the boys, holding the hose.

"Here you go," Joe said, presenting it to them with an extended arm.

ADVERSITY

The boys exchanged glances and rolled their eyes. Was this some sort of joke? They stared back at him, and Joe waved the hose in front of their faces, as if to say, "Who goes first?" They instinctively knew they were thinking the same thing: *What a bastard.*

Eric grasped it first and chugged the water that poured from the end. He passed it to John, who did the same. Their thirst remained unquenchable as they passed the hose between themselves. The water was warm and had a strange metallic taste, but they didn't mind.

"That's enough!" Joe walked up to the tap and turned it off. "You can piss off home now."

Eric bit his lower lip. They had worked hard in the scorching heat, and now they were expected to be grateful for some warm water from a fucking hosepipe. What the fuck was all this about? There was no please, thank you, or kiss my arse… nothing. He hadn't anticipated any gratitude anyway.

John returned the tools he had been using to the shed, and after a brief tidy-up, they both headed home. They couldn't wait to get away from him, get home, eat some food, and catch up with their friends, but there was no escaping him for long.

Joe stayed at the allotment for the next few hours, drinking his way through his bottles. He got up from his armchair; opening the drawer in his workbench, he put his hand to the back, grabbing a metal tin. Putting it on the bench, he opened it. It was full of notes that didn't belong to him.

He counted them and bundled them up into rubber bands, putting them back inside the tin, closing the lid, and hiding it back in the drawer.

SEVENTEEN

It was just another ordinary day. Annie was in town running errands, and running late. Every time she left the house and ventured out to do some shopping, she would always bump into someone she knew, and they'd stop and natter for a while before carrying on with what they had to do. Inevitably, she would meet someone else, and the process would continue. Instead of running errands, she would run through a gauntlet of gossip, idle chit chat, and rumours, and Annie loved it as it distracted her from her own life.

She loved hearing what others were doing, how they felt, and who did what to whom. Despite this, Annie would always respond to questions about her life with her tried and trusted response: "We're all good, thank you." The only person she confided in was Peggy, her one true friend, who was more like a sister than a neighbour.

Annie had been to the post office to buy some stamps and had stopped to chat with the old postmistress behind the counter. She was eighty years old and had worked in this small, unremarkable place her entire life. She had a craggy, weathered, lived-in face. It was a face that had met a million customers, had heard a million stories over the decades, and had a million stories to tell herself. She always swept her grey/white hair behind her head, securing it with a bun and a few hair clips.

Curvaceous and always dressed in black, she earned the moniker 'Queenie' for her vague resemblance to the late Queen Victoria, despite her true mourning for her late husband, who had passed away some years earlier. Many customers found her brusque and impatient manner off-putting, but Annie considered her endearing. After all, with a friend like Peggy, she was used to a person like this. This pillar of the community was as small and unremarkable as her workplace.

Luciano Pirisi was a lovely man. He always had an eye for the ladies and a gift of the gab that could get him into all sorts of trouble, but his customers flocked to his shop, not only to buy his fruit and vegetables but to be charmed and entertained by him. He had honed his craft over many years since leaving his native Italy with his wife, Monica, and their three boys. He was a short, stocky man with a thick mane of snow-white hair that looked like candy floss atop his athletic shoulders and had a very bright twinkle in his piercing brown eyes.

His generosity was as big as the wide smile on his face, and he would often give his favourite customers more than they wanted at no extra cost. While an apple and a few carrots may have seemed insignificant to him, they could mean the world to those who were struggling to stretch their housekeeping budget. Despite his advancing years, his velvety Italian accent and ruggedly handsome features mesmerised Annie, and she eagerly anticipated her weekly pilgrimage to buy his produce.

After several encounters with the good, the bad, and the beautiful, Annie finished paying for her shopping and left his shop. The bags were heavy and cumbersome, and as she headed home, she struggled to carry them, their weight cutting into her hands, turning her knuckles white and her fingers purple. As she huffed her way along the busy high street, she recognised a familiar-looking face. During her weekly shopping trips, she had often seen this handsome man. They would exchange a quick nod of the head and a half-smile, and that was it. They had always made eye contact but had never spoken one word between them. But that was about to change.

He stood outside a barbershop and casually puffed on his cigarette, watching the world pass by in front of him. Annie, her arms straining from carrying her heavy bags, shuffled past him, but instead of the usual silent acknowledgement, he flicked his cigarette away and approached her.

"Need a hand with those bags? They seem heavy," he said in a husky voice.

Annie smiled coyly at him; his piercing blue eyes stared back at hers. "Oh, no, I'm alright, thank you. I can manage; I don't wanna put you out."

"Well, you seem to be struggling," he countered, reaching for the bags. "Here, let me help you."

Annie nervously looked around to make sure nobody was watching. "It's okay; I only live down the end of the road."

He smiled and managed a small laugh, saying, "It's not too far to drop you home then."

Annie looked at him more closely now. His tall frame, neat appearance, and the way he carried himself exuded an undeniable charm. It brought back memories of how Joe used to be and how he used to treat her.

He smiled at her warmly, quickly taking the bags from her and leading her to his car parked only a few yards away. He opened the door and put the shopping bags on the back seat. Then he walked round to the passenger side and opened the door. She climbed in, and he climbed in beside her, looking at her like nobody had done in a very long time. For a brief moment she wasn't Annie Maxwell. She felt like she was somebody completely different, like something had ignited inside of her. She hadn't felt like this in a long time, and she didn't want this feeling to end.

They set off down the busy road. Looking out of the window, she watched life whizz past her eyes in a hazy blur of colour and noise, a split-second moment in time that vanished as quickly as it arrived.

"You live at the end of this road?" Edward asked Annie. She

remained engrossed in her own thoughts, unaware that he had spoken to her. He coughed into his fist in a blatant attempt to catch her attention.

She looked at him coyly. She didn't live at the end of this road or indeed in this particular area. Home was a mile or so away, and she would usually catch the bus if she had lots of shopping to carry—like today—or walk back if the weather was fine. However, she was thankful for the lift, and after a short drive of a few hundred yards, her intrepid chauffeur discovered that her home was significantly farther than he had previously assumed. But that didn't matter.

Eventually she found herself in familiar surroundings. "You can just drop me at the top of the road," she said.

"You sure? I don't mind dropping you right outside."

"Yeah, I'm sure. I am married, y'know."

He nodded, "Okay, I'll pull up over here."

Annie turned her head, closing her eyes and biting her lip in frustration. *God, why did I just say that? I'll probably never see him again.*

"Thanks for the lift," she said.

"Don't mention it," he said cheerily as he leaped out of the car, grabbed her bags, opened her door, and assisted her. "By the way, my name's Edward," he said, passing her the bags.

"I'm Annie. Annie Maxwell."

They exchanged smiles, each not knowing what to do or say next. In the distance she noticed two women chatting to each other. Both stared back over at her and her mysterious companion before carrying on with their conversation. At that moment, a wave of anxiety washed over her.

What am I doing? I'm standing here with another man in my street, and people have seen me. I must be crazy. I'm married to Joe Maxwell, for fuck's sake, and he'll kill me if he finds out.

Edward leaned in closer. "Annie, are you okay?"

"You shouldn't have given me a lift home; you don't know my husband. Please, just give me my bags and go," she said, panicking.

"I was only trying to be helpful," Edward said, a confused look on his face.

"Please, just go!"

Edward respected Annie's wishes. "Don't go carrying all those bags by yourself next time, alright? I'm sure I'll see you around," he said. His expression was warm and genuine. He got in his car and sped off up the road. Annie stood on the pavement, laden with heavy bags and mixed emotions. Part of her didn't care if Joe found out because, apart from her boys, she didn't have much to care about. After all, she'd done nothing wrong, but he wouldn't see it that way, and there'd be no doubt he would take it out on all of them.

EIGHTEEN

The curvy woman in the red coat, she's definitely a secretary, answering phones all day and typing important letters. The man with the two-piece suit and pipe is a policeman, or a detective. He has an inquisitive face and suspicious eyes. The young, slim girl with the high heels and knee-high skirt works in a shop. Or she's a model. Yes, definitely a model.

John's imagination was in overdrive, as always. He was sitting in his dad's car, patiently waiting for him to return. With the immortal words, 'I'll be back in ten minutes,' ringing in his ears, this short period of time had now turned into a long, tedious twenty minutes and counting. He pressed his nose firmly against the window and sighed. Not only was he bored, he was becoming increasingly agitated.

He'd learned not to ask about his father's somewhat ambiguous business. Joe flitted from one place to another, running errands and bringing John along to make him appear less inconspicuous. Joe made it clear that he had to remain in the car at all times.

Twenty minutes at his age seemed like an hour, and he was not only running out of things to do, he was running out of patience too. He had already pretended to drive the car, bitten his nails to the quick, and fashioned shapes from the clouds that were gradually moving across the sky.

The car door suddenly opened and startled John; his dreamlike thoughts had now dissipated, and he was back to reality. Joe threw a small leather bag onto the passenger seat. The weight of whatever was inside the bag was evident as it thudded upon landing. He clambered into the driver's seat and half-turned to face him. "Right, I've got one more thing to do, and then we'll head home," he said as he started the engine and crunched the gear stick into first.

John nodded back with a blank expression on his face. His role as a passenger in his father's Morris Minor was to maintain silence, follow instructions, and obey. Something of which John was an expert at.

To say his relationship with his dad was fractious was an understatement. In fact, he had no relationship with him at all. He was a cold, heartless individual with a fiery temper and a dark, sinister soul.

They drove through the grey, shabby streets for a short while. John sat in the back, gazing out of the window as life passed by; as he did every week, the world was a seemingly colourless place with intermittent flashes of red buses, yellow lorries, and green patches of grass trundling by. This was no place for a conversation, not that John was expecting one any time soon. He had grown accustomed to the long, tense silences while Joe conducted his business.

The car pulled off the main roads and weaved its way through the cramped side streets until it eventually stopped and parked across the road from a double-fronted barbershop with a red and white striped pole spinning outside the door. Joe reached into his overcoat pocket and produced a small brown paper bag and a bottle of lemonade. "Right, stay here; I won't be long."

John stared at the shop, oblivious to his dad's command.

"Hello! I'm talking to you, boy. Did you hear what I said?" Joe shouted.

"Yeah," he whispered, his mind elsewhere.

Joe grabbed the bag from the passenger seat, got out of the car, and slammed the door. He crossed the road, but instead of going for a haircut, as John presumed, he headed down an alleyway next to it and disappeared from view.

And it was back to square one for John, alone in the car and with time to kill.

He opened the bottle of pop, took a hearty swig, and swallowed it down, followed by a loud, roaring belch while sucking on his sherbet lemons. The minutes ticked by, and before long, he had drunk most of the lemonade, and the pressure on his bladder told him he needed the bathroom.

After a few more moments of indecision, he hesitantly got out of the car, looking around to see if anyone was watching, and then slammed the door and headed across the road.

He peered through the window of the barbershop, looking for his dad. The sound of scissors snipping and the rhythmic hum of manual clippers filled the room as men in flat caps and wool coats chatted in low, muffled voices while leafing through well-worn copies of *The Daily Mirror* or *Radio Times*. Despite the absence of his dad, he ventured down the dim alleyway, eager to discover what or who he might encounter.

Walking cautiously, he came across an inconspicuous red-brick building. He twisted the door handle, and to his surprise, it opened after he had checked around and over his shoulder. He hesitated for a moment, unsure whether to enter or not, but he'd come this far, and there was no turning back. He gently pushed the door open and peered inside.

The inside was darker than he'd expected. A row of dimly lit, Baroque chandeliers with tassel lamp shades cast harsh shadows along a narrow corridor that stretched out ahead of him, lined with closed doors on either side. The floorboards creaked beneath his feet as he stepped inside.

To his left was a room that resembled a reception area. The only furniture in the room consisted of a large desk adorned with a small lamp, a telephone, and a couple of chairs. Opposite, there was a lounge with two sofas, several comfy chairs, and a coffee table with magazines and newspapers strewn across it.

Lamps adorned the room, their red shades casting a scarlet glow beneath them. It was a mishmash of patterns and textures, a clandestine, decadent sign of sleaze and disrepute.

John continued slowly down this half-lit corridor, now desperate for the bathroom. There must have been ten rooms, five on each side, with a number above each door. It was reminiscent of a hotel or boarding house John had stayed at with his brother and parents when he was very young.

There in front of him was a staircase. He carried on walking slowly; his breathing became shallow, and his heart started to pound, unsure whether to turn back or carry on into the unknown. But he was too far inside the belly of the beast to turn back now. He had to proceed with trepidation, not crippling apprehension. He was filled with thoughts about what he might encounter, but most importantly, what would happen if his father discovered him sneaking around the place?

He noticed a slightly open door, so he decided to take a look. Only a rickety old metal bed, a wooden chair, a small sink, and a shower cubicle in the corner furnished it. He could hear muffled voices coming from a few doors up, so he decided to explore further.

Walking towards the door, the noises became more intense. Placing his hand on the handle, he took a deep breath, opened the door slightly, and peered through the crack.

Rooted to the floor, he gasped, his eyes widening with revulsion. Just a few feet in front of him, a man on all fours, stark bollock-naked, had his face firmly pressed into a pillow.

A studded collar sat tightly around his neck. His hands were cuffed to the metal bedpost; he wasn't going anywhere. A curvaceous woman, clad in stockings and suspenders, stood behind him, her nipples adorned with tassels and a large strap-on dildo around her waist.

John had only seen pictures like this in magazines he'd found in his dad's shed. He couldn't believe that he was seeing the real thing with his own eyes; he only came here because he was bored; his curiosity had got the better of him, and he needed a wee. But here he was, no longer needing a wee, as his John Thomas was standing to attention.

She vigorously thrust in and out of him, riding him like a horse. She raised her arm in the air, mimicking the motion of a jockey, and delivered a forceful slap to his rear end while holding a wooden paddle. He jerked backwards, suddenly lifting his sweaty face from the pillow before letting out a long, throaty grunt in ecstasy. The cuffs rattled against the metal posts.

John's excitement was short-lived. Nearly falling through the door in shock, he couldn't believe what he was seeing. Instinctively, he clasped his hands over his mouth to stifle any noise. He was unable to breathe; he was afraid to breathe because this was not just any man.

It was his father.

Joe closed his eyes tightly as the dominatrix grabbed his hair at the back of his head and pushed his face firmly back into the pillow. "You fucking love it, don't you?" She shrieked at him humiliatingly, "You filthy bastard! You love being dominated, you weak, pathetic excuse of a man, don't you?" She grabbed him by the hair again and snapped his head back.

"Yes, I do, mistress," came his weak, breathless reply.

It was both a painful and pleasurable experience for Joe. He threw his head back and shouted for the woman to go faster and harder. She deliberately slowed down and told him to shut up. "I control the pace, not you. You're at my mercy, and you do as you're told!"

John stood in the doorway, watching on in horror. He knew exactly what was going on in front of him, and he felt repulsed by it. He turned, and looked down the dimly lit corridor. He knew he had to get out, but at this point he didn't know how. All he could see was a sea of doors down the corridor closing in on him. He began to panic, but then he heard a faint voice in the distance. He headed towards it, hoping that it would lead him in the right direction.

John rushed into the dark corridor, but in his haste, he collided with someone exiting one of the rooms and skidded to a standstill. They both collapsed on the floor, surrounded by towels. They scrambled to their feet, fighting for breath, the wind knocked out of them. "I'm sorry, I didn't see you," John said as he bent down to pick up the towels.

She knelt alongside him to help. He looked at her and was surprised to see a pretty, young girl not much older than him. She had bright, inquisitive eyes and long hair that flowed over her shoulders in an untidy braid. She gazed at him with a hint of hesitant curiosity. "It's okay. Hey, I haven't seen you here before; have you come about the job?"

"No, no, no, I'm... lost," he said anxiously. "I just needed to use the toilet."

The girl gave a smile. "I can take you if you like."

"Nah, I need to get out of here. My dad is in the barbershop."

"Oh, so why didn't you go in there instead of coming here?"

John was unable to think of anything to say.

"Actually," she replied, "you don't need to answer that. I think you were just being nosy, weren't you?"

"Yeah, something like that."

She chuckled, "We get lots of boys coming in here, checking the place out. Come on, I'll show you out."

"What about those?" John pointed to the remaining towels.

"Don't worry; I will pick them up when I return. I'm Elizabetta, by the way. And what's your name?"

"John. So you work here?"

"Yeah. I keep the rooms tidy and take care of the washing."

"What, and you know what goes on?"

"Of course I do; this place belongs to Daddy. He has lots of businesses around here." She approached the door and opened it. "Well, here we are. You can escape now."

John nodded sheepishly and headed out the door. "Maybe see you again sometime?" Elizabetta called out, giggling as she closed it behind him. He ran down the alleyway and across the road toward the car. He leaned up against it and looked up to the sky, trying to calm his racing heart and make sense of what he'd just seen.

He could have kicked himself. Had he remained in the car, he would have remained oblivious to what he had just witnessed. He should have remained in the back seat of the car, bored and restless but with his innocence intact. But no, he had to stick his nose in and let his curiosity get the better of him. And now he couldn't unsee what he had just seen. It was yet another experience that would be indelibly burnt into his memory forever and another secret to keep with all the others.

Once he composed himself, he got back into the car and slumped down on the back seat. He grabbed his bottle of pop, suddenly developing an unquenchable thirst. His hands shook as he twisted the top off the bottle, and as the adrenaline coursed through his body, the bottle slipped out of his hands and landed on his lap. If the day couldn't get any worse, it just had. Now drenched, he forgot all about the waiting in the car, the boredom, and the horrific scene he had just witnessed.

He started to mop up the mess with the sleeves of his jumper, popped a sherbet lemon into his mouth, and sat back, gazing at the clouds in the sky. He was unable to form an image from the clouds, especially in light of what he had just witnessed. He sat in silence, awaiting his dad's return. How was he going to react when he saw him? He wouldn't be able to look him in the eyes, not after this.

But in the back of his mind, the memory of Elizabetta's smile lingered—brief, kind, and fleeting, like a light in the darkness.

The car door opened, breaking his concentration. John immediately sat up straight and composed himself. Joe, looking flushed and dishevelled, climbed gingerly into the front seat. He slammed the door shut as usual, threw his bag on the passenger seat, and turned to address John. The windows steamed up, and the smell of stale sweat and sex filled the car.

Joe set his gaze upon John's crotch. "Why are your trousers wet?" He said angrily. He didn't give John the opportunity to answer. "You dirty little shit, you've pissed yourself, haven't ya?"

"Erm, no, I spilled my drink, actually," John replied, his eyes looking to the floor, not wanting to make eye contact.

Joe raised his hand and growled at him. "Who the fuck do you think you're answering back?" John cowered and braced himself for what was to come. Joe clipped him straight across the head; he jolted backwards.

"Don't ever take that tone with me, y'hear? It better not be on the seat; otherwise, you'll be clearing it up when you get home," Joe muttered under his breath, the car jerking to life as they pulled away from the kerb. John stared out the window, a vacant look on his face. This was his dad, back to being the brutal bully he is, and yet not fifteen minutes prior, he was on all fours, chained to a bed with a woman telling him he was weak and pathetic.

He'd seen despicable things and been subjected to the very real horrors life had thrown at him. These bitter, traumatic memories swirled around in his young mind like a tornado of turmoil and emotion. The scars would never fully heal, but as long as he had hope, his mother, and Eric, he knew deep down that he would be okay.

NINETEEN

Eric was helping his mother cook dinner in the kitchen. He sat on a chair, a metal bucket filled with water at his feet and a large sack of potatoes by his side. He'd been peeling them for a while, but the bag never seemed to empty. With precision and dexterity, he cut through the pile with a small and extremely sharp knife. Annie had assigned him this task as she prepared the other veggies on a thick chopping board on top of the counter.

She danced to songs playing from a small wireless on the windowsill. He sat there laughing, watching her prancing around as if nothing mattered. They were both in their own private universe, and when Joe wasn't home, it almost felt normal—whatever that was.

When they heard the front door open, their fun came to an abrupt halt. Annie promptly turned off the wireless, and the kitchen fell silent. It was no longer a place full of music and conviviality. The atmosphere changed quickly, as it always did, and a cloud of anticipation hung in the air.

Annie's eyes were full of anguish as she glanced at Eric. They heard heavy footsteps pounding up the stairs, followed by the slamming of the front door. Joe appeared at the kitchen doorway, glanced at her, and gestured towards the fridge.

"Get me a beer, will ya?" He spoke in his usual harsh and arrogant tone. "The ones at the back, 'cause they'll be colder."

Eric shifted in his chair, watching as his mother succumbed to this nasty, repulsive man. He really wanted to get out of his chair, grab it, and smack it right around his head. As he lay on the floor with the chair scattered around him, he would bend over and snarl, "Why don't you get it yourself, ya lazy cunt!" Instead, he sat on the chair, head lowered, peeling the potatoes and thinking, 'One day...'

Annie reached into the back of the fridge, as directed, and pulled out a bottle of Fuller's London Pride. She took a bottle opener from the drawer, popped the cap, grabbed a pint glass from the cupboard, and gently poured it into the glass, just as he liked. She handed it to him. "Is that cold enough for ya?"

"I dunno, I ain't had a swig yet," he said before taking a large gulp.

Eric rolled his eyes and pondered, *'Why does she tolerate this behaviour? Why don't we just leave?'*

"Where's John?" Annie enquired.

"You ain't gonna believe it. The stupid little bastard dropped a bottle of pop into his lap. Well, he said it was pop, but I reckon he pissed himself, the dirty little shit." He shook his head, snorting through his nose. He walked into the lounge, turned on the television, and slouched into his armchair. And that was where he would remain, as he hadn't shared a bed with Annie in years. Eric tightened his grip around the knife. Annie sensed he was becoming agitated. She rested her arm on his shoulder and gently pushed him back into his chair. She shook her head. "Keep peeling those spuds, darlin'. I'm just going upstairs to make sure that your brother is alright."

Eric grumbled. "Mum!"

"Shh! Not now! I'll be back in a minute, so keep peeling!" She replied, unable to ignore the accusation.

She walked up the stairs, the heels of her shoes knocking against the bare wood and creaking with each step. She gently rapped on his door with her knuckles. "Only me, love, can I come in?" she asked.

"Yeah," he replied quietly. When she entered the room, she found him lying on his bed, arms behind his head and staring at the ceiling.

"Are you okay?" She asked tentatively, her eyes reading his body language, knowing something had happened but not knowing what.

He replied without looking at her. "Yeah."

Her motherly instinct told her that something was wrong. She had the impression that Joe had upset him. As she approached him, she caught a glimpse of his wet trousers crumpled on the floor. She sat alongside him on the bed and gently lifted his chin; he closed his eyes. "Come on, look at me. I know what happened because your dad told me."

He stared blankly at the ceiling, not wanting to make eye contact with his mother for fear of giving away the game. He lay still, his head a jumble of fear and despair. His ashen face was as pale as the walls around him, and his eyes were red and bulging. The shock of seeing his father in such an uncompromising situation, the frustration of constant belittlement and ridicule, the fear of being on the receiving end of his father's rage, and the sadness of witnessing the emotional torture his mother and they endured made him want to cry, but he struggled to find the right words. "Dad said that your trousers are wet."

John stared at her. "I suppose he told you that I'd wet myself?" He averted his gaze from her, unable to look her in the eyes after what he had witnessed. "It isn't pee; it's lemonade. I tried to explain what had happened to him, but he didn't listen, as he never does.

She rubbed his back, reassuring him. "Look, I know it's not pee; I know it's lemonade, so it doesn't matter what he thinks. I'll just take them downstairs and wash them."

She stood up from the bed and grabbed his trousers off the floor. "Dinner won't be long, so come down when you're ready."

He remained silent as she closed the bedroom door behind her. She paused for a bit, then lifted the trousers up to her nose and sniffed. The distinct sweet, citrus smell of lemonade overwhelmed her senses, proving that John would never wet himself. She sighed with relief, anger bubbling beneath her calm exterior, and thudded down the stairs with the wet trousers nestled in the crook of her arm.

Something inside her had awakened, and she decided she couldn't take this any longer. Was this due to the attention she'd received from another man, which made her feel special for a few moments and helped her realise she deserved more in life? Or was she simply trapped in an unhappy and unpleasant marriage, feeling her life was stagnating and knowing she needed to stand up to him? Whatever it was, she was not going to tolerate it. With each step, she whispered to herself, "I'll show you, ya bastard, making me and the kids feel like this all the time."

John felt overwhelmed with shame as he opened his bedroom door and gazed down the stairs. He felt guilty because his mother was engaged in a battle he knew she would lose. If she was this angry about his father believing he had wet himself—imagine how upset she would be if she learnt the truth. This was one secret he had to keep to himself. If that wasn't awful enough, things were about to get far worse.

John walked tentatively down the stairs and paused in the living room doorway. He watched as Annie stormed past Joe and stood in front of the TV, holding up the wet trousers. He ignored her as if she were not there. "See these? He didn't wet himself; it's lemonade, and he told you so. But guess what? You would not listen to him, would you?"

Joe stared blankly at her. She bent down and turned off the TV without looking away from him.

Eric loitered in the kitchen doorway, stunned at what he was seeing; the boys had never seen her like this before. Fear gripped them, aware that the outcome would not be favourable. She was generally submissive and non-confrontational, a victim of oppression and abuse. She knew she was going to make him angry, but she didn't seem to care this time. Her shaking was more due to frustration and anger than fear. Her maternal impulse was to protect her children at all costs—especially since she knew they had done nothing wrong—and confront this aggressive and unpredictable man who should have been doing the same. The boys could sense their father's rage rising beneath the surface, ready to erupt at any time. But she stood firm.

"Look at me when I am talking to you."

Joe breathed through his nose; his face darkened at Annie's defiance.

"You didn't believe John when he told you what happened, did you? You never listen to anyone, do you? Well, I've had enough, and one of these days, me and the boys are going to bugger off and leave. And what will you do then?"

Joe could hardly believe what she was saying. She had never spoken to him in this way before, and he was seething. He leaped up from his chair, immediate and explosive, causing his glass to tumble to the floor and beer to flow into the carpet. He pounced at her, grabbing her by the hair, and flinging her around the room like a rag doll. She started screaming at the top of her lungs. "Let go of me! Let go of me, ya bastard; you are hurting me!"

Joe dragged her violently across the room. He growled at her. "Leave me? You said you'd fucking leave me?"

Eric shouted at the top of his voice, "Get off her dad, you're hurting her!"

"You can shut the fuck up, or I'll paste you across the wall as well."

Annie kicked and fought with all her might, but her strength was no match for him. He slammed her face into the TV screen with one hand on the back of her hair and the other on the back of her neck, squashing and disfiguring her against the glass. "Do you see this? I paid for this. In fact, everything in this house belongs to me, including you. Do you understand?"

Annie yelled in desperation. "Get off me, will ya?" Joe continued to impose his power over her, tightening his grip.

"If I want to watch TV at home, I'll watch the fucking TV. You would not have any of this if it weren't for me!"

Eric stood in the doorway, clutching the knife in one hand. His whole body was screaming at him to do something to protect his mother, but the threat in Joe's voice held him back. He knew what his father was capable of and what would happen if he made a move. He wanted to run over and stick the knife in him, to make him pay for everything he'd done, but he was powerless. Instead, he watched as his father used nearly superhuman strength, driven by hatred and outrage, to brutally drag Annie across the room and into the hallway.

John backed away from the doorway and stood halfway up the stairs, terrified. Annie cried in agony as Joe dragged her over to the phone, which lay on top of a little table near the front entrance. He snatched the phone and shoved it hard against her ear while still clutching her hair. "Why don't you call that nosy bitch across the road? She'll help you! Oh, you can't, can you? Because, you know what, she doesn't even have a phone, does she?" He smashed the phone against the wall, before releasing Annie from his clutches.

The wave of abuse and physical assault was finally over. He hovered over her and panted heavily, attempting to catch his breath after such an enormous effort. Beads of sweat collected on his wrinkled brow, and a few stray strands of his meticulously slicked-back hair draped over his eyes.

John looked down at his mother, who was crying on the floor. His bottom lip began to quiver, and tears welled up in his eyes. Joe looked up and noticed him on the steps. "Are you happy now, boy? You, ya little bastard, are to blame for everything, not me! This is all your fault!" His voice was as loud as a cannon. "She comes down here yelling at me about your fucking trousers? The silly bitch is standing in front of my TV, threatening to leave me? Who the fuck does she think she is?"

Joe picked up his jacket and stepped over Annie, who was sobbing on the floor. He opened the front door and faced John before slamming it behind him. Tears streamed down John's face, and his heart ached as he saw his mother lying on the floor in a crumpled heap. Eric stood in the doorway, his eyes blank and his heart heavy. "Mum… I'm sorry, this was all my fault."

"It's not your fault, love. None of this is your fault." Annie replied softly.

Both boys sat down on the floor next to her. Eric caressed her face and stared into her eyes. "We can't live like this; please listen to me: he is going to kill you one of these days, I'm telling you." Annie sat motionless, head lowered, gently weeping, with John sobbing on the floor beside her.

Annie brushed her tears away with her palms while looking at Eric. "I promise you, we will leave one day. It's not the right time yet; I'm waiting until I have enough money saved, but when I do, I promise you both that we'll get as far away from here as possible and start a new life."

They both leaned in and held her tightly. Eric closed his eyes. He knew this couldn't go on. They could not continue to live under this constant onslaught of violence and anger. Something had to change. Though his mother would find it hard, he knew they had to leave.

TWENTY

Eric stood up straight and resolute, hands behind his back and chest puffed out like a pigeon. He could have been a soldier preparing to receive an honour for his valour on the battlefield, a graduate preparing to receive their degree or doctorate from a wily old professor, or a humble individual who had recently received an OBE for charitable work from her Majesty.

But this was not something to be proud of.

His thin legs were bruised, his knobbly knees scraped and bloodied. Several blades of grass protruded from his hair, and his eyes darted about the room in nervous anticipation, knowing what was going to happen. He was in the headmaster's office, in serious trouble, and awaiting his punishment. The headmaster sat back in his enormous leather chair and announced, "Day four of term, and you're already here, Maxwell! So, what happened? Who did you pick a fight with this time?"

Eric did not flinch. "Nobody, sir!"

"Nobody, sir?" He shouted. "Are you going to be one of those boys who will never learn? You've been sent here because you've been fighting, yes?"

"Yes, sir!" He responded firmly. The headmaster widened his eyes and motioned for him to continue. "Terry Kitchener was picking on Lawson Bartlett for no reason. I told Terry to leave him alone because Lawson's my mate, but he wouldn't listen; instead, he kept calling him names, which annoyed me. And Lawson's shy and would never hurt anyone, and this isn't the first time he's picked on him, so he needed to be taught a lesson. And I was the one to teach him. That's how I ended up here, sir."

The Headmaster paused for a brief moment. Clasping his hands together, his fingers interlaced, he began twiddling his thumbs. Eric stood as stiff as a sentry, awaiting his fate. He got up from his chair, circled his desk, and approached Eric. "I respect you for standing up for your friend Maxwell, but the school does not support this behaviour, nor will it condone any form of fighting or violence. Do you hear me?"

"Yes, sir!"

"You've only been back five minutes, and you're already in trouble. I have a feeling that this will not be the last time you stand in front of me. I will not allow vigilantes in my school to impose their own form of punishment, do you understand? As Headmaster of this school, it is my responsibility to set examples and standards."

"Sir!" Eric replied.

"Be outside my door at 1 pm. I will deal with you then. Dismissed."

The standard punishment for children was the cruel and barbaric 'Six of the Best.' Regardless of how minor the offence was, fear was the only way to instill respect in these kids. Most of the time, these acts were trivial at best, and being caned was an entirely unnecessary form of punishment, but that was how things were. Swearing, smoking, fighting, or being late to school would send the offender up to the office, where they would join the miserable queue of other sorry-looking souls awaiting their fate.

This practice typically took place shortly before afternoon classes, marking the start of a psychological torment that everyone in the school perceived as a strategy to maintain discipline.

Anyone who was invited to a meeting with the headmaster in

the morning would have to wait until 1 pm to find out what was in store for them. Trying to concentrate on classes while knowing what anguish lay ahead made the wait even more excruciating.

They would frequently assemble several students together, each anxiously anticipating the opening of the office door and the call of their name. A big clock on the wall ticked slowly above their heads, serving as both a timely reminder of where they were and a metaphorical countdown of what lay ahead.

The door opened, and the headmaster emerged. He was a gaunt, terribly thin man with pitiless eyes and a contemptuous and deprecating expression on his face. He seemed to relish inflicting agony on them; it appeared to be the highlight of his day.

"Maxwell!" he cried at the top of his lungs, his voice booming across the corridor, giving the others waiting another brief respite. Eric stepped boldly into the room with his heart thumping. He was shitting himself, but he reminded himself that this situation was not as dire as the one he was experiencing at home with that bastard, and he was eager to get it over with.

He heard the heavy door close behind him. "Bend over and face the window." Eric had been here before, so he knew what to expect. As he took his position, he braced himself for what he referred to as the 'six of the worst.' He felt a sharp swish of air behind him, followed by what felt like a cutlass slice across his buttocks.

Eric jerked bolt upright and winced in searing pain, the wind knocked out of him, but he drew a deep breath and refused to give him the satisfaction of knowing how much it hurt.

"Did I tell you to stand up?" The headmaster commanded forcefully, "Now bend over."

Whack!

The strike landed in the exact spot as the previous one—almost with pinpoint accuracy. Eric stood bolt upright again.

"Bend over."

Whack!

The searing agony radiated through Eric's body with excruciating intensity. Two strokes of the cane would have sufficed to reprimand any student and prevent them from misbehaving again. But the headmaster persisted with unwavering ferocity, almost enjoying the savagery of the situation.

After a few minutes, the door opened and Eric shuffled out into the corridor. Every movement he made sent a wave of agony through his entire body. He winced with each step, his shorts chafing against the raw skin beneath. His eyes were burning as he walked back to class.

The other kids who were still waiting their turn looked at him in utter amazement. They all knew who he was and what he stood for. He had a reputation as a tough kid, but he wasn't a bully looking for trouble. He wasn't troublesome, but he was a troubled soul, and God forbid that anyone did him or his brother wrong.

As he tentatively made his way back to the classroom, he heard the headmaster bellow out the name of the next boy; his voice reverberating through the corridor, and the process began again.

While the teacher spoke to the class, John stared out the window. He was exhausted from the frequent shouting and abuse his father hurled at his mother, but he also despised school. He was bored listening to his teacher ramble on about things he had no interest in. His difficulty in concentrating was not due to a lack of interest in the subject matter. He was in fact a clever and popular lad with a sharp sense of humour; he was creative and had an inquisitive imagination. He hated the stuffy, regimented routine of talk and chalk learning—and the discipline of following instructions.

He showed a complete disinterest in every subject. He couldn't understand how algebra worked or when he'd ever use it. The dulcet and monotonous tone from one teacher reading the works of Shakespeare out loud to the class was about as stimulating as watching the bloody wretched thing at the theatre. However, John did like one thing about school, and that was his history teacher, Mrs. Chapman, not just because she was lively and enthusiastic, but because she had an enormous pair of tits.

The only subject in which he excelled was woodwork. He was fascinated by the vices that perched at the end of the workbenches, these enormous metal crocodiles that gripped their prey in their steely jaws with an unmatched display of strength and authority. He loved the lathe machine, a massive green behemoth that sat in the corner of the room, gnawing and chewing its way through the wood.

Even the most basic tools at his disposal encapsulated him. The hammer and chisel were the standard bearers of the woodworking world in his eyes since they reminded him of himself and his brother. Eric was the hammer—forceful, strong, and dependable—and he was the chisel—sharp, creative, and useless without the other.

He was fascinated by how these basic blocks of wood could transform into a chair, a bird box, or anything else he could imagine, creating something out of nothing with a few tools.

"Maxwell! Are you joining us today, or what?" Mrs. Wilberforce shouted, her voice echoing around the classroom like a church bell.

"What?" He jolted from his seat.

"Do you care to join us today, or are you going to spend the whole lesson dozing? I could get someone to fetch you a pillow and a blanket if you like, as I seem to be causing you some inconvenience," she remarked sarcastically.

The entire class laughed in unison. John's cheeks reddened from embarrassment. "Erm, sorry, Miss."

He couldn't stop thinking about his father, shackled to the bed, and a woman rogering him with a rubber cock. It happened weeks ago, yet it still haunted him. He hadn't told anyone about that day, and he never would, including Eric, whom he trusted and confided in. Besides, it was hardly a casual topic to bring up over the breakfast table.

'Hey, did you know that Dad is a violent and utterly repulsive bastard who treats everyone like shit, especially Mum—who's a woman, by the way—and makes everyone's life absolutely miserable? It turns out he enjoys being bummed by a strong woman while shackled to the bed wearing a dog collar.'

No matter how hard he tried, he couldn't focus on the lesson. He fidgeted in his seat, fiddled with his fingers, and bit what remained of his nails instead of writing down everything on the board. When he grew bored with that, he began scratching his name onto the old wooden desk with a protractor. He became restless, which then made him disruptive.

He ripped a page from his book and tore it into strips, then rolled them into little balls. He placed them in his mouth, chewed them, and then flicked them at the back of Kimberley Featherstone's head, who was sitting in front of him. Again and again, he picked, chewed, rolled, and flicked these tiny paper missiles at her head while she remained completely unaware.

John reached into his desk and took out another piece of paper. He folded it and turned it into a paper aircraft. The teacher was writing on the board with her back to the class when John got up and flung this paper bird across the room. As soon as it left his fingers, it soared vertically into the air, almost colliding with the ceiling lights before taking a turn and heading towards Mrs. Winterbourne.

As she turned to address the class, it smacked her square in the face. The entire room burst into laughter. She glanced at the paper plane lying at her feet before addressing the class in a furious tone. "This is no laughing matter. Do you all hear me?" She knew who the offender was right away; she'd been watching him during the class.

"John Maxwell, come here immediately!" she exclaimed, gesturing to him.

"It wasn't me, Miss," he said, trying not to smirk.

"Don't you dare backchat me, boy! Get here now!"
He stood, kicking his chair back, and slowly made his way to the front of the classroom, dragging his feet and drooping his arms by his sides. As he passed, a few kids giggled quietly at him. To a select few, he was always the class clown, making everyone around him laugh. This was his way of dealing with his inner grief.

Mrs. Winterbourne held a different opinion of John; she disliked him. She was aware that he was a problematic and disconnected boy, but she didn't care because he had humiliated her in front of the class.

He approached the front of the room and stood facing her. She scowled at him. She was at the end of her tether, angry over the umpteen amount of chances she had given him. He never seemed to learn anything in this class, or any previous ones. She found him to be a major pain in the arse. With all eyes on him, he realised he had gone too far this time, but he didn't really care.

"Maxwell, how long have you been back? Four days? And you've already disrupted my class twice! It may have been the excitement of returning to school, or you were just trying to show off to the young ladies in the class, so I gave you the benefit of the doubt on that one."

In her caustic, authoritative style, Mrs. Winterbourne spoke to the entire class. "Alright, everyone, pay attention. I think it's time to show John here that I will not stand for any kind of disruption in my classroom. In fact, I hope that everyone will learn a valuable lesson from this."

John bit his lower lip, knowing what she meant.

She approached her desk, opened a drawer, and took out a wooden ruler. She approached him slowly, as if on purpose, to heighten the suspense and extract every last drop of fear from him. The entire class sat quietly in their chairs, making it impossible to hear anything else.

She said forcefully, "Hold your hand out, now."

He did exactly what he was told. He held his scrawny arm out as far as it would reach, palm upturned. Shaking with anxiety, he swallowed hard and glanced at her with merciful eyes. His face was the focus of twenty-nine pairs of eyes, anticipating his reaction.

Whack!

John was taken by surprise. He anticipated a countdown of some sort, but instead, she struck him twice across the palm of his hand, without warning. The pain that followed was excruciating. Once his hand began to throb, it quickly heated up and began to sting. The class looked on, the other boys open-mouthed and the girls wincing in their seats.

To their surprise, though, he remained silent throughout the ordeal. A small frown spread across his face as he tightened his jaw, and a few beads of perspiration formed on his forehead. Mrs. Winterbourne returned to her desk and put the ruler back into the drawer. She squinted at John. "Go back to your seat now." He lowered his head and placed his palm under his arm to alleviate the pain. She addressed the class, "Does anyone have something to say? No, I didn't think so. Shall we carry on with the lesson then?"

TWENTY-ONE

Joe mounted the kerb and parked outside the local newsagent's. It wasn't a convenient nor a safe place to stop, but he was so arrogant he didn't actually give a shit. Several onlookers—mainly middle-aged ladies—tutted and looked on in disgust at his disregard and lack of respect. He opened his door, and a gust of wind almost took it off its hinges. He stepped out, slammed the door shut, and adjusted his collar and cap. He glanced at the gossiping women as they glared at him. He gave them a wry smile, knowing that this would annoy them and give them something else to moan about. He crossed over the road and made his way towards the shop.

Fred saw him approaching through his shop's window. He sighed a little and braced himself as he knew exactly what Mr. Maxwell was coming for. The door opened, and Joe heard the tinkling sound of the bell above his head. He walked towards Fred, who stood behind the counter. "I'm not happy it's late. I came last week, and you weren't here. Ya missus said you were out. Maybe it was a coincidence, but I think you were hiding out the back."

Fred started to stutter nervously. Joe continued, "You know what day I come, and you know what time I come. You miss a payment again, and I'll torch this fucking place with you and ya family in here, you hear me?"

"I...I'm sorry, Mr. Maxwell; I had a family emergency."

"I don't care what emergency you had. You owe money; you pay it. And you pay it on time." Fred rang the till, pulled out several notes, and handed over the money. The bell tinkled again, and a woman walked into the shop. Joe recognised her. "Hello Mildred, how are you?"

Mildred smiled warmly at him. "Oh hello, Mr. Maxwell, I'm very well thank you, how are you?"

"I'm fine, Mildred, thanks for asking. I've just been chatting with Fred here, and he said the one-hundredth customer who walks in here today will get their shopping for free! And guess what?"

Mildred was elated. "What, really? Oh my goodness, that's amazing; thank you very much. I can't believe my luck."

Joe smiled broadly and looked over to Fred. "Today's her lucky day, innit, Fred?"

Fred smiled through gritted teeth. "It certainly is, Mr. Maxwell."

"Right, well, I best be off; have a good day." Joe folded the money up and tucked it into the inside pocket. He grabbed two bars of chocolate from the display on the way out. He sauntered across the road towards his car, climbed in, and drove off down the road.

As Edward drove off in his car, Stan locked his front door. He had seen Annie get out of a stranger's car and stand talking to him. In this close-knit community, where everyone knew each other's business, anything out of the norm wouldn't go unnoticed. Stan wasn't the type of bloke who got involved with all that titter-tatter. He was as straight as the day was long and wouldn't impose himself or his opinions on anybody unless asked. Every day at midday he walked to the local pub and spent a few hours playing dominoes and cards with a few other men over several pints of bitter.

The Crown boasted sparse furnishings and an unsavoury reputation, drawing an eclectic mix of patrons from tough, working-class men to various low-lifes, hangers-on, and even certain members of the criminal underworld. Between the hours of 11 am and 2 pm, there were usually some regulars dotted about the place, each seeking solace from the burdens of work, their wives, or general everyday life.

The old and familiar faces were as much a part of the furniture as the mahogany bar they propped up. Regulars included Bobby Peters, who worked for the Royal Mail, and Frankie Townshend, the local milkman, who both enjoyed having a few loose ones after their busy rounds before heading off to bed for the afternoon.

Gerry Ferguson worked nights as a railway porter and would often disappear down the back lane with one of the 'ladies of easy virtue' before returning to his pint of Guinness and his game of dominoes before heading home to his wife.

Stan was halfway through his second pint when a familiar figure entered the pub through the side door. Joe walked straight up to the bar and ordered his drink. "Pint of bitter," he ordered sharply. This place was his local and so familiar to him. He had so many memories here; he always felt Doris's presence when he walked through the doors, even though she had been gone for years. It took him back in time.

Joe fondly remembered how she had helped and supported him when he came out of the army. Most importantly, she helped him secure a job, not just any job, but one that involved working for Ronnie. And in his eyes, he owed her everything. She was the only woman he had ever shown total respect for. Doris had suddenly upped and left and started a new life somewhere else; nobody knew where or why, apart from maybe one person, Franco, who had also disappeared suddenly. She had left her daughter Elizabetta behind, whom Ronnie adopted as his own daughter.

Even after all these years, the place was still exactly the same. The only difference now was that a miserable bastard was running it. The landlord poured Joe's drink and handed it over to him. Joe noticed Stan playing cards with three other men and quickly made a quick bee-line towards them. "Budge up, lads; room for one more, eh?"

Whether they wanted him to join them or not, he grabbed a stool and sat down, knowing that none of them would ever say no. Gerry raised his eyebrows and glanced over at Des, who seemed unfazed by his status as the local piss head. Tommy took a long drag on his cigarette and sipped his stout. Stan and Joe were neighbours, and although they didn't really know each other on a personal level, Stan certainly knew he was an unsavoury character and had a bad reputation.

The lads looked at each other, then at Stan, each waiting for someone to speak up and tell him they didn't want him to play. As usual, nobody had the guts to do so.

"Alright, Joe?" Stan said, much to everyone's surprise, "Always room for one more."

Joe smirked, and the lads shuffled about to make room for him. Joe turned towards the landlord. "Round of drinks over here when ya ready."

"I need a word with you, Joe," the landlord said, "but in private."

"What about?"

"Well, like I said, in private." He beckoned Joe over to the bar. Joe stood up and walked over towards him. The landlord leaned over the bar and spoke quietly. "Your tab's overdue."

Joe looked him dead in the eyes. "And…?"

"Look, I hate to be telling you this, but the brewery is starting to ask questions," he stuttered. "If you don't pay it, then they'll start sniffing about, and I'll get into trouble and…"

Joe didn't blink. "Okay, well, you should have said so." He

reached into his coat pocket and pulled out a five-pound note. He handed it over to him. "This should cover it."

The landlord's eyes widened, and he nodded enthusiastically. "Yeah, that's great, thank you!"

"Good. Now fetch us a round of drinks and keep them coming."

A few hours had passed, and Joe, Stan, and the others were still playing poker. The pub had officially closed for the afternoon, but Joe insisted on keeping the drinks flowing, and they continued to play on. Since Joe was determined to recoup the five pounds he had just paid the landlord from Ronnie's shop money, the bar had turned into a lock-in, with no one leaving. Joe knocked another whiskey back and slid the glass across the table next to him with the other empties. He glanced at his cards once more before tossing them in the centre of the table with a look of disgust and a frustrated yell. "Fuck's sake!"

Des, an old, weathered, and wizened gentleman of Jamaican descent, roared with glee as he reached over the table and scooped his winnings up in his wrinkly, cigar-like hands. "Lovely!" he muttered in his dark, gruff voice, "That'll pay my rent this week and keep my old lady off my back!"

Stan and the others chuckled quietly, but Joe didn't find it amusing; he was a terrible loser and was growing increasingly annoyed. Tommy chimed in as he poured the remaining beer into his glass, saying, "Well, I think that's you done, isn't it, Joe?"

Joe reached into his coat pocket and pulled out his last fiver. He slapped it down hard on the table."I ain't finished yet, and nobody tells me I'm done. You hear me, Tommy?"

Twenty minutes later Joe was down to his last pound. He drained another whisky and gasped loudly as it burnt the back of his throat. His right elbow rested on the table, his fist buried deep into his cheek, while his left hand flicked the corner of his cards, all while observing the game and the table. Tommy folded, quickly followed by Stan. Jerry turned his cards over and sorted them on the table. "Three of a kind," he remarked hopefully as three sevens lay in a straight line.

Good.

Joe turned his cards and fanned them out on the table in front of him. A king, ten, eight, seven, and five of clubs. "I think you'll find that's a flush." Joe sat back in his chair, looking down at his cards and then at Gerry. He smiled in a cocky manner, knowing his hand would be difficult to beat.

Des widened his eyes and nodded in approval. It would take something special to trump Joe's hand. He stared at his face-down cards for several moments, then carefully turned them over onto the table and fanned them out. With three aces and two threes—a full house—Des's hand had everyone's attention. "I think you will find I've trumped ya," Des said as he sat back in his chair and started laughing, almost mocking Joe and gloating over his incredible poker-playing skills.

Joe had been well and truly fucked. Gerry flung his hands in the air and shouted, "You lucky bastard!" Tommy poured another drink and lit a cigarette, while Stan sat still and silent. Out of the corner of his eye, he glanced at Joe, his eyes darkening as if the devil had taken control of him. In a fit of rage, he flipped the table into the air, the money, cards, ashtray, glasses, and bottles flying all over the room. "You fucking cunt!"

He was out of control, screaming and shouting at the top of his voice. Nobody dared get in his way as they knew he would beat the shit out of them. The red mist finally cleared. He grabbed his coat and walked out, leaving the disarray behind him.

TWENTY-TWO

"Two teas," the café owner said as she placed them down onto the table. Annie smiled warmly in appreciation and gazed across the table at Edward, who was finishing off his piece of chocolate cake. He chewed his food slowly and deliberately as he glanced out the window. He looked like his mind was somewhere else.

The sounds of the coffee machines hissing, whistling, and whirring; the clunking and clattering of dishes from the kitchen; and the incomprehensible chatter from the other customers in the cafe were loud and persistent. She reached over the table and grabbed his hand, trying to get his attention. He turned and smiled at her.

"You seem deep in thought; are you okay?" She asked.

"Yeah, I'm fine; I was just thinking about Joe." Annie looked confused, as always when he mentioned Joe, which he seemed to do frequently when they met up, but she didn't say anything.

Over the past few months, they had settled into a quiet rhythm. It started simply enough: meeting at a local café for tea and cake, where their light-hearted conversations filled the air with laughter and warmth. But as the weeks went by, what had begun as friendly companionship turned into something more. There was a magnetic pull between them—unspoken but undeniable.

The café was small and cosy with warm lighting and checkered tablecloths, offering a brief escape from the harsh realities of her life with Joe. Each time she met Edward, she felt like she was stepping into a different world, one filled with the possibility of happiness.

Sitting across from each other at their usual table, their eyes met constantly. She found herself drawn to his charm, the easy way he smiled, the softness in his voice that was such a contrast to the harshness she endured at home. Edward made her feel safe; he made her feel alive in a way she hadn't in years.

They would often take leisurely walks around the park's lake, feeding the ducks and swans as they sat on benches and talked endlessly about anything and everything. She had not told a soul, not even her closest friend Peggy, about what was going on or what she was up to; this was her time—her time to be Annie and to escape from her sad world.

Over the months they became close. Annie was falling in love and was hoping Edward felt the same way. She felt free and alive with him; she hadn't felt like this in years. Edward was everything Joe used to be. She hung onto every word that poured out of his mouth—a mouth she had kissed with her lips, a mouth that had whispered sweet nothings in her ear. He understood how deeply unhappy she was, and he promised to rescue her from her miserable life, promising to love, cherish, and care for her and her boys forever.

It was just a matter of time before they would all leave and be a family together.

Between the cups of tea and the chit-chat, the conversation was light-hearted and enjoyable. She knew it was easier for him as he was single, had no children, and had not even been married. He continued to live at home with his mother in a cramped two-up, two-down cottage in an affluent area of town. He had harboured dreams of joining the army until he discovered he had a hearing defect and was colour blind. Drifting in and out of jobs, each as dull and monotonous as the other, had taken its toll on him until some auntie he hardly knew died and he received a fairly healthy inheritance that he'd lived off ever since.

It was time to go, and Edward drove her home in complete

silence. It was their way of readying themselves to get back to normality. Annie would use this time to prepare herself to return to her world. Similar to an actor putting on makeup and getting ready for the curtain to rise, she needed to change from the giddy, carefree woman she felt when she was with Edward to the quiet, subdued, and lonely woman she was.

Edward had warned her she had to be normal at home; she could not change her behaviour, or Joe would know something was going on. She breathed deeply, knowing Edward was right in what he was saying: she had to be calm and composed when she got home. He pulled up to the top of her road and caressed her cheek, looking deep into her eyes.

"Look, it won't be long before we can all be together. I love you." She closed her eyes and sank back into the seat. She couldn't believe what she was hearing. She opened her eyes and looked at him, her face beaming. "How can I possibly act normal at home now that you've just said that?" she asked, her eyes wide with shock.

"Well, you have to promise me you will, as we don't want him knowing; if he found out, he would not make this easy for us, so if this is what you want, you have to do this for us."

"It is what I want, I promise."

"Come on, you better go. I'll see you soon." He leaned down and planted a kiss on her lips, after which she closed her eyes. As he withdrew, she smiled and turned to open the door.

"Looking forward to it already."

"Remember, you don't want him to notice anything unusual."

Annie climbed out of the car and was about to close the door when she leaned over towards him to have one last word. "I'm not going to risk anything. I love you."

Edward stared into her eyes and smiled. She looked at him and felt reluctant to leave but knew she had to. He nodded, and Annie closed the car door. She peered through the glass to catch one last glimpse of him and gave him a goodbye wave before making her way down the road. She arrived at her front door, fumbling in her bag for her keys. She looked up the road, but he had already driven off.

TWENTY-THREE

Ronnie had called a meeting with Joe and several other members of the firm. Joe had been working for Ronnie long enough to realise that something serious was coming, and today was one of those days. Ronnie tugged on his cigar and tapped his ash into the ashtray. He leaned back in his chair, blowing a thick cloud of smoke into the air before addressing the room. "Okay, listen up everyone. There's a shipment of guns arriving in the next few weeks—real heavy-duty, army-grade stuff."

Ronnie wasn't his usual relaxed self; there was a sharper edge to his gaze, a tension that made everyone in the room sit up and listen.

Joe's face remained impassive, but he felt a knot form in his stomach. He knew exactly what kind of people were involved in arms deals, and they weren't the sort you crossed lightly. Still, he didn't show hesitation, knowing that any sign of doubt would only weaken his position with Ronnie.

"What's the plan?" Joe asked, his voice steady.

Ronnie leaned back in his chair, studying Joe carefully before speaking again. "I have already assigned a crew to remove the guns from the ship. But once they're off, that's where you'll come in. I need you to oversee the transfer—make sure everything goes smoothly. Then, you'll stash them somewhere safe until I give the word."

He took another drag and exhaled slowly. "But listen carefully, these people we're dealing with—they're nasty bastards—so don't fuck it up 'cause they don't take kindly to fuck-ups. If they find out someone's intercepting their shipment, it could turn ugly. Fast."

Joe nodded, understanding the weight of what Ronnie was saying. The stakes were more significant than anything they had faced previously. The docks were constantly teeming with security, and the focus wasn't solely on removing them from the boat but also on evading potential observers, both within and beyond the law.

"Where do you want them hidden?" Joe enquired without any delay. If Ronnie had called him in for this job, it meant he trusted him. It was a chance to prove his worth.

"There's an old warehouse in the east end. Out of the way, barely anyone goes near it anymore. You stash them there, keep it locked down, and don't tell a soul. I'll have more details when I get them. Right, off you go."

Ronnie added. "I can't take any chances with this one, fellas. This is too big. The shipment comes in, and once it's off the boat, you make sure it disappears."

Ronnie held up a hand and pointed as they began to flow out the door. "Oh, I want a quick word."

Joe pivoted. "Yeah?"

"Not you; with Roy."

Joe left the room, curious about what they were discussing.

"Close the door behind you."

He lingered behind the door for a moment, filled with paranoia and anxiety, yearning for a drink as he sensed they were about to discuss him.

Roy moved to the desk where Ronnie was sitting. "All okay?"

Ronnie reclined on his seat. "Something's not right with him."

"Who?"

"You know who I mean. Joe. Just make sure you're there for the shipment; that's my top priority. I've got someone sorting him."

"Yeah, you know me; I won't let you down."

Ronnie picked up the phone and dialled. "It's me. It's sorted. He'll be there, you just make sure you do what you've gotta do."

TWENTY-FOUR

John and Eric walked in the back door. Their mum was cleaning the kitchen table. "Hi boys, you two had a good day at school?"

Silence.

They both appeared ashen-faced and with no reply, Annie knew something was wrong. She paused and looked at them with a puzzled expression. "What's going on?"

Eric blurted out "Well, I was given the cane today."

"Why, what have you done?"

"You know my mate, Lawson? He was getting picked on by Terry Kitchener, who thinks he's a top dog at school, but he's just a dickhead," he ranted.

"Um, language, Eric! You've just had the cane, but I will give you a clip round the ear if you carry on saying words like that." She folded her arms. "Right. So let me guess, you ended up fighting with him?"

"He deserved it. I hate bullies; I see enough of that here at home."

She listened to what he had to say. He was animated and agitated, and although she knew what he'd done was wrong, she understood why.

"I'm telling ya, he is a coward, Mum; all bullies are." He looked at her, knowing she understood who he was talking about. He then continued with his rant. "He started it; he threw the first punch, so I punched him back, we got into a scuffle and then we got caught."

"Show me," she said with a flick of her head.

"Show you what?"

"Your bum."

He undid his trousers and pulled them down to below his waist before hitching his underpants up. She could see the marks on the top of his cheeks; there were several very painful-looking reddish marks along his cheeks, and the bruising was also visible. Annie inhaled sharply through her teeth. "Go and have a bath; that should help soothe it, and then when you get out, I will put some cream on it." He nodded and pulled up his trousers.

She looked at John. "And what have you been up to?"

"I got the ruler today." He held his hand out to her, revealing the marks on his palm. "Look, she whacked me so hard."

"For God's sake, not you 'n' all. So what did you do then?"

He stood in front of Annie, his thoughts racing with what reason to offer. "School's boring, Mum; I hate it." Of all the excuses he could have chosen, he picked this one.

She fixed him with a harsh look. "I know you don't like it, but you haven't got a choice; you need to go. But you still haven't told me what you did to get the ruler."

"I made a paper plane and threw it in the air, and it hit the teacher in the head."

Eric sniggered.

"And it's her fault, 'cause if her lesson was interesting, then I wouldn't be making them, would I?" John added, trying to justify and seek approval for his actions.

Annie puckered her lips, trying not to giggle. "Jump in the bath after Eric, and I'll give you some cream too." She couldn't express her anger toward either of them. She felt a sense of responsibility, knowing that if she had left Joe, their behaviour would have continued anyway. She was fully aware the school wouldn't tolerate this, as they were all victims of Joe's temper, and she felt she had failed them. "Don't tell your father about this, okay?"

The boys exchanged nods. Eric responded: "We wouldn't tell him because he doesn't even talk to us anyway." She grabbed the cloth and resumed cleaning the kitchen table as they disappeared upstairs.

*

Annie was having a well-earned rest. All was quiet and settled, and this was how she liked it. She sat in the living room and flicked through a magazine while puffing on a cigarette. The clock on the mantelpiece ticked away, the only noise. Everything was immaculately clean and in its place. She wouldn't want it any other way.

She had arranged the plump and shapely scatter cushions at curious angles, complementing the sofa's contours. Both the mahogany coffee table and the rug on the floor aligned parallel to the hearth. There was not a single speck of dust, crumb, or ball of fluff in the place. Annie was very house proud.

She took one last drag and stubbed it out in the ashtray on the small side table next to her before putting her magazine neatly away with the others on the corner of the coffee table. She lived on her nerves, never knowing what version of Joe she would encounter when he walked through the door. She cast her mind back to how he used to be.

When did it all change, and more importantly, why?

In the early days he wasn't a drinker. He occasionally enjoyed a drink and may have indulged in excess during events such as weddings and funerals, but who didn't? She reflected about the early days of their relationship, before the criminal world had completely consumed him. Joe used to smile more and even laugh quite a bit, but she hadn't heard him do either of those things in a long, long time.

She actually didn't know what had changed him, what had made him start to drink, gamble, and be such a horrible bastard. Was it Ronnie? Was it the work he did for him that finally tipped him over the edge? She might never discover the truth, as it remained unspoken and unpermitted. In Joe's eyes, Annie and the boys were meant to be seen and not heard.

Joe led a double life; at home, he was miserable and a bully, but once he left the house, he transformed into a completely different person. He was a gentleman, opening doors for the ladies, giving the kids playing in the street a few coppers, and generally keeping his head down and going about his business.

Most family homes likely operated this way, with the exception of Peggy's, where she held the position of authority and poor Albert simply followed her instructions. Men were the breadwinners, and women were the homemakers. They didn't live in a big house in a smart area, as that would bring unwanted attention from neighbours and the boys in blue. They led a comfortable lifestyle, with regular influxes of cash from the smartly dressed men who frequented the house.

The living room would often be filled with several men smoking endless cigarettes and talking business in hushed tones as she busied herself making pots of tea and sandwiches. Their home had transformed into a criminal fortress. Joe welcomed visitors into their home for meetings, including guys she didn't know or trust.

Annie would turn a blind eye to all the comings and goings and a deaf ear to the whispered conversations. She knew what they did was wrong, but she also liked the fact that they didn't struggle. The only thing she did struggle with was the fact there were guns under her roof where her boys lived. She tolerated everything else that went on because she had no other choice. She had no control over the universe Joe had introduced into their lives, and there was nothing she could do about it.

She exhaled deeply, her heart throbbing with the weight of the memories. She desired more for herself and her sons. But now, it appeared like they were all just trying to survive.

She sat back on the sofa, her mind scrambled. She always felt exhausted due to her troubled mind. She just needed to stay strong, save as much as she could, and think about her future with Edward and her boys.

It was a bright, sunny day. The sun was beaming through the window, and she could feel the warmth on her face. Her eyes were closed. The ticking of the clock further relaxed her; she could sense her eyes growing increasingly heavy. Fighting to stay awake, she finally succumbed; her eyes blinked a few times, and she drifted off to sleep.

The sound of the front door opening and closing abruptly woke Annie. Her body jolted as she sat upright and rubbed her eyes before realising where she was—and, more importantly, what time it was. Her heart leapt in her chest, panic gripping her for a moment. She jumped up from the sofa and rushed towards the kitchen, thinking, "Shit, it's Joe, and I haven't made his dinner."

As she began to rummage through the cupboards, Joe approached the kitchen. She braced herself, expecting his usual foul mood, the angry muttering. However, tonight was different.

"Who wants fish 'n' chips then?" He announced, strolling into the kitchen with a parcel wrapped in old newspapers and tucked under his arm like he was carrying a rugby ball. "Annie, get the plates out, will ya?"

Hearing their father's voice, the boys made their way downstairs and hesitated in the doorway, unsure how to respond. They both looked at Joe as if he were a stranger.

Joe turned to face them. "I got us all dinner. Thought I'd treat you all."

Annie exchanged a glance with the boys, who appeared just as perplexed as she was. Was this actually happening? Was

Joe attempting to be kind? She felt a glimmer of hope, but soon pushed it down, afraid of becoming too comfortable. With Joe, these moments of peace were always fleeting, and always followed by a storm.

The boys sat down at the table and Annie served their dinner. The fried fish, chips, and peas may have been a simple meal, but it was a real treat compared to their normal dinners.

Joe tucked straight in and started to chat, his voice lighter, his mood excitable. "Tuck in before it gets cold."

Annie nodded, but a sense of apprehension persisted. This wasn't the man who berated, belittled and bullied her. This man, seated at the table, smiling and offering food, was a stranger.

As they ate, the tension in the room increased, but no one dared say anything. The boys remained quiet, exchanging glances now and then, apparently perplexed by their dad's abrupt change in behaviour. Annie attempted to eat, but the meal felt heavy in her stomach. She hoped that Joe had turned a corner and that this rare generosity would remain. But deep down, she knew in her heart it wouldn't. She had learnt not to rely on these moments of normality. They were usually followed by something worse.

After dinner, Joe sat back in his chair, stroking his stomach with satisfaction. As the boys cleaned up, Annie stood by the back door, peering out at the darkening backyard. She felt Joe's gaze on her, but she did not look around. Instead, she concentrated on the sound of the boys' voices as they washed the dishes, the clink of plates, and the rush of water.

Joe reached into his trouser pocket and pulled out a wad of cash. "This is for you," he said, tossing several notes onto the table. "Here's some housekeeping for the next couple of weeks." He handed some change to the boys. "Here you go, boys; go get yourselves some sweets or something."

The boys tentatively took the money from Joe's enormous

hand and thanked him under their breath. Annie looked at them and raised her eyebrows, knowing too well that this would be short-lived.

TWENTY-FIVE

Joe entered the living room to find Annie curled up with a magazine and the lads engrossed in front of the TV. "Right, Eric, I want you at the allotment with me today, so get ya boots on quick smart."

"I can't, Dad; I've got homework to do."

He grumbled as he glanced over to John, "Bloody homework, since when did you do that shit? Right, well in that case, John, you can come with me instead."

Eric jumped up off the sofa. "No, I'll come." He didn't want John to go to the allotment alone with him. He was aware that it was unsafe for him to be alone with him, and he felt a strong need to protect his brother.

"You've just told me you've got homework to do, so John'll come with me."

"Nah, it's okay; I can do it when I get back. Anyway, he will be useless. Anything you need help with, I will do it."

John piped up. "Oi, you! Who are you calling useless? I'll go if you have homework." There was a reluctance in his voice. Eric shot him a look.

"No, John, I've said I'll go now, so you stay here."

Joe was growing impatient. "Just bloody sort it out, will ya? I'll be in the car, so whoever's coming had better get a bloody move on."

Annie looked through the window and watched him get into the car and start the engine. "Thank you for keeping the peace, son," she said softly as Joe beeped the horn, impatient as ever. "You'd better go; best not keep his Royal Highness waiting."

"Better hurry," John said. "You better not keep the miserable git waiting."

Annie yelped. "John, language!"

It was a glorious sunny day. Eric had been diligently toiling away for an hour or so, ensuring he kept himself occupied and out of the way by turning the dirt over with a shovel on a small patch of land and removing weeds and stones into a nearby wheelbarrow. Working on the hard, brittle dirt caused blisters and pain on his hands; the labour was heavy and exhausting. Joe, meanwhile, stood outside his shed with a bottle of scotch in his hand, staring unblinkingly as perspiration ran down Eric's hot, crimson brow and over his face.

Eric was on his hands and knees, picking worms out of the soil, his baggy shirt covered in dirt and sweat, and his spindly legs sticking out from beneath his shorts. He could feel Joe's eyes burning into the back of his head, and as he glanced over his shoulder, he saw him taking a swig with one hand and rubbing his crotch over his trousers with the other.

A sick feeling crept into Eric's stomach. He'd anticipated this moment would come at some point, and a feeling of dread washed over him. Joe shouted over to him. "Come in the shed; I need your help." Eric clambered to his feet, but he was apprehensive. He knew he couldn't say no. He closed his eyes, took a deep breath, and walked towards him.

"What's up? What do you need me to do?" He asked, pretending everything was okay.

After gulping down a shot of scotch, Joe stepped to one side and gestured to Eric to enter the shed before following him. Joe gently closed the door behind him and leered at him. "Come over here," he gestured with a tip of his head.

"No, I've got the digging to do; that's what you brought me up here for, innit?"

Joe lunged forward unsteadily and grabbed Eric's crotch. Eric tried to push him away, but Joe overpowered him. Joe held onto him tightly, twisting his balls. "Dad, please don't. You're hurting me." His eyes watered. "Please no, not again."

"Shut up, I'm not gonna hurt you; you enjoy it." He relaxed his grip on Eric, but he did not let go and pulled him closer. He took a seat in his chair, unbuckled his trousers, and finally released his grip. He took out his cock, which stood to attention in his hand. "On ya knees, boy... It ain't gonna suck itself, is it?"

"Dad, please don't. I don't_" He pleaded with his dad as he recoiled, but he shouted over him.

"Shut that fucking door and get back over here! It's either going in ya mouth or up ya arse, your choice!"

Eric's heart raced, his mind whirled, but he was grateful that he had come instead of John. Eric braced himself as he walked over to him, dropping to his knees and reluctantly taking his old man in his hand. He didn't like either option, but he knew that this would be less painful.

"Getting brave, ain't we, son... think you're a big man?" Joe scowled as he grasped Eric's head tightly and thrust his cock into his mouth. "I'll show you what a big man is. And don't even think about biting it."

The sound of someone whistling a tune and the approaching heavy footsteps halted Joe's pleasure. He quickly pushed Eric backwards onto the floor. "Don't say anything." Joe stood up, straightened his trousers, and peered out the window to see who it was. "It's Nigel. Don't make a fuss, you hear me?"

Nigel was a doddery old man who owned the plot next to Joe's. He was a cheery old boy with two arthritic knees that made him waddle like a duck, and you could smell him before you could see him with his pipe permanently nestled in the corner of his mouth. Joe flung open the shed door and closed it behind him. "Alright, Nige, what are you doing up here today? You don't usually come up here this early." Joe was irritated as he thought nobody would interrupt his dirty little antics.

Sitting on the floor of the shed, Eric could feel the tears dripping down his cheeks as he spat into his palms and wiped the distaste from his mouth. He couldn't believe his dad had just jumped up, gone out, and started talking to Nigel as if nothing had happened.

"I've just come up here to potter about and get away from the missus; she's driving me mad, if I'm honest. You as well, eh?"

Joe replied nonchalantly. "Yeah, something like that."

"Here, I couldn't borrow a shovel, could I?"

"Yeah, of course you can." Joe opened the shed door and gave Eric a sinister look. "Can you grab Nige a shovel?"

Eric gathered himself and got up off the floor. "Yeah, of course." He grabbed it and held onto it tightly. He would have loved nothing more than to smack it straight over his dad's head and tell Nigel everything. Flushed with emotion, he brushed past his dad and handed it to Nigel.

"Thanks, son," Nigel said, grabbing it out of his hand.

"No problem," Eric replied sheepishly, avoiding eye contact.

Nigel raised his eyebrows and smiled. "You're a good lad, ain't ya, helping your dad out on a hot day like this."

Eric dropped his head, and he wiped his mouth with the back of his hand, mumbling, "Yeah, something like that."

Joe pulled him in closer. "Yeah, he loves to help his dad, don't you, son?"

"Good lad," Nigel grinned. "Right, I best get on. Thanks for this. I'll bring it back when I'm done."

Eric walked back towards the muddy patch, picked the fork

up, and started to turn the soil again, stabbing the ground with real vigour and aggression. His heart pounded in his chest as the sweat dripped off his forehead; all he could think about was digging his dad's grave and burying him in it. "One day, you bastard," he muttered to himself, "One day."

Eric, wearing a hangdog expression, shuffled into the kitchen. Annie stood at the oven, cooking dinner, while John was setting the table. "Hello love, how'd ya get on?" She asked, "Where's ya dad?"

Eric, hot and bothered and covered in muck, snapped back. "I don't know and I don't care."

"Why, whatever's the matter? What happened?" She noticed every time Eric came back from the allotment, his mood was always different. He was distant, angry, and aggressive. He hesitated for a second and then let his frustrations pour out of his mouth.

"He asked me to help him, but did he help me? Did he bollocks! All he did was drink while I broke my back all day digging his patch. I should've dug a big hole and pushed him in it." He held his hands out, palms up, to show his blisters. "Look at these, all because of that lazy bastard!"

"Language, Eric."

"No, I don't care, Mum; I'm fed up with him." He wiped his mouth, his eyes vacant and empty. "If he's not beating the shit out of us, he's drinking all the time. He wanted some help in the shed, so I went in, and… and…" Eric was flustered; his breathing became shallow, and then he started panting like he was about to have a panic attack.

He paused momentarily, realising that his emotions were overwhelming and that he needed to stop before he said too much. Every time something like this had happened, he tried to reveal the evil that he was being subjected to, but he just couldn't bring himself to say it. He knew it would destroy her.

"What's the matter?" She asked with a deep, concerned look on her face, "Sit yourself down and breathe."

His sad eyes filled with tears as he took a seat at the table. He closed his eyes and shook his head. "It doesn't matter. His drinking is getting worse, Mum," he said.

She put her arm on Eric's shoulder and gave it a reassuring squeeze. "Try not to upset yourself, love. It's been a hot day, and I can imagine how hard you've worked; you must be exhausted. Have a soak in the bath after dinner; that'll help no end."

Eric held his frustration in, as this was his answer to everything: have a bath or a cup of tea. Everything will be alright. And yet they all knew it was never going to get any better and nothing would ever change. He gave a half-hearted nod.

John gazed over at him. Deep down in the pit of his stomach, he knew something had happened; he was not accustomed to seeing his brother so anxious.

Eric wiped his eyes, took a deep breath, looked at his mum and said, "Yeah, you're right; a bath might help. But you know what might help more: if you leave him, then none of us will have to put up with this shit anymore."

"I'm trying to love, and we will one day, but I can't at the moment. I try my hardest to make you boys happy," she responded reassuringly, knowing he was right.

"We know you do; this ain't about what you do for us; it's about what he *doesn't* do and the way he treats you like the shit on his shoes. You think that's okay, and it's acceptable for him to beat you? Can't we just pack our bags and go while he's not here?" Eric's voice was firm, hopeful.

She sighed in frustration. "I can't; it… it's complicated."

Eric pressed on. "What's complicated about packing our stuff and going somewhere safe?"

"Don't ya think I haven't thought about this? Even Aunt Peggy has said we can all go to hers, but it's not that simple," she yelled and shrugged her shoulders, "You know what he's like and what he's capable of. We can't just up and leave; where are we gonna go, huh? And even if we had somewhere to go, he'd come looking for us."

With her words echoing in their ears, the boys lowered their heads. She composed herself and continued. "I've been putting money away for years—just a few bob here and there—but it all adds up. Just give it time. It won't be long, I promise. Just trust me."

It was late. The boys had been in bed for over an hour, but despite being tired, they were both still wide awake. No matter how many times Eric tried to get comfortable and get some sleep, it didn't work. He fidgeted and huffed and puffed as the weight of what had happened in the day sat heavy on his shoulders and played out like a movie in his mind. His restlessness also hindered John from falling asleep. "You can't get to sleep either?" John said.

"Nah, not tonight," he replied.

"What happened today?" John asked quietly, "'Cause I know something did."

Eric's heart skipped a beat as he lay on his back and stared at the ceiling. He knew this moment was coming—John was always curious, always wanting to know everything. But Eric couldn't bring himself to tell him the truth. How could he? John was still just a kid, and the thought of burdening him with the darkness that their dad inflicted on him felt unbearable. "Nothing."

John knew that his brother was not being truthful. Eric remained deep in thought, thinking up an excuse to tell him because he didn't want to tell him what had actually happened. "You know what he's like. He got mad at something, grabbed me by the throat, and wouldn't let go. I thought he was gonna choke me or even worse, kill me, but luckily Nigel turned up, so he let go, and Dad, being Dad, walked out of the shed and started talking to him like nothing had happened."

John gasped, knowing there was more to it. He'd seen his dad's temper. He'd seen the bruises on Eric before, the way Eric withdrew after spending time alone with him. John wasn't naïve —he knew what their father was capable of. "What did he get mad about?"

"I told him I wanted to come home and not be up at his shitty allotment."

"He'll do it again, won't he?" John replied, worried.

Eric's bravado faded. He felt the fear rise in him, the helplessness he felt when his dad had cornered him in that shed. But he pushed it down. He had to be strong—for John, for himself. He couldn't show weakness. "Yeah, probably," he replied.

John shifted uncomfortably on his bed, his heart sinking at Eric's words. He hated seeing his brother like this—defeated, angry, but keeping it all bottled up. He wished he could do something to protect him the way he had always protected him. "I hate him."

Eric looked over to his brother; the anger inside him flickered back to life. But this time, it was different. This time, it was cold and calculated—a simmering rage rather than a burst of emotion. He was tired of living in fear. He was fed up with his dominance over every aspect of their lives. "If he tries it again… I'll be ready," he muttered.

John was confused by the sudden steeliness in his brother's voice. His tone tonight was different from his usual anger. It was as though he had made some kind of decision, one he wasn't fully sharing with him. "Ready how?"

Eric's mind was already spinning with thoughts of revenge, of standing up to Joe once and for all. He couldn't tell John everything—he didn't want to drag him into the mess that was brewing in his mind. Not yet. "Doesn't matter. Just… trust me. I'm not going to let him keep doing this."

John sensed a shift in him. There was something more going on, something Eric wasn't telling him, but he didn't press any further. Instead, he just nodded, feeling a strange mix of fear and admiration for his older brother.

The two brothers sat in silence for a few moments, each lost in their own thoughts. The faint sound of the radio playing downstairs drifted up through the floorboards, a reminder that life went on, even when everything felt like it was falling apart. Eric stared up at the ceiling, his mind racing. He knew he'd made a promise—to himself, to John—that he had to keep. Joe's reign of terror couldn't go on forever. And when the time came, Eric swore to himself that he'd be ready to do whatever it took to stop him.

But for now, he kept those thoughts to himself. John didn't need to know the details—not yet.

TWENTY-SIX

Eric put his hand in his pocket and jiggled the loose chain. He walked down the busy street with a few pals, looking for places to go and something to do.

Norman was a bit of a troublemaker at school. His mop of red hair matched his fiery temper, and he was handy with his fists on account of his impoverished upbringing. His dad was in prison and wasn't coming out any time soon; nobody really knew why he was in there and what he had done. His mum struggled to cope with the six kids she had to bring up on her own; she had no support or family to help, and money was very tight. The neighbours helped her a lot with regular handouts.

Mushtaq—or Mush, as he was known—was the same age as Eric. His parents were from Pakistan, but he rebelled against his religion and his very strict upbringing. He had been born and raised here, and therefore he considered himself to be English. He wanted to live a westernised life, much to the disgust of his family. Mush was a bit of a tough nut and was able to take care of himself. His father owned the local corner shop, and while he was busy with his customers, Mush would pop out to the storeroom in the back and help himself to cigarettes, sweets, and pop and sell them on. What he didn't sell, he shared with the lads.

He was a cheeky little bugger with light fingers and a real gift of the grab.

Spencer, standing six feet tall and nearly fifteen stone, was a formidable opponent. He was the joker of the group; they found him funny; they liked having him around. Nobody really knew much about him; he didn't say much.

They were a boisterous bunch that sometimes appeared to be in the wrong place at the wrong time.

They all bundled into Carter's fishing tackle shop. It was such a dark and gloomy establishment; it made everything in the place look green in colour. The place stank of a heady mix of wet straw, damp floorboards, and musty old shelves that hadn't been cleaned in years. But the overriding stench emanated from the proprietor himself.

Mr. Carter appeared at the counter upon hearing the little bell tinkle above the door, letting him know someone had entered. He was a short, stocky man with glasses that perched on the end of his nose; his face was round, and he had a handlebar moustache that had so much wax in it even a force ten hurricane wouldn't move it. He appeared as though he hadn't bathed in weeks, and his scent suggested that he had been dissecting bodies in the back room.

"Alright, lads? What can I get for you today?"

Eric glanced at Mush, Norman, and Spencer, and they immediately took action. Mush headed over to the counter, making a show of examining a rack of fishing rods, while Norman wandered toward the lures, deliberately knocking a few off the shelves. "Sorry, mister, I'm so clumsy."

Carter walked out from behind the counter, grumbling about these clumsy kids as he bent down to pick up the scattered lures.

Mush took a quick look around to see if anything could be pinched but averted his eyes as Carter stood up.

"Are these rods any good?" Norman shouted, "I've been looking for something for river fishing, but I'm not sure about the strength."

Carter sprung into action, leading them over to the big display on the far wall. "Well, you've come to the right place!" It was obvious that he hadn't had a single customer enter the shop all day. It was also obvious that he liked to chat, as he started telling the lads all about his love of fishing, how long he'd had the shop, etc.

Eric hung back near the front door. He watched as Carter and his mates disappeared from view, then crept towards the large glass cabinet by the wall in front of him. He looked in, and something caught his eye. On the bottom shelf, nestled amongst the expensive-looking reels, lay a large Swiss army knife, a sleek, polished model with multiple blades splayed out like a shiny explosion of stainless steel. Under the cabinet lights, its red casing gleamed like a precious ruby. Eric wanted it, and he was going to have it.

He looked to see where Carter was and what he was up to. His mates surrounded him, feigning interest as Carter droned on and on, fully immersed in conversation with his small audience and completely unaware of any distractions. He wasn't coming up for air any time soon.

Eric needed to grab the knife, and he needed to do it now. He quietly popped the latch and bent over, the crack of his arse peeking out the top of his trousers. He checked over his shoulder one more time, and with quick hands, he snatched the knife and slipped it into his jacket pocket.

As he stood up and closed the latch, the bell above the door tinkled again, and a father and his young son entered. Eric puffed his cheeks and called out to his mates. "I've just realised the time, lads; we'd better get a move on 'cause we don't wanna be late."

Carter was slap bang in the middle of showing the lads an array of rods when he was suddenly interrupted. "You're going? But I've got loads more to show you." The lads turned to see who had entered and then glanced at Eric, who shook his head at them.

"Sorry, mister, we've got to go, but we'll come back another time," he said as they headed for the door. Leaving Carter to deal with his next customers, they stepped outside, and Norman was the first to pipe up.

"For fuck's sake, if that bloke and his son hadn't come in, we could have rinsed the place."

"Maybe it was a blessing in disguise 'cause I was losing the will to live listening to him prattle on," Mush added.

The lads giggled. "C'mon, let's go to Woolies, see what we can get from there." Eric said. Now wasn't the time to tell them what he had stolen; that could be kept for later.

Norman and Spencer stood at the edge of the riverbank throwing stones into the water. Eric and Mush sat slightly up the bank, taking turns having a drag of a cig. Eric lay on his back and blew a plume of white/grey smoke into the air; it danced in the wind, contorting and swirling as it rose and dispersed. Beside him lay the fruits of their labours: two record albums, a set of screwdrivers, a twin pack of white school shirts, and several pocketfuls of pick 'n' mix sweets. He reached into his front pocket and produced his newly acquired possession. "Oi lads, look at this." Something flickering in the sunlight blinded them as they turned to take a look.

"What is it?" Spencer asked, his hand shielding his brow from the sun's glare as he took a closer look. Eric sat up, and with the cigarette dangling out the corner of his mouth, he held the blade out for all to see.

"Wow, where did you get that from?" Mush asked. Eric smugly glared at it, running his finger along the sharp edge of the blade.

"Where the bloody hell do you think I got it from, your dad's shop?" he said sarcastically.

Mush had a vacant look. "My dad doesn't sell them."

"Durr, I know that. Did you not hear what I just said? While you Divs were busy looking at fishing shit and listening to that smelly old bastard's life story, I slipped this little beauty into my pocket."

"Give it here; let me have a look." Norman stretched his arm out, palm facing upwards as he wiggled his fingers impatiently.

Eric closed the blade and tossed it towards him. Norman effortlessly caught it with one hand. He looked at it closely; he opened up all the different sections, and it revealed the corkscrew, the scissors, and the file, as well as the flashing blade itself. "Bet that would've cost a few quid."

"Yes, it did; that's why I put it in my pocket," Eric said with pride, a glint in his eye. They all stood around looking at it shining in the sunlight.

Spencer stood beside Norman, his eyes wide and bright. "Are you going to keep it or sell it?"

"I'm not sure yet," Eric pondered briefly, "I'll probably keep it. It might come in handy someday."

Over the ensuing weeks, the gang continued to pilfer from shops using the same distraction technique every time. Why pay when they could just help themselves? As a result, Eric's confidence and bravado increased. He was the fearless leader, the one everyone looked up to.

Out here, he was untouchable. But every time he made his way home, the thrill of the theft would fade, the knot would tighten in his stomach, and the looming dread of home would suffocate him once more

TWENTY-SEVEN

A few days later, there came a harsh rap on the front door. Eric shovelled another bowl of cornflakes into his mouth and continued to read one of John's comics. He heard two more raps on the door, but this time they were much louder. He put his spoon in the bowl and slowly chewed his cereal while turning the page.

Bang, bang, bang!

The boom resonated throughout the home, as if the door were ready to cave in. "Hello, anybody home?" said a deep voice from the open letterbox.

"Get the front door, will ya, Eric?" Annie yelled out from upstairs.

He huffed, got out of his chair, and walked to the front door. When he opened it, he was surprised to discover two of Her Majesty's finest constables, dressed in pristine uniforms, standing in front of him. They appeared enormous and towered over him, their eyes burning a deep hole into Eric's from beneath the peak of their shiny helmets. "Mr. Maxwell?" the first one enquired. Eric immediately felt apprehensive. He slipped his hand in his pocket, clutching the stolen knife as he gulped anxiously. "Erm, yeah, it is."

"Joe Maxwell?"

Eric relaxed somewhat and removed his hand from the knife in his pocket. "No, I'm Eric; I'm his son."

"Is your dad in?"

"No."

"Where is he?"

"Dunno."

"When will he be back?"

"Dunno."

"You don't know much, do you?"

Eric stared at them with soulless eyes.

"Well, when you do see him, tell him we'll be back, okay?"

Annie shouted from upstairs. "Who is it?"

"It's the police. I think you should come down." He shouted upstairs.

Joe stood in the corner of the bedroom, waving his arms and beckoning for silence with one finger over his mouth. He murmured, "Tell them I'm not here, okay?" She nodded, flinging the window open, and leaning out with her hair in curlers.

"Can I help you?" Her demeanour had shifted from weak to confident.

The copper gazed up at her. "Sorry for interrupting you, Madam, but I am searching for Mr. Joe Maxwell. Is he in?"

"What's the problem?"

"Well, that's what I need to speak to him about."

"Did my son not tell you he's not in?"

"Yes, he did."

"Okay, there you go. There's your answer: he's not here. He left very early this morning, and I don't know when he will be back."

"Could you tell me where he was going?"

"I'm not sure; work, I suppose. He never said anything, and I didn't ask."

"Oh, work, you say?" He smirked. "Well, let him know we'll be back."

"Will do." She closed the window firmly behind her.

Eric grinned at him as he closed the door. His gut had almost fallen out of his arse as he thought the policemen came around to nick him. He pulled the knife from his pocket, kissed it, and returned it, feeling relieved.

Joe breezed past Eric, clearly in a hurry, and left the house through the back door.

John entered the kitchen, pulling his school tie on. "What's going on?"

"The coppers have just been round looking for Dad."

"Why, what's he done?" came the response.

Annie was about to ask Joe what was going on upstairs, but in typical fashion, he had vanished. She bounded down the stairs. "Has he gone?" she asked Eric, who was back at the kitchen table eating breakfast.

"Yeah he's just left. What do you think they wanted Dad for?"

She responded with a deep sigh. "I dunno, and to be honest, I don't want to know. Now, could you and John please get off to school? I have errands to run and things to do."

They collected their bags, kissed their mother on the cheek, and left for school. Just as they were about to shut the door, she said, "Please behave yourselves today, boys. I don't need more stress today. I have enough going on with the police showing up early this morning looking for him and us having to lie."

"Alright, Mum, we'll try," Eric said.

"You won't try," she yelled. "You will, understand?"

As they locked the door behind them and set off, John spoke with Eric. "What do you think they wanted?"

"Fucking hell, I don't know, do I?" Eric complained, throwing his arms up in the air, "All I know is, it's a good thing you didn't open the door, 'cause you would've told them he was upstairs!"

John responded blankly, "And that would've been a bad thing?"

Annie finished applying her lipstick, grabbed her coat and bag, and left the house. She walked up the road to catch a bus into town, completely unaware that Edward had parked his car down the street and was monitoring her house.

After finishing her shopping, she walked to the cafe where they would usually meet and ordered two cups of tea. She took a seat at their regular table in the far corner. Edward soon arrived along with the tea. Before they sat down, they exchanged hugs and a brief kiss on the cheek. "Good morning, how are you? Are you okay? You had a busy morning?" he enquired.

"Yeah, you could say that," she rolled her eyes, scrunched up her face, and tutted. "It's been manic, thanks for asking. I had the bloody police come around first thing this morning."

"The police? That sounds serious. Who were they looking for?" Edward edged forward in his seat.

"Well, Joe, who else?"

"Bloody hell, what has he done?" Edward pushed on.

She threw her cup into the saucer, almost breaking it. "Look, I have no idea what he has been up to, and to be honest, I don't care. I'm not sure why the police want him now, but I do know one thing. I am so exhausted by this whole thing."

Edward took her hand and squeezed it reassuringly. "I know this is difficult for you, and I realise how exhausting it must be. Just hang in there."

"I don't know if I can anymore," she said. "I want all this to stop;

I just want to be happy."

"I know you do, and I am working on it, I really am. After I finish tying up a few loose ends at my end, we will be able to leave."

She nodded, sighed, and smiled because she felt comfortable with him and was thrilled to have him in her life; she couldn't wait for him to meet her boys; she knew they'd like him and they'd have their happily ever after.

"I've saved some money up, and me and the boys… we're ready to go when you are."

He shifted in his chair, gazing deeply into her eyes. "Look, we'll finish our tea, I'll drop you home, and I'll be in touch, and then we can make plans."

TWENTY-EIGHT

It was a cold, dark night. It had rained on and off throughout the day, but it was now pouring down. A burst of white lightning lit up the sky in the distance, followed by a deep rumble of thunder, signalling the upcoming arrival of a storm that was gathering in more ways than one.

Joe had decided to go into hiding for a bit because the police were after him. Using an alias, he checked into a B & B, a modest place on the outskirts of town. He had intended to isolate himself in his room, keep his head down and his mouth shut, but his impatience and insatiable thirst made this a fruitless exercise.

Joe had gone downstairs and asked the landlady, Mavis Collier, to open the bar, but she had made it clear that the guest house had strict rules that must be followed at all times and that the bar would not open until 6 pm. Joe, true to his nature, was determined to have his drink. Producing a crumpled old ten-pound note and waving it in front of her face was a deal breaker, and with the place empty throughout the day, he spent his time drinking in a quiet area near the window.

Mavis' husband, Sidney, had taken over bar duties. As the day wore on, the place started to fill up, and by early evening, the drink had begun to take effect on Joe. The room began to spin through his blurry, bloodshot eyes, but instead of keeping his head down and mouth shut, or more importantly, heading off to bed, he started to get gobby.

A young man strolled in and headed to the bar. He wore a large overcoat over a pair of oil-stained overalls and hobnail boots that thumped across the bare wooden floorboards. "Hello, Brian, a pint of the usual?" Sidney chirped, exchanging pleasantries as he pulled his pint.

Across the room, Joe ran his eyes over him. He stood up from his table and headed over to the bar. "Can I get you a drink?" he slurred.

Brian looked at him in bewilderment. "What?"

Joe sidled up to him. "I said... I'll buy you a drink."

"No, you're alright, mate; I've just ordered one," came the reply.

"Well, I'll get you another."

"I don't want one, thanks." Brian felt a sense of annoyance and unease having just gotten in from work and an inebriated stranger staring directly at him.

Joe made a grab for his arm. "C'mon, have a drink with me?"

He moved away from Joe, brushing his arm away from him. 'Look, I've told you twice now, I don't want one, so can you just fuck off?"

Joe was angry, furious in fact. He grabbed his arm again, tighter than before. His eyes narrowed, still bloodshot, his brow furrowed, and he scowled at him. "Do you know who the fuck I am?" The place fell silent as everyone turned towards the bar to find out what was causing the noise. He should have been keeping a low profile, so this move wasn't a good idea.

Brian attempted to break free from his vice-like hold, but he was too powerful. "What are you doing? Get your fucking hands off me, will ya! I don't know who you are, and frankly, I don't give a fuck. So, fuck off will ya. I've come in here for a quiet drink, not to have some pissed up twat hassle me!"

"You what? Pissed up twat? I'm Joe Maxwell, and I work for Ronnie, Ronnie Fitzpatrick."

Sidney glared at him. "I suggest you sit down Joe and shut the fuck up, he's not interested who you are or who you work for, you hear me!" His voice bellowed from the other side of the bar with everyone looking at them.

Joe let go of his arm and put his hands out in front of him. 'Whatever you say."

Sidney walked out from behind the bar towards Joe and stood inches from his face. "I want a word," he uttered through gritted teeth. He walked towards the table where he had been sitting; Joe followed him. He pulled out a chair; placing his arm firmly on his shoulder, he pushed him into the seat. He leaned in towards him. "Right, listen to me; Ronnie would not appreciate you shouting your fucking mouth off. You know this is the place to keep your head down when shit's going down, not let every fucker know who you are by shouting your mouth off. You never know who might be watching or listening."

Sidney, like him, was undoubtedly on the payroll, just like every other fucker in this town.

Joe stared him in the eyes. He hated being told what to do. He would like nothing more than to smash the place up and paste every cunt in the room. But he knew he couldn't. Sitting back in his chair he grabbed his glass, but it was empty. Sidney glared at him, "I think you've had enough." Grabbing the glass from his hand he headed back to the bar.

When things began to close in on him and he felt himself losing control, which was a common occurrence these days, he headed to the place where he felt safe—the allotment. Armed with 2 bottles of whisky and a few packs of cigarettes, he looked around to see if anyone had followed him or had spotted him in the vicinity. He fumbled through his keys to unlock the padlock as the rain whipped around his face, his cold hands struggling to find the right one in the darkness. He finally unlocked the chain and headed up the path towards the shed.

He opened the door, turned, closed it behind him, and propped a plank of wood against it to prevent it from opening. He took his wet coat off and hung it up. He slumped down into the chair and opened one of the bottles. Popping two Valium in his mouth and taking a hearty swig, he let out a throaty gasp. The flashes of lightning started to quicken, and the rumbling sound from the thunder grew closer and louder, announcing the storm was forthcoming.

His pulse was racing, his heart was thumping, and he couldn't tell if the rain or the sweat seeping out of every pore had soaked his brow. The pills eventually started to take effect, and, disorientated by the drink and deafened by the explosive noises ringing inside his head, he started to shake uncontrollably. Throwing himself to the floor, he crawled under the workbench for cover.

He took another long drink from the bottle, feeling the alcohol burn all the way down into his gut. Feeling drowsy, his mind started to wander, transporting him to places and moments he wanted to forget but couldn't. The dim light of a hanging lantern distorted his face with memories too painful to bear as he closed his eyes and started to drift off.

The shed suddenly vanished around him, and he found himself hunkered down in a narrow slit trench in the middle of a muddy field. The downpour of mortars and grenades lit up the sky around him; the earth underneath him trembled as distant bombs exploded as the booming sound of thunder rumbled on. Joe hid in the sludge, his quivering hands holding his rifle, as the rain turned into bullets. He could hear the voices of the men he had fought with and the screams of the ones who hadn't made it home.

His entire body trembled as he attempted to gather himself, but the terror and horror of the situation overwhelmed him. In the midst of that war-torn landscape, his mind wandered to Doris, the first person he met after returning from the front line.

He recalled how her pub had served as a refuge, a place where he could drown his memories of the war in drink. At first all he could offer was the rough, broken parts of himself, but over time they had developed a mutual respect between them.

He thought about Ronnie—who gave him a purpose thanks to Doris—when no one else would. After the war, there was no place for men like him; he was damaged goods, too violent. However, Ronnie acknowledged his potential and taught him how to channel his violence.

The criminal world had become Joe's new battlefield, and Ronnie was his commander. In this world, people appreciated and admired his brutality, and intimidation and control ruled. And as the years passed, he got greedier, wanting more and more, pushing him further and further into the abyss.

And then there was his wife, the marriage that was built on deceit and lies, covering up all that he truly was.

Yet the most profound secret, the one that troubled him the most, remained untold to her, his boys, or even to himself. He had always been aware of his sexuality and he had always carried the accompanying sense of shame.

He wasn't made for the life he was living. He wasn't made to be a husband, a father, or a soldier. He never intended to become a criminal. He was something else, someone he was terrified of and had spent his entire life avoiding.

The whisky bottle slipped from Joe's hand and rolled across the floor as the storm outside continued to rage on. The drink and the drugs had caused him to fall into a deep stupor, and subconsciously, he recalled the altercation he'd had with Franco all those years ago.

TWENTY-NINE

It was around 1 am when Joe arrived at the club. The last of the punters had left around midnight, and the staff had filtered off home. Only Errol and Franco remained at the bar as Joe walked in. "How was it tonight?"

"Same as every other night," Franco replied, flicking his cigarette ash into an ashtray. Franco didn't like Joe, nor did he appreciate his questioning.

Joe pulled a stool out at the bar, knowing this would wind him up. He turned to Errol. "Pour us a drink, will ya? I've had a helluva night. Ronnie has had me running around all over the place."

"Bar's closed," Franco muttered. Errol looked at him, unsure of what to do.

Joe said, "Pour us both one, then you can get off, Errol." He pulled his stool towards Franco.

They both sat quietly for a moment, a hint of tension between them. Franco was on the verge of taking a sip from his drink when Joe met his gaze, eager to start a conversation. "You've always had a bit of a problem with me, haven't ya?"

Franco lowered his glass and stared at him. "I don't have any problem; I just don't like you, and I don't fucking trust you. But you've always known that. I don't know why Ronnie wanted you in the firm, 'cause personally, I know what you've been up to, and I think you are a liability."

"Well, I applaud your honesty," Joe scoffed, grabbing his glass and rubbing it against his lips. "But your memory ain't too clever, is it?"

Franco snorted. "What the hell are you on about?"

"Trust," he replied. "I'm surprised you know the meaning of the word after what happened that night."

Franco slammed his drink down hard on the bar. "What happened that night was *your* fault, not mine! I mean, what doorman lets a bloke into a club carrying a shooter for fuck's sake?"

Joe quietly laughed to himself. "Your memory really is shot to shit. Let me remind you of what actually happened. As Ronnie's right-hand man, second in command, head of security, or whatever the fuck your job was, you should have been more thorough and diligent. But you weren't—you were too busy eyeing up the ladies to even fucking notice. If it weren't for me once again picking up the bits you fuck up, well, Ronnie would have been shot."

Franco snapped, seizing his glass and shattering it on the bar. Joe leapt from the stool. Grabbing his wrist with one hand and the back of his head with another, he rammed it hard onto the bar. Joe's grip on his hand was so tight that blood was dripping onto the floor as he pushed it into the broken glass on the bar, causing him to yell out in agony. Joe leaned in towards his face as he towered over him. "And that's why I'm doing your job now."

Franco tried to pull away, but Joe pressed harder on his hand. He clenched his teeth in agony. "And you can thank Doris for that. I can understand why she fucked off, but I will never know why she left Elizabetta with you."

Franco writhed in agony as he tried to escape his grip. "You know what? I can see straight through you, you bastard. I know exactly who you are and what you are up to. Mark my words, Ronnie will find out one day, and you'll be sorry."

Joe pulled his head up from the bar; he didn't take kindly to his words. "Oh, will you now? We'll fucking see about that, won't we?" He let go of him, grabbed his jacket, and headed towards the door. Franco shouted after him. "I know all about your dirty, sordid little secrets."

Joe continued walking away.

"All the men you took up to your room—the money you gave Doris to keep quiet. I know everything, Joe. I've been waiting a long time for this, and now's the time to let people know who you really are."

He heard the door slam. He walked behind the bar, grabbed a bar towel, and wrapped it around his hand. He poured himself another drink, knocked it back, wiped his mouth with the back of his hand, and gave a loud shout. "You're finished, you hear me? Fucking finished."

He walked slowly to the back office, grabbing his coat and keys before locking up and leaving through the club's back door. Stepping out into the thick, foggy night, he looked left and right, as he always did, and took a drag on a cigarette before setting off up the cobbled street to where his car was parked. At this time of night—or morning—it was usually quiet, the odd rumble of traffic coming from the main roads in the distance.

He took one last drag on his cigarette and tossed the butt into the gutter as he approached his car. He exhaled a plume of smoke. He turned the key to unlock the door and heard a familiar voice behind him.

"I'm finished, am I?" Joe spat, holding a gun to his head. His knuckles whitened as he gripped the handle of the gun, the cold steel pressing against his head. Franco started breathing heavily, his hands raised in a gesture of desperate surrender. As the gun barrel pressed deeper into his skin, sweat trickled down his brow. He closed his eyes tightly.

"Joe… Joe, listen to me," Franco stammered, his voice quivering. "You don't need to do this."

Joe's expression remained icy, his jaw tight, and his eyes, dark with a simmering rage, fixed on him. "You haven't given me a reason not to." His voice was low, almost a growl. "You think threatening to tell Ronnie the truth bothers me?"

Franco swallowed hard, his hands trembling. "I only said that to provoke you. I swear, Joe, I wouldn't have said a word. I didn't mean for any of this to go this far."

He leaned in closer, the gun pressing harder into his head. "Oh, I think you did."

Franco started to pant, his panic rising. "Please, Joe, you don't have to do this. We both want the same thing, don't we?" Joe's grip tightened on the gun.

Joe stared at him for a moment, his breathing slow and measured. "It's too late for that," his voice was deathly calm.

Franco's eyes widened, pure terror washing over his face as he begged for his life. "Please! I'm begging you; I'll do anything! I'll leave town, I'll disappear, I'll never bother you again—please, don't do this! You don't want this on your conscience."

Before Franco could say another word, a deafening *bang* echoed through the air. His body slumped to the floor, a pool of blood quickly forming beneath him. Joe lowered the gun, staring at his lifeless body. His face remained emotionless as he grabbed the body and lugged it into the boot of his car.

There was no room for mercy in this world. Not anymore.

Joe switched the wireless on and started singing along as he drove down the road. He was running on adrenaline and had no remorse whatsoever; as always, he loved the feeling of being in control. Seeming like he had been driving for ages, he reached the forest on the outskirts of town and slowed the car to a crawl. He had been here before and knew exactly where he wanted to dump him.

Pulling into a secluded area, he got out, opened the boot, and grabbed hold of Franco. Dragging him out and throwing him over his shoulder, he grabbed the spade and set off into the forest mumbling, "You cunt. I'll show you. Nobody threatens me and gets away with it."

He shook him off, his body crashing to the ground with a deafening thud. He rolled his shirt sleeves up and started to dig. Once the hole was deep enough, he dragged his body over to the edge and kicked him into it. If that wasn't dignified enough, he then unzipped his trousers, flopped his cock out, and pissed all over him.

"Who's had the last laugh now, you dirty fucking spick?"

THIRTY

With his hands crossed in front of his body, Joe stood at the entrance to the club, surveying the crowd that was gathered outside. It was a typical Friday night, filled with the usual people eager to enjoy themselves.

He felt a tap on the shoulder from one of the other doormen, Ray, who motioned for him to follow him into the main room. He pointed at a man who was leaning against the bar. "You see him over there, the geezer sitting in one of our booths with that bird?"

"Yeah?"

"I don't trust him. He's from a rival firm. Franco said he saw him selling pills in our club, and I think you need to go and sort him out."

Joe lifted an eyebrow, understanding the situation. Up until now he hadn't really done much; he just stood at the door taking a pay cheque. Now was his chance to show Ronnie what he could do over all his other flunkies. This was his chance to stand out and make a name for himself, and there was no way he was going to fuck this up.

He broadened his shoulders, tilted his head back, inhaled through his nose, and strolled over to the booth. "Excuse me, sir," he said quietly, sidling up beside him, "Can I have a word with you?"

"Looks like you already have," he said in frustration. Mehmet was Turkish, and he was well-known in some circles for selling marijuana and the infamous Jacks—heroin tablets that were still circulating in the city's underbelly. He looked at Joe and didn't like what he saw. They had originally been obtained legally on a doctor's prescription from a clutch of chemists around London but were now a valuable item on the streets.

"What is this about?" Mehmet asked.

"A little birdie told me you're selling pills in here."

He laughed, "So what are you going to do about it, throw me out or what?" He placed a pill in his hand. "Or do you want a bit of this?"

Joe's eyes widened, slightly tempted to grab the pill out of his hand, but he knew Ronnie had eyes everywhere, and the one person who would be watching him would be Franco, who didn't like him. This wasn't just about selling a few pills; Mehmet was part of a larger network that didn't like being pushed out of their manor. But Joe recognised an opportunity—one that would benefit him more than simply throwing him out on the street.

"Listen," Joe murmured softly, leaning in so that she couldn't hear. "I know what you are doing—or should I say, *we* know what you're doing. And Mr. Fitzpatrick—that's Ronnie if you're on first-name terms, like me—wouldn't take too kindly to it."

"What do you think I'm doing? I'm here, having a night out with my woman."

"Erm, I don't think so. You're peddling your shit and whatever else you have. You can't be doing this in Ronnie's place; he hasn't given you permission."

"I don't need anyone's permission, only permission from who I work for."

"Do you, now?"

Mehmet's eyes narrowed. "I do not take orders from people like you… Are you a doorman? If you throw me out, they won't be happy, and they'll come. And you don't want that trouble around here. Not in this part of town anyway." His voice was threatening, but Joe did not flinch. He sat back and grinned. "I'm not barring you; I'm making you an offer," he laughed.

Mehmet looked puzzled. "What do you mean?"

Joe lowered his voice. "Look, they sent me over here because they know who you are and are aware of your actions and intentions. I recommend that you pay attention to what I have to say, as you have two options: either you leave or you cooperate with me, in which case I will handle the situation."

"What do you mean?"

"I'll move the stuff for you; you get your cut, I get mine, and everyone will be happy. Nobody needs to know anything."

"How can I trust you?"

"You ain't got a lot of choice, 'cause you're either in, and you walk out and make it look like I've told you to leave, or I fucking sling you out."

Mehmet took a few minutes to assess the situation. "What if I say no?"

Joe's eyes darkened, and he leaned in closer. "We both know you ain't gonna say no. We both just wanna make money, regardless of who we work for."

Mehmet stared at him for a long time before finally nodding. "Okay, we'll do it your way."

Joe grabbed his arm. Unhappy that her evening had ended abruptly, the woman began to make a scene. Franco watched on from across the room as he escorted them out.

Joe saw this as a huge opportunity to make more money; his greed always prevailed. Joe didn't return to the main room; he stayed on the door, as that was his job. Franco's curiosity compelled him to enquire about the events, leading him to approach Joe.

Joe's mind was already working on his next move when he felt a tap on his shoulder. He turned around, but before he could say anything, Franco jumped in. "So, what was all that about?"

"I was doing your job. And so was Ray by the looks of it. He told me to deal with it, so I did. Looks like we're both doing your job, and from where I'm standing, that ain't gonna take long. You're gonna be where I am, and I'm gonna be where you are." He smirked.

Franco grabbed his arm in frustration. He put his other hand inside his jacket and rested it on his gun. Joe looked at him, his eyes narrowed. "I don't fuckin' think so. I'll shoot you here and now, and I don't give a fuck who's looking, including Ronnie. That's the difference between me and you; you care, and I fuckin' don't! So I suggest you get your fuckin' hand off me and go and do the job you're paid to do, you cunt."

*

Joe's arrangement with Mehmet initially went smoothly in the first few months. He acted as a middleman, making a tidy profit while evading suspicion as the drugs moved covertly through the club. He kept everything under control, despite Franco's eyes always watching. He told Ronnie that he didn't trust Joe, but it fell on deaf ears. There had been no trouble in the club for a long while, which meant nobody was watching Ronnie, who considered him as a valued member of this firm.

Ronnie began to see him as someone who could manage himself. He was impressed by him, and Joe knew this, feeling he was in a position of power. He made himself visible at all times, especially when Ronnie was around. His name was mentioned frequently within the firm, but without anyone realising, he was operating as a gatekeeper for a lucrative drug operation.

But as with anything in the underworld, things eventually began to unravel.

Franco opened the door to the staff toilet to find Joe standing in front of the sink, tucking something into his inside left jacket pocket. "Did I startle you?"

"No. Why?"

"Shouldn't you be on the door?"

"I'm going now."

Franco had his suspicions about him for quite some time. He was aware that there was an ongoing situation in which he was directly involved. "Well, just beware; I'm watching you."

"Yeah, you've said that before," Joe smirked.

Upon noticing the surge in demand, Mehmet became greedy and began taking shortcuts. Without Joe's knowledge, he began to escalate the situation by pushing stronger drugs and blending them with other substances to enhance their potency. Rumours quickly spread that someone was using Club CasaNova to sell heroin and amphetamines. Joe wasn't aware of what was going on; he assumed they were still dealing with what he'd agreed on.

The money kept rolling in until one of his regulars overdosed in the club's toilet. Roy discovered the man slumped in a cubicle, his mouth foaming. This was a serious situation. Ronnie wouldn't want his name, or club, to be associated with dodgy drugs and certainly wouldn't want the coppers to come and snoop around. He went and had a word with Franco, who ordered a cleanup operation to get rid of the body.

Joe was at the door, and Roy approached him. "I need your help. Someone has overdosed in the toilet, and we need to sort this out before anyone finds out. Franco's been suspecting somebody has been selling dodgy drugs in the club for a while. Although he couldn't pinpoint the individual, he harboured his suspicions.

Joe remained calm. "What do you need me to do?" This was the least of his problems. He had to get rid of the drugs and Mehmet as soon as possible, as he knew Franco was already sniffing around him.

Roy whispered in his ear. "Help me take the body out the back.

Franco has contacted Eddie; he's on his way to meet us, and he'll sort it from there. If anyone asks what happened, you tell them the geezer had a heart attack, okay?"

Despite his best efforts, Joe's problems did not end with the overdose.

Things had quieted down in the club over the past few weeks. Despite it being a nice little earner, he'd decided to end his involvement with Mehmet and stop selling drugs. He had also made sure Mehmet wouldn't ever return to the club; his body was dumped thirty miles away in a forest where nobody would ever find him.

Joe stood at the door, chatting to people as they were entering. He had clocked the car across the road with four guys in it. He was aware of their identities and everything was proceeding according to plan. The guys piled out of the car and headed towards the club. As they reached the door, Joe put his arms out in front of him. "Sorry, fellas, you ain't coming in; we're full."

"You let them in before us, didn't you? So we're coming in."

Roy knew trouble was brewing. Stepping forward, he said, "C'mon guys, he's already said you're not coming in, so go somewhere else."

At that point, one of the men raised his fist and took a swipe at Roy. Meanwhile, the other two jumped on Joe and started grappling with him. With the chaos going on and the other punters screaming, the fourth guy made his way into the main room. He walked straight past Franco, made his way to the booth where Ronnie and Virginia were sitting, and pulled out a gun. Pointing it at Ronnie, Joe ran through the main room, leapt in the air, and tackled the guy to the ground.

The gun went off.

Everyone started screaming and running for cover. Ronnie watched on as Joe restrained the guy on the floor, managing to get the whole situation under control. Joe dragged the guy to his feet, twisting his arm around his back, and marched him towards the door. He looked at Franco. "Start clearing this place with the others. I'll sort this out." He barged through the doors and headed outside up the road and around the corner where the other guys were waiting in the car. He opened his jacket and pulled out a wad of notes. Peeling a few off, he handed them over. "Good job, lads, now fuck off out of here." He headed back towards the club.

Inside, the lights were up and the last of the punters filtered out. Once clear, Ronnie ordered everybody to the main room. He paced up and down, the anger emanating from him as he took a long drag on his cigar, and walked towards where Franco was sitting. He leaned in toward him, blowing the smoke into his face, and bellowed. "So what the fuck were you doing? How the fuck did you let this happen?" He started poking him in the shoulder. "Someone walked into my club and pointed a fucking shooter at me? I want to know who that cunt was and how he had the audacity to do that!"

Franco just sat there. He couldn't say anything, and what pissed him off even more was he knew Joe was involved with this somewhere along the line. He stood up and pointed in Joe's direction. "This has something to do with him, I'm telling you. We have never had any problems in this club until he started working on the door. I've been telling you this, and you haven't listened."

Ronnie pulled his gun out and pointed it at him. "I suggest you sit the fuck down. I think you've forgotten who runs this fucking firm. I run it—not you—so shut the fuck up and listen. And that goes for all of you." He pointed the gun at Joe. "Just to let you know, there will be some changes around here, so you can piss off while I think. We'll have a meeting tomorrow morning, everybody here at eleven."

They all got up and started to filter off. Ronnie headed towards the bar to pour himself a drink when he turned to the guys. "Erm, not you, Joe, I want a word."

THIRTY-ONE

Annie was in a buoyant mood. The only chore left for her to complete was vacuuming the living room. As she pushed and pulled the vacuum back and forth, she started to dance and sing to herself; her body swayed and wiggled in time with each thrust. Usually this type of housework would be boring, but not today. She had an extra spring in her step and an extra twinkle in her eye, for today was the day she was meeting Edward.

She eagerly anticipated meeting him, especially after his promise to take her and her boys away and begin a new life together.

She took the bus into town. With her face pressed up against the window, her breath pulsed against the glass, creating a throbbing patch of condensation in front of her mouth. She watched the world outside whiz by with a blurry kaleidoscope of colour. A couple of rows in front of her, a young girl stood on the seat next to her mother, watching a young couple pull funny faces at her as her baby sibling cried. On the opposite side sat several older women dressed in long overcoats and headscarves discussing the day's gossip. The bus conductor merrily meandered up and down, happily dishing out his well-rehearsed patter to the newer passengers while giving out their tickets.

Edward was waiting for her at the bus stop. She hopped off the bus as it pulled over and stopped, immediately surprised and taken aback by his greeting.

Back at the allotment, it was late in the afternoon when Joe started to stir, not that he was aware. In fact, he didn't have a clue what day it was, let alone what time it was. He slowly hauled his heavy body up from the chair and steadied himself. He felt dizzy and nauseous, and his hangover showed no sign of relenting.

The sound of an out-of-tune orchestra crashing and banging in his head was a jumbled crescendo of indecipherable noise. His mouth was dry; he coughed and sputtered before producing a ball of phlegm that he spat out onto the floor. He looked at his reflection in the windowpane as he rubbed his eyes and dragged his fingers through his tatty hair. He opened the shed door, and the fresh air filled his lungs.

He appeared dishevelled, mentally drained from the vivid dreams he'd experienced and the memories that would forever torment him. His drinking was making him increasingly paranoid, which in turn was making him more violent and unpredictable.

Then it hit him.

"Fuck! Fuck!"

His heart sank as he checked the time and date on his watch. He had missed the shipment at the docks. The plan had been to meet the others in a quiet spot about a mile away, pick up the shipment of firearms, then take them to the lockup across town. However, due to the police snooping around and paying him a visit, he had decided to go to ground. He looked to the heavens, and a wave of dread washed over him. He realised he had made a significant mistake and was facing serious consequences.

Did the others take the shipment and cover his arse, or did they sling him under the bus? Deep down he knew the answer.

He picked up his keys and hurried down the path towards the entrance to the allotment. His shoulders sagged when he realised his car was parked at the B&B, and he had a mile walk ahead of him. With a plethora of excuses swirling in his mind, he set off, his collar pulled up around his face and head lowered to avoid detection. He managed to return unseen.

Driving through the streets, he decided to get washed and changed at home before heading to Ronnie's. But, unbeknownst to him, things were about to get a whole lot worse.

The boys were sitting at the table having something to eat. Joe came out of the bathroom with only a towel around his waist. He'd had a shave and a quick wash around his armpits with the flannel and ran a comb through his wet hair. He didn't acknowledge them—not that he would've anyway, not now that he had a thousand excuses on his mind—as he marched through the room and went upstairs to get dressed.

Edward and Annie had spent their time together meandering around town, taking in the sights and sounds and chatting about this and that. They walked past an ice cream parlour filled with parents and young teenagers. "C'mon, let's get an ice cream," chirped Annie, "my shout."

Edward checked the time on his watch. "Oh shit, look at the time. I'd love to, but I've got to head off. I've got some work commitments that I have to attend to, and I completely forgot. You do understand, don't you?"

Annie felt a bit perturbed. He hadn't mentioned a thing about work, and now suddenly, he casually mentioned he had to head off. It was quite unexpected; however, she accepted it, knowing that they would soon be spending every day together. "Of course, you do what you need to do."

She walked through the front door and shouted through the house. "Hello boys! Where are you?"

"We're in the kitchen," came the reply from Eric. She took her coat off, the smile on her face wide and bright. She glanced up the stairs and saw a pair of shoes on the top step. The sight of Joe standing there shocked her. He hadn't been home for days, but here he was.

He gave Annie a thunderous look. "What are you so happy about?"

"I'm not." Once again, she could never do anything right. When she was feeling miserable, he moaned. When she was happy, he moaned. He drained all the confidence she had and sucked the life out of her. But in the forefront of her mind, she kept telling herself over and over, *Not long now, girl. Not long.* She walked through to the kitchen and kissed the tops of the boys' heads. She smiled at them both. "Not long," she said. They both looked at her confused.

"Not long? What do you mean?" Eric said. Before Annie could respond, there was a tremendous hammering on the front door, almost in a frenzied manner, pounding away like a battering ram against a portcullis and sending reverberations through the walls of the house.

"Who the hell is that?" Annie snapped, "Okay, okay, I'm coming!"

Joe froze on the stairs, as he knew that was no ordinary knock.

John spotted something out of the corner of his eye and shouted. "Mum, two policemen have just come into our backyard!"

"Fuck's sake!" Joe seethed.

Annie opened the front door, and the sweet smile she had worn on her face suddenly turned sour. Edward stood on the doorstep in front of her, flanked by two uniformed policemen. Her heart sank; she felt sick to her stomach, and her whole world instantly came crashing down. A million questions started running through her mind, which she needed answers to. She looked at Edward with tear-filled eyes and a confused look on her face. At that moment she realised everything he had told her had been a pack of lies.

He didn't look at her—he couldn't—instead, he looked straight past her and stared straight at Joe standing in his line of vision. "Alright, Joe?"

"Well, look who it is." Joe spat back.

"Mind if we come in for a bit? You know the drill."

"As a matter of fact, I do, Eddie."

Annie's throat tightened; she tried to blink away the tears trickling down her cheeks. Not only was she feeling betrayed; she now knew Joe and Edward had encountered each other before. She realised that all the time she spent with him was just an ulterior motive to get information about Joe. Yet another man in her life had deceived and disappointed her.

Edward brushed past her, clutching a piece of paper in his hand. Several police officers filed into the house after him. "You know what this is," he flashed a blank piece of paper in his face, "so we're gonna have a mooch about."

"Do you wanna tell me what this is about?" Joe asked nonchalantly.

"I think you know full well what this is about."

Joe looked at him with a blank expression on his face. "Oh, do I? Well, even if I don't know, I'm sure you'll explain."

"We believe you have an illegal stash of firearms hidden in this property," Eddie declared

"Firearms? You must be joking!" Joe replied, astonished at the accusation.

"So we can either take you back to the station and tear this place apart, or you can sit quietly on the sofa while we conduct our search. Your choice."

Joe was a seasoned pro when it came to police matters and

knew how to play the game. "Where's your search warrant? 'Cause that shitty piece of paper in your hand ain't one. I'm sure you need one to be able to search for whatever you're looking for."

Edward smiled. "I'll sort one out later. Let's go, fellas."

Edward and his officers started to disperse around the house. Annie stood motionless; she leaned on the wall to steady herself. All she could hear was the muffled sounds of the boys coming from the kitchen and the officers instructing one another. She tried to comprehend what was happening, but nothing made sense. What she did understand was that the man she'd fallen in love with was meant to change her life, but she never imagined it would be this way.

With the family camped in the living room with two officers for company, the police began their extensive search of the property. They meticulously searched every drawer, cupboard, wardrobe, nook, and cranny, leaving no detail overlooked.

An hour or so passed when Edward entered the living room. "The key to the coal shed, where is it?" He demanded with an outstretched hand.

Joe sat back in his armchair and dragged on a cigarette. "I ain't giving you the fucking key. You've wrecked the house, so you might as well wreck the yard 'n' all." The boys looked at each other and bowed their heads. Annie sat motionless, her heart shattered into countless fragments.

"You said it." Edward was getting increasingly frustrated with Joe's games. Joe remained silent, completely ignoring Edward's gaze. Edward turned his head towards the kitchen, where several officers were standing. Beyond them a couple of officers were loitering in the backyard. "Kick the door in, lads," he shouted with an air of authority. Annie looked at him, but Edward didn't reciprocate. She hadn't seen this side of him, so hard, cold, and a completely different person from the guy she had gotten to know over the months.

Within minutes, an officer appeared in the living room's doorway. "Guv," he said, gesturing to him to follow him outside. Edward walked outside. Joe could hear whispered conversations coming from the next room and sensed that something was about to happen. Edward walked back in with four officers in tow. "Right, Joe, we've finished our search."

"I told you I didn't have anything, didn't I?" He interrupted, a satisfied grin on his face, "Fucking wrecking my house, upsetting my wife." He put his hand on Annie's shoulder; she pulled away, and looked at Edward. "Look, you've clearly upset her... and my boys, 'n' all."

Edward retaliated. "Cut the bullshit, Joe, and save the sentimental stuff for someone who gives a fuck. We all know what you're like. Explain what this is." An officer behind him produced a battered old Post Office bag with several rifles and shotguns inside.

Joe's face dropped. He jumped out of his chair. "What the fuck? There was nothing in there, I swear!"

"Yeah, right. So if there was nothing in there, how do you explain this?"

"You've set me up, ya bastards," Joe yelled and launched himself at Edward. The room erupted into chaos as several policemen swarmed in. Joe barely had time to land a punch. The heavy thud of boots against the floor echoed as they charged at him from all sides, their voices a mix of sharp commands and urgent warnings.

In an instant, two officers lunged at him, tackling him to the ground, but they struggled against him, his raw strength making it difficult for them to pin him down. His muscles tensed as he thrashed wildly, kicking out and trying to throw them off. One officer grabbed his arm, twisting it behind his back with a firm grip, while another tried to hold down his legs. Joe let out a furious growl, his body convulsing as he resisted.

"Hold him down!" one of the others yelled, rushing forward to help. Joe's breath came in ragged bursts as he fought with everything he had, his eyes wild with fury. His fists clenched as he struggled, his body writhing under the sheer weight of the officers on top of him.

It took three of them to restrain him as Joe fought them off. Finally, one of them managed to get the cuffs on his wrists, yanking his arms behind him with a grunt of effort.

"Stay down!" He shouted, pressing his face into the floor, his knee digging into his back.

"Get the fuck off me!" He snarled, his muscles tensed as he tried to free himself. But the weight of them on him was too much. They had him pinned, and the fight was over.

The room buzzed as they finally subdued him, Joe breathing heavily, his chest heaving as he lay motionless beneath them. His eyes still burned with rage, but he knew it was over. The fight drained from his body as they hoisted him to his feet, holding him firmly on either side.

"Good work, lads!" Edward shouted.

"This is a setup, you bastard, and you fucking know it."

"How can this be a set-up? We—or should I say I—have been watching you for months now, haven't I, Annie? We know you're a wrong 'un' and what you get up to." Annie wanted to run over towards Edward and slap him straight round the face; she felt embarrassed and hurt that she had been used in this way. "Put him in the van, lads; we'll deal with him back at the station."

They dragged him toward the door, his legs barely able to keep up, but Joe's mind was still racing. They had caught him, but he was far from finished.

"You won't be seeing him for a while," Edward said to Annie, treating her as if nothing had happened over the past few months. Annie was in a state of shock. She sat at the bottom of the stairs; she couldn't believe the arrogance of him.

Edward picked up the phone in the hallway and dialled a number. "It's me... I told you I'd sort it, and I have."

Ronnie relaxed back into his office chair. "Cheers, Eddie. Good work."

Edward's expression was unreadable as he hung up. Annie sat on the stairs, observing him intently. For the first time, she knew he was up to something much bigger than simply manipulating her to obtain access to Joe. And she was scared of whatever it was. He smiled slyly at her as he left, slamming the door behind him.

Her heart raced; she sat motionless, her hands trembled; her heart shattered into a thousand pieces.

'How could I be so stupid?' she murmured to herself. The man who had captured her heart, whom she felt she could trust, had misled her, like everybody else she'd ever known.

Her eyes welled up with tears, as she realised the promise she had made to her boys wasn't going to happen.

THIRTY-TWO

A few weeks had passed since Annie had been completely heartbroken. Everything had changed yet somehow remained the same as it always had been. The late summer days had been filled with bright blue skies peppered with cotton wool clouds, the chirping of the birds singing their songs in the warmth of the sun, and the almost ethereal experience she felt as she watched the pink/purple pastel evening blanket drape itself over the daylight and succumb to the dark night sky. All of these things reminded her of the happy, carefree times she had spent with Edward.

However, it was now late autumn, and for the next few months, the skies, veiled in a grey/white cloak, would remain so. The days were shorter and the nights tortuously long. Every day had become sterile and desolate, just as it had the day before and just as it would be the day after. Her outlook on life mirrored the changing of the seasons and had become a metaphor for how she had been feeling.

Any confidence that had been built up by Edward had been destroyed by his deceit and lies; it wasn't her he wanted; she was just a pawn in his game, someone who had been chewed up and spat out. The door to happiness—or freedom—the excitement of whatever lay ahead had been firmly slammed in her face, and she found herself back to square one. Joe's absence and the fact that he wouldn't be around for a while were the only positives.

Her emotions had become erratic and unpredictable. She experienced betrayal, humiliation, and scorn. In her fragile mind, all men were bastards, and she detested every single one of them. They looked like they were made on the same factory line and distributed to the sad, desperate, and the downright unlucky.

She felt a surge of anger, directed not just at him but also at herself for having placed herself in such a precarious situation to begin with. How could she have been so stupid and naive? How could she ever think she'd be whisked off her feet and live the happily ever after life she always wanted? The world was harsh, hard, and brutal, and any such fairytale dreams should have remained in books and on the screens. Just as the world had come to terms with President Kennedy's assassination, Annie also felt a profound sense of loss as if she too was mourning a loved one's passing.

Eric walked into his mum's bedroom with a cup of tea. The only light in the room came from the door he'd just entered. He placed the cup on the side table next to the bed and tapped her on the shoulder. "Mum?"

Annie didn't move. He shook her shoulder again. "Mum, time to get up." She blinked a couple of times, then slowly opened her eyes and let out a long, heavy sigh. "Are you still feeling poorly?" He asked.

"What time is it?" She asked, rubbing her eyes with her hands.

"It's time you got up," he insisted, "I made John's breakfast, and he's gone off to school. I've washed the dishes, and I've peeled the potatoes, so please, can you get up, 'cause I'm gonna be late for school again?"

She pulled the blankets over her head and muttered, "Ten more minutes." With a forceful swish, he opened the curtains, allowing the room to flood with sunlight. He shook her vigorously until she snapped. "Just leave me alone, will ya? Can't you see I'm not feeling well? Go and bugger off to school."

"No. You've got to get up and get out of bed, Mum." He tugged the blankets off her. "I know you feel safe in bed, but you need to get up. Please! It's not good for you, lying in one room all the time like Dad."

"I can't ever do right from wrong in this place. And I certainly don't need you picking on me. I had enough of that from him!" She barked in frustration. "Close the curtains and shut the door on your way out."

Eric replied firmly, "I'm not going until you get up."

She threw her blankets back and sat up, spun herself round, and planted her feet firmly on the floor. With great effort and little energy—and feeling like she had nothing left to give—she stood up and pointed at Eric. "Are you happy now? Now, piss off and go to school."

She got straight back into bed as he walked towards the door. She leaned over to her bedside drawer and produced a small half-empty bottle of vodka. She took a swig, shook her head, and forced it down; this had become her only friend. Eric looked over at her and frowned. "Mum… please." Annie shot him a filthy look.

Closing the door behind him, he stood outside in utter bewilderment. His mother had only ever shown love and affection for them both, but now, he had never seen her so cold, uncaring, and detached. Her eyes appeared hollow, nearly lifeless, and she had transformed into a mere shadow of her former self. But he didn't know the exact reason why.

It had been weeks since she had seemingly given up and had taken to her bed. Usually she would have been up before everyone else, but she couldn't muster the strength to leave her bedroom anymore. Her growing depression, the monotony of everyday life, the debts that had been piling up, and the abuse and disappointment of men had exhausted her. Her heart felt heavy in her chest, leaving her with little to no energy. She didn't have the flu or a heavy cold, or a stomach bug for that matter. In fact, she hadn't been feeling poorly at all. She felt lost and empty; she was spiralling into oblivion.

Eric headed downstairs feeling heartbroken. His mother was whiling her days away in bed in some incoherent fog through the booze and pills while he desperately tried to hold the fort but was unable to do anything to help. He grabbed his coat and bag and headed up the road to school.

Walking up the street, a car pulled up beside him, and the window opened. "Are you Eric?"

"Yeah, why? Who wants to know?" He felt on edge, stooping down to see who this stranger was and what he wanted.

"Are you off to school? Jump in, and I will drop you."

"Fuck you, ya dirty old perv!" he sneered.

"You're a cheeky little shit, aren't you?"

"Well, you're the one who pulled up beside me asking who I am. Bit weird, innit, you driving about the streets looking for young boys?"

He leaned over toward Eric, who could now get a clearer view of who he was talking to. "My name is Roy, and I work for Mr. Fitzpatrick, an acquaintance of your dad's. You know him, don't you?"

"Yeah, of course I do."

"He has sent me round to make sure everything is okay, see if you need anything."

"We're fine."

"Mr. Fitzpatrick thought your mum would be struggling with a few things since your dad's been locked up."

"Well, I told ya, we're just fine."

"Shut up and just get in the car," he replied bluntly.

"No! I'm not getting in. I said we're fine. I've got to go." He continued walking, but Roy was unyielding; the car slowly moved alongside him.

With force, he said, "Look, get in," demonstrating his unwavering persistence. "I'm not asking you this time; I'm telling you. And, if you don't, I'll fucking drag you in."

Eric knew at this point he had to get in. The car stopped, Roy leaned across and opened the passenger door. Eric climbed in, and they drove off. "I've got a few errands to run, so you're coming with me."

"Why?" Eric felt uncomfortable when he ignored him. He didn't even know this man, and how did he know if he even knew Ronnie? They drove out of town, the hum of the engine drowning out the silence between them, and they soon turned a corner and headed into an undesirable-looking area. Eric still didn't know what the hell he was doing in the car and where they were heading. He turned and looked at him. "Where are we going?" he said, despite his inner turmoil.

Roy's eyes were fixed on the road. "You wanna earn yourself a bit of cash?"

Eric was apprehensive but the money was too tempting. "How much?"

"Fucking hell, you're a cheeky little shit, aren't you? You didn't want to get in the car a minute ago, and now you're asking how much you'll make without knowing what you're doing."

Eric sat back in his seat. "Well, as long as it's not sexual, I'll do anything."

Roy looked at him, surprised. "Fucking hell, it's nothing like that, you silly bastard."

Eric felt relieved. It was bad enough that it had happened to him by his dad, let alone a stranger. "Where are we going then?"

"Can you shut up for a minute?"

Eric realised he had gone too far, so he chose to remain silent for the remainder of the journey.

They pulled up outside a dingy shop. Roy opened his car door. "Wait here."

Eric nodded and watched him disappear into the shop. He glanced around nervously, wondering if he had made a mistake. A couple of minutes later, Roy returned, holding a small package wrapped in brown paper. He got in the car, and passed him the package. "Take this to the address I'm about to give you," Roy said, starting the engine. "Don't open it, just deliver it."

Eric stared at the package in his lap, wondering what was inside. Drugs? Money? Something worse? He didn't ask. He just nodded, his mind racing. This was it—his first job for Roy, for Ronnie. As much as he wanted to turn away, something inside him kept pushing forward.

Eric looked out of the window. He knew if he wanted things to change in his life, he had to do something about it, and now was the time to earn some cash - some serious cash - and finally fuck school off altogether.

THIRTY-THREE

Annie never considered herself to be a drinker. With the exception of Christmas and occasional parties, where she occasionally indulged in a glass of wine or sherry, she typically abstained from alcohol. But these days were far from usual. She drank—and she drank a lot—to the point where she relied on alcohol to get her through the day. When she eventually managed to rise from her bed, she sipped on a large glass of vodka, which was akin to her first cuppa of the day. She took a cheeky sip to rouse herself, followed by another to wash down the paracetamol she had taken to alleviate the persistent headaches she was experiencing.

It was two-thirty in the afternoon. She was still in her nightie making a cup of tea in the kitchen. She put the milk back in the fridge and opened a cupboard above her head. She reached in and produced a small bottle of rum, which she tipped into her tea before putting it back where it belonged. Peggy entered through the backdoor, making Annie jump.

"What the hell do you think you're doing, strolling in here like that?" Annie remarked. Peggy found her rudeness shocking.

"And a good afternoon to you too! Bloody hell, what's up with you? I haven't seen you for a while, so I came over to see ya, and this is the welcome I get?"

Annie glared at her. "So you thought you would stroll through my back door, did ya?"

"Your front door's locked—for some reason—so I thought I'd come round the back. Is that such a crime?" Peggy softened.

"Look, Annie, I'm worried about you."

Annie's words slurred. "Yeah, well, don't be. I survived when you weren't living across the road, and I'm sure I can survive now that you are."

"You haven't been right since he went away. This isn't like you."

Annie became animated; she flung her arms in the air and became more and more aggressive. Peggy had never seen her behave like this; she was always so understanding, so considerate. She didn't recognise the person standing before her. "You think it's to do with that bastard? Just shows how well you know me, doesn't it! It runs deeper than him, let me tell you. All the things he's done to me don't even come close to what I've been through these last few months."

Peggy tried to calm her down. "What's happened?" she asked, grabbing her arms to offer a crumb of comfort. Annie shied away. "Talk to me; you can tell me anything; you know that! We have been friends for years. I only want to help."

"Friends for years, really... Do you think so? You... you've always been jealous of me!"

Peggy scoffed, "Jealous? Why would I be jealous of you?"

"Oh, c'mon, you're not stupid; look at us. For example, I've never struggled financially. We've got a car, a television, a telephone...most people haven't got any of these things, especially around here. I've always been able to get by, whereas you've always struggled to make ends meet, hence me paying off your bloody debts."

"What? I didn't ask you to do it, but you did it because I thought we were friends." Peggy explained.

Annie continued. "I've always made an effort to look good, but you wear the same clothes every day, no matter where you go. You've never had any ambition, have ya? You had all your life in front of you; you could have been anything you wanted to be, but instead you married your childhood sweetheart, popped a few babies out, and have lived a dull, boring life ever since. But the main thing is you're jealous 'cause you've always wanted to *be* me, haven't ya?"

"What? Don't flatter yourself, darlin'," Peggy spat back. "Let me tell you something. You've had your say; now listen to me for a change."

Annie stood with her arms folded, ready to listen to whatever she was about to say.

"All I have ever done is listen to you moan about everything and talk shit. Oh, you have a bloody nerve, you do. First things first, I've never been jealous of anybody, let alone *you*. I have treated you like you were my sister since we were little, and now look at ya? Y'see, Annie, for all ya lovely dresses and fancy hairdos, ya sparkly jewellery, and ya posh telly and telephone, I've got something you don't."

"What's that then?"

"A loving husband."

Peggy's words resonated with Annie, bringing back all of her emotions. Of course, Peggy was right, but Annie didn't want to admit it. Backed into a corner, her only form of defence was to attack. She pointed her finger at Peggy. "Your Albert has always wanted me, y'know, and you've always known this, haven't you?"

Peggy erupted into laughter. "He might have fancied you when we were kids, but he's definitely never wanted you, and he certainly wouldn't now. Look at the state of you; you're a bloody mess! Oh, and one more thing: seeing as we are telling our truths, my husband has never so much as laid a finger on me. It's a shame the same can't be said for that bastard you're married to. You think you have it all? You don't have anything!"

Peggy knew she had to tell her a few home truths, hoping this would help her; she also knew this was not her best friend talking; this was the booze, and she was at breaking point. Rather than continue to tear a strip off her, she walked towards the back door, but before she walked out, she turned to face Annie and shook her head. "You're out of order, you are! You're gonna end up killing yourself if you carry on like this. Imagine how your boys would feel. Take a good look at yourself, Annie. You're a fucking mess, and the answer to your life isn't hidden in a bottle. So on that note, I'm gonna go. Think about what you're doing to yourself. You know where to find me when you need me or, better still, want to talk."

Annie swigged her tea in one gulp and let out a flagrant, exaggerated gasp. She remained silent and defiant, aiming a blatantly obvious two-finger salute at Peggy, along with an obligatory 'fuck you!' thrown in for good measure. Peggy shook her head. Feeling hurt seeing her like this, she slammed the back door behind her. She stood out in the yard and breathed an almighty sigh.

Annie grabbed the rum from the cupboard and headed off upstairs. Sitting down at her dressing table, she looked at her reflection in the mirror. Staring back at her was someone she didn't recognise—a gaunt-looking, pale-faced shell of the woman she used to be. With dark circles under her eyes and a few extra lines on her furrowed brow, she was shocked at how much older she now looked. She reached over to a small bottle of pills, opened it, and shook several into the palm of her hand. She paused for a moment before putting them on the dresser.

Looking back into the mirror, she grabbed a lipstick and applied it liberally across her lips until they were a thick, waxy mess. Using the back of her hand, she then smudged it all over her mouth and cheeks. She stared into the mirror again. With her grey complexion and a scarlet gash daubed across her face, she looked like a clown. Angered by this, she growled under her breath. "I'm a mess, am I, Peggy? I'll fucking show you."

THIRTY-FOUR

Annie woke up that morning feeling a flicker of determination she hadn't felt in weeks. Her life had been chaotic for far too long; she needed to get herself together and try to restore some order. Peggy's harsh but honest words had been echoing in her mind, gnawing at her through her depression.

Peggy had been right. Annie had everything but the one thing that truly mattered—peace. And she realised that if she didn't pull herself together, she would lose everything else too. Her boys needed her. She had to be there for them, for herself, no matter how broken she felt inside.

The prospect of another gloomy, empty day was too much for her to take, so today would be the first day of the rest of her life. No more, she swore to herself; she would not give in to her feelings of shame.

It became clear to her that she needed to make a change because things had spiralled out of control. Getting the house in order was the first step in making it a more pleasant place to live. Additionally, she was aware that she needed to apologise to Peggy, but she was not looking forward to doing so.

She started with something simple. She got out of bed, pulled on some clothes, and stared at her reflection in the mirror. She didn't look her best, but there was still a glimmer of life left in her.

She began by collecting the empty spirits bottles lying around the house and pouring them down the sink. She then set out to clean the house. She collected all the rubbish, placed it in rusty metal dustbins, and carried it into the lane for the dustmen to pick up. Washing and scrubbing the cracked paving slabs until they were immaculate and scattering a few potted plants around the yard added a splash of colour to the once dull space.

By the time she was done, the house looked like it used to, back when she had cared, when she hadn't let her life spiral into chaos. It was late afternoon, and she felt a pang of exhaustion, but also pride. She had done it.

She had started to pull herself out of the hole she'd been sinking into for so long. She decided to make dinner—nothing fancy, just something hearty and warm. She put some chicken in the oven, boiled some potatoes, and prepared vegetables.

The familiar act of cooking grounded her, reminding her of simpler times when her boys were younger and Joe was away more than he was home. She used to take pleasure in small things like this—making a home—and for the first time in a long time, she allowed herself to feel that again.

The boys made their way home from school. They rarely talked because they had little to talk about other than school, which they didn't want to discuss. The thought of returning home had begun to fill them with dread. John, affected by his mum's emotional state, had grown more reserved and quiet, and no matter how hard Eric tried to encourage him, he refused to talk.

On the other hand, Eric was taking on all the responsibility at home, looking after and attending to all his mum's needs and wants. He had shown great maturity at such a young age. He would attend the register in the morning, then bunk off school with his mates to go shoplifting or doss around the empty houses on the wasteland. Whenever he did stay at school, he would frequently doze off during class, act disruptively, get into fights with other boys, and inevitably wind up in the headmaster's office. This, however, all changed when Roy started to take him out on jobs and he started earning money. Good money.

Eric stood on the front doorstep and grabbed the handle. He inhaled deeply, bracing himself to be surprised by what version of their mum they were going to get today. Lately, each day had become monotonous and repetitive; he felt a sense of being trapped, a hamster on a wheel, yearning to progress without ever getting anywhere.

Even when his dad wasn't in prison, life was tough, but at least they had a wonderful mum. However, since he had been sent down, her condition had deteriorated; a fog of depression had settled over her, and neither of the boys really understood why. They had hoped that his incarceration would make her happy, but it seemed to have the opposite effect.

Eric opened the front door, and they were met with the aroma of the most mouth-watering home-cooked meal they had not smelt in a long time. They inhaled deeply and closed their eyes, reviving their senses as they savoured the moment. Suddenly, their taste buds started to tingle, their mouths started to salivate, the sound of the radio became audible, and a faint, melodic voice could be heard coming from the kitchen. However, the aroma was unlike anything they had ever encountered before.

John grabbed Eric's arm. "Mum's out of bed... and she's cooking! You know what that means, don't ya?"

"It means I don't have to eat your shit food anymore," John joked.

Eric grinned. "You cheeky bastard. Listen, just walk in normal, like we always have, and don't say anything, okay?" With a nod they entered the house and closed the door behind them.

"Hello boys!" Annie called out from the kitchen. They hadn't heard her upbeat voice in what felt like forever. "Dinner won't be long." At the foot of the stairs, Eric closed his eyes and stared up at the ceiling. He grinned as he wiped away a few tears with the sleeve of his sweater, overcome with an enormous sense of relief.

Stepping into the kitchen, she turned around and smiled at them—a real, genuine smile. They hadn't seen their mother like this in weeks. She had washed, blow-dried, and set her hair. Her skin shimmered under the ceiling light, and her emerald eyes sparkled with a little hint of makeup. Her pinafore concealed a knee-length skirt and a chunky, cosy sweater. Instead of the gaunt, sunken-eyed wreck who had spent her days moping about the house, here was their familiar, beloved mother.

She looked beautiful.

"Alright, Mum?" John cautiously enquired. She approached him, grabbed both his cheeks, and planted a gentle kiss on his forehead. "I am, my darling."

She did the same to Eric, but after kissing him, she pulled him in close and whispered in his ear. "Thank you. Thank you for all your help over the last few weeks. I don't know what I would have done without you."

He looked deep into her eyes. "You're my mum. I'd do anything for you." The three of them embraced each other. She didn't feel lost anymore. With Joe gone, she was determined to rebuild her life and establish a sense of normality for her boys, fully aware that every day would bring new challenges.

Annie reconnected with her boys during dinner. They had started talking about how tasty it was and shared a giggle over Eric's happiness at not having to do all the chores anymore. She asked the boys about their day and how school had gone.

"It's boring," was John's typical reply.

Eric, however, remained silent. She had a feeling that something was bothering him, but she was unable to pinpoint it.

"And you, Eric, how was school today?"

He gave a shrug. "It was okay."

John looked at her and then at Eric. "He bunked off school today. He's done it for weeks."

"Shut your mouth, John!" He said angrily, and then punched him in the arm.

"Ow, get off me, will ya? Mum needs to know the truth," he shouted.

"That's enough, boys, stop it!" her heart sank, but her voice stayed composed. "Is that true, Eric?"

His eyes flickered in defiance as he looked at her. "What does it matter, anyway? School is pointless. I would much rather be working and earning money than sitting there wasting my time. I have no interest in learning anything useful there. You were drinking, and somebody had to pay the bills, so I had to get a job."

"Doing what? Who do you work for?"

"Mr. Carter's fishing tackle shop. I ain't going back to school and you ain't making me. Dad's not around anymore, and you need somebody to keep paying the bills."

She paused for thought but she couldn't argue with his reasoning. "I suppose you're right."

"Hey, does that mean I can get a job 'n' all?" John interjected.

Eric smiled.

"John, Just eat your dinner."

With the washing up finally finished, it was time for one more thing to address. Putting her coat on and applying a fresh coat of lipstick in front of the mirror, Annie opened the front door and set off across the road.

Annie was just about to knock on Peggy's front door, her hands quivering just a bit in nervous anticipation. Weeks had passed since her last visit, and their previous conversation had been filled with tension. Since she unleashed those painful words at her best friend, the guilt has been persistently weighing on her mind. After emerging from her deepest despair, she recognised the need to make amends. But the worry remained: what if Peggy no longer wanted anything to do with her?

Her heart raced as her knuckles rapped against the door. She contemplated turning around and leaving, as the wait appeared to stretch on endlessly. However, the door swung open.

Peggy stood there, her face glowing with astonishment. "Hello, Annie."

Even with the immense feeling of relief, Annie remained acutely aware of the burden of guilt. She couldn't meet Peggy's gaze and instead focused on her hands. "I came to apologise," she said softly. "I was horrible to you, no matter what I said, and I'm truly sorry. You didn't deserve any of that."

Peggy's manner softened. She extended her hand and gently touched Annie's arm. "Oh, Annie. Don't be silly. We've all been through difficult times. There's no need to explain."

With tears brimming in her eyes, Annie looked up. "I can't quite explain what happened to me... I felt completely lost and overwhelmed by everything, and I took everything out on you. You have been a wonderful friend to me, and I'm so sorry I yelled at you."

Peggy beamed, her eyes full of affection. "Love, you were going through a really tough time. I was worried about you. But I'm glad you're here now."

"You mean that?" Annie enquired softly. She remained astonished that Peggy could show such forgiveness.

"I certainly do," Peggy replied, swinging the door open wide. "Come in, my dear. I've just brewed some tea."

Annie stepped inside and instantly experienced the comfort that had been absent from her life for far too long. Peggy's home, adorned with delicate floral wallpaper and filled with the aroma of freshly made tea, welcomed her with its comforting warmth.

In the living room, Peggy had thoughtfully arranged a charming little tea set on the coffee table. Peggy said, "I was hoping you'd come around eventually," as they settled into their seats. "I had a feeling you just needed some space."

Annie gazed at Peggy, and a tightness gripped her throat. "You are too kind to me."

Peggy carefully poured a cup of tea for Annie and placed it gently on the table. "You were suffering, love. It's common for people to express their emotions when they are in pain. I could sense that it wasn't you speaking."

Annie felt a comforting warmth as she savoured her tea. "You've been there for me for as long as I can remember. I don't deserve your kindness."

Peggy waved her hand dismissively. "Shut your bloody mouth, will ya? That's what friends are for. We'll be there for one another no matter what. It takes a lot of courage to come here and apologise. I really appreciate it."

For a while, they enjoyed their tea in comfortable silence. Annie felt a sense of ease for the first time in a long while. She surveyed the room, noticing the subtle details she had missed before, like Peggy's framed photo collection on the mantelpiece, the knitted blankets draped over the sofa, and the soft ticking of the wall clock. Everything felt so... ordinary, and that was exactly what she had longed for.

Annie whispered, "I've missed this."

Peggy radiated joy. "I've missed you, 'n' all. But what really matters is that you're back now."

For hours, they reconnected and shared the details of their lives, discussing everything that had happened between them. Peggy told Annie about the simple things, like how Albert had finally mended the squeaky door that had been driving her crazy and how the neighbours were doing. Listening to her stories gave Annie a sense of belonging she hadn't had in a long time.

Over the course of the evening, Annie felt lighter than she had in a long time. Peggy had welcomed her back with wide arms, as she always had, and this gave Annie the courage and strength to keep going.

Before departing, Annie faced Peggy. "Thank you for forgiving me. I don't know what I'd do without you."

Peggy held her tightly. "You won't ever have to find out, my love. I'll always be there for you."

Annie felt a sense of fulfilment as she made her way home. She knew she had a long journey ahead of her, but she was no longer alone, and perhaps everything would be okay after all.

THIRTY-FIVE

Annie woke up abruptly in bed upon hearing the distinct sound of clattering downstairs. For a moment, she was disoriented, unsure if it was real or just another of her unsettling dreams. But then the noise came again—louder, more deliberate. Something, or someone, was definitely moving around downstairs.

Her heart raced, and she fumbled for the bedside lamp, but her hand froze halfway when she heard the soft padding of feet approaching. It was Eric, his face pale and tense as he stood in the doorway, peering at her with wide eyes.

"Mum, what's going on?" he whispered.

Annie blinked, trying to shake off the sleepiness in her eyes. The house was pretty dark, but she just had this feeling that something was wrong. She kicked off the blankets and swung her legs over the edge of the bed. She reached under the bed, and her fingers brushed against the crowbar she had stashed away— just in case. She didn't trust a lot of things these days, but she trusted the weight of that tool in her hand.

"Stay here," keeping her voice low but firm.

Eric frowned. "Mum—"

"I said stay," she cut him off, her eyes blazing with determination. "I'll be fine."

Eric stepped back reluctantly, watching as she moved purposefully toward the bedroom door, crowbar in hand. Descending the stairs slowly, her heart pounding in her chest, every step filled with trepidation. As she reached the bottom, the dim light from the back lane outside barely illuminated the kitchen. She could see the silhouette of a figure rummaging through the drawers, and cursing.

"Get out of my house!" she yelled at the shadowy figure bent over the sink. She gasped when he suddenly turned to face her, and a familiar voice barked back at her.

"What are you doing, you stupid bitch?"

"Joe?"

"Who else did you think it fucking was."

Annie's body tensed at the sight of him. What was he doing here? He should have been in prison. She hadn't seen or heard from him in weeks, and yet here he was, tearing through the kitchen like a madman.

"Joe," she said, her voice strong but a bit shaky at the end, "what are you doing?"

Joe didn't look up at first. He was too consumed by his frantic search, slamming drawers shut and tossing utensils and papers aside. "Where's the bloody key, Annie?" he growled, his voice tinged with desperation.

Annie stepped further into the kitchen, tightening her grip on the crowbar. "Key to what?"

"The coal shed!" Joe barked, finally turning to face her. His eyes were wild, bloodshot, and hollow. He appeared more unshaven and gaunt than the last time she had seen him, resembling a man unravelling from within. "Where is it?"

Annie stared at him, trying to make sense of his frenzied state. "What's in the coal shed? What are you looking for?"

But Joe ignored her question, brushing past her as if she didn't exist. His entire focus was on finding that key, his hands trembling as he yanked open more cabinets, his frustration growing by the second.

Upstairs, Eric had returned to his bedroom, but he wasn't alone. John, wide-eyed with curiosity and fear, stood beside him, peeking out through the door. Together, they listened in tense silence as Joe stumbled outside, fumbling with a torch as he made his way to the coal shed.

"What's he doing?" John whispered, his voice shaky.

"He's looking for something." Eric replied, his eyes narrowing. He didn't trust his dad one bit, and whatever his intentions were sent a shiver down his spine.

The boys crept toward their bedroom window and peered out into the backyard. They could see Joe outside, cursing under his breath as he banged on the door to the coal shed. The old wooden door groaned as he forced it open, revealing the small, dusty space inside. Eric and John exchanged a glance—this wasn't the first time they had seen their father act like this. He'd always been erratic and prone to outbursts and wild schemes. But tonight felt different. Desperation clung to him like a second skin.

"What do you think he's looking for?" John asked nervously.

Eric shrugged, but his stomach churned. "Whatever it is, it can't be good."

Joe began pulling things out of the shed and tossing them carelessly onto the ground in his frantic search for something. The storm clouds overhead had yet to break, but the wind had started to pick up, swirling leaves, coal dust, and debris around the yard. He was oblivious to it all, his attention fixated on finding whatever he was looking for.

Annie stood in the doorway, watching him from a distance. Her earlier resolve had begun to falter. This man she had once believed in had become a stranger, consumed by whatever darkness had taken root inside him.

"Joe, what are you looking for?"

He didn't answer. He had emptied the contents of two bags of coal and found a small, locked toolbox in the corner of the shed, half-buried under the coal dust. His hands shook as he yanked at the lock, but it wouldn't budge. He cursed under his breath, looking around wildly for something to break it open.

"I know he's hid it here… that fucking Eddie… trying to set me up again." He grumbled to himself as he tried smashing the lock open.

"I hope you're gonna tidy all this shit up," she said sternly.

Luckily, Joe was too frantic to hear what she had said, because if he had, he would have belted her.

"In case you hadn't notice, I've been in prison, 'cause those fuckers—especially Eddie, that slimy, two-faced bastard—set me up, and I need to make sure they haven't put anything else in there."

She took a deep breath. Eddie, or Edward as she knew him, penetrated her soul. Joe slammed the box on the ground, determined to break it open. The sound echoed in the darkness, and as she stood there, watching him wreck what was left of their messed-up lives, she realised that whatever was in that box wasn't just a secret—it was the final piece of Joe's broken soul.

Without saying a word, she headed back inside. She could feel her mood changing as she trudged upstairs. Eric hung over the bannister waiting for her to come up, however he was lost in his own thoughts. He realized something he hadn't fully grasped until now—he had another secret. His dad had always been the one running around doing shady jobs for Ronnie, And yet here he was, stepping into the same murky world as him. "He's out, then."

"Clearly."

"I knew this peace wouldn't last for long," he said, noticing an instant change in his mum's demeanour.

She brushed past him. "Go get in bed now," she said firmly, walking into her bedroom and closing the door behind her. Eric knew how mentally fragile she was, and anything could tip her over the edge. He walked back into the bedroom, John still standing on his bed and peering through the window.

"What's going on?" He asked loudly.

"Shush, will ya? Keep ya noise down; you don't want him coming up here."

Joe was filthy, covered from head to toe in black soot as he made his way back into the house. He showed complete disregard for what Annie had said, leaving a huge mess behind. The boys quickly closed the curtains and got back into their beds. They pulled their blankets over them and looked at each other. "What do you think he's up to?" John asked with some trepidation.

Eric shook his head. "I have no idea, kid. But now he's back; who knows what's gonna happen?"

THIRTY-SIX

"Just to remind you," Annie said, her back turned to Joe as she finished washing the last few dishes, "it's Peggy's birthday on Friday. She's having a little get-together with the neighbours. Me and the boys are popping over to have a few drinks and some food."

He looked at her and shrugged his shoulders. "Drinks? But you don't drink."

"I don't." She spoke with a hint of defiance in her voice. "I know you come back every few days for clothes and to see who's been asking for you, but I thought I would tell you because if you came back and we weren't here, you'd go mad, seeing as you seem to be treating this place like a hotel at the minute."

John looked over to his dad and panicked for a moment, burying his nose further into his comic, waiting and anticipating the worst because his dad would usually fly off the handle if Annie dared to answer back.

"Well, I won't be back Friday; I'll come Saturday, so make sure my washing is done for then and don't go fucking gossiping or telling anyone you've seen me." He picked his keys up from the worktop and went out the back door. John lowered his comic and looked at his mum, relieved his dad had left and didn't start fighting; Joe couldn't hang around or be seen in the area, which was a good thing because if Annie had spoken to him like that in the past, he would have battered her.

For the first time in a long time, she said what she wanted and didn't seem to care. Having a clear mind and not a fuzzy one from the drink gave her a newfound strength and confidence she hadn't had in a while. Perhaps she had finally broken free of the shackles that had weighed her down and found her voice. Or maybe he just wasn't listening because he knew he had to get in and out.

Eric walked into the kitchen to find John still sitting at the table. "Alright, where's Mum?"

"She has gone to get her hair done." He remained engrossed in his comic. "Where've you been?"

Eric grabbed a glass from the cupboard, opened the fridge, and poured himself a drink. "I've been out and about. Here, I got you something." He reached into his pocket and tossed a bar of chocolate over to him.

"Thanks! I suppose you got this out of your wages from your Uncle Ronnie, did ya?"

"Do you want it or not?" Eric snapped, reaching out to grab it back from him.

"Of course I do! I can't believe Mum let you leave school, and I've still got to go. If she knew who you were working for, you'd have to go to school. Working in the tackle shop… my arse!"

"You ain't gonna say anything, 'cause we're all gonna benefit from this. So I suggest you shut the fuck up and eat ya chocolate."

A few hours later, Annie arrived home from the salon, her hair wrapped in a headscarf. She hung her coat up and walked into the living room where the boys were sitting watching TV. "Well, what d'ya think?" As she took her headscarf off, she twirled around.

They both said in unison."It looks lovely, Mum."

"Thank you, my darlings," she replied, smiling as she checked the time. "We've got an hour before we go over to Aunt Peggy's, so make sure you're ready by the time I've finished getting dressed. And Eric, make sure you hurry John along; you know how he likes to dawdle."

"Yeah, alright," he laughed as she disappeared upstairs.

In her bedroom, she sat at her dressing table and applied her makeup. She knew deep down that the way she was acting was a façade, a mask she was wearing to conceal the deep pain and sadness in her heart. She was determined to ensure that no one would ever find out.

Upon opening the bottom drawer of the dressing table, she found a bottle of vodka staring back at her, the only one she had forgotten to discard during the extensive cleanup. The temptation to reach down and grab it pulsated through her body. Unscrewing the lid, she raised the bottle towards her nose, taking a sniff and closing her eyes. A hollering from downstairs interrupted her just as she was about to place the bottle to her lips and take a swig.

"Mum?" John yelled, standing by the front door with Eric and peered up the stairs, his patience wearing thin.

She paused. "Yes, love?"

"How long will you be? You told Eric not to let me dawdle, but you are doing exactly that. We've been waiting ages. Can we go and meet you over there?"

"No, I will be down in just a minute." She was thankful he called up the stairs at that moment, as she was so close to giving into temptation. Screwing the lid back on the bottle, she placed it back in the bottom drawer.

The boys could make out, through the half-light on the top of the landing, a set of long, thin legs coming down the steps after a pair of feet in black court shoes. Then came the dress—a black, short-sleeved dress with a button on the front and a waist belt to accentuate her lovely curves. She came into full view, a gold crucifix glistening around her neck. With her makeup, she looked stunning. She sashayed down the stairs, carrying herself with effortless elegance.

They gasped and stood open-mouthed. They hadn't seen her looking so stunning in such a long time. "Wow, Mum... You look beautiful."

She placed her hands on their shoulders, giving them both a squeeze. "Thank you. Right, you ready?"

"Well, we have been ready for ages." Chirped John.

She walked towards the front door; they stepped aside, allowing her to pass in between them and reach for the handle. She paused for a moment to check herself out in the hallway mirror. With her hair immaculately coiffed and lipstick and makeup meticulously applied, she opened the door, and stepped out into the cold night air. They trailed behind her, shut the door, linked arms, and proceeded to cross the road.

"Only me!" Annie chirped, closing Peggy's front door behind them and walking into the living room. It seemed as though half the street had been invited; the room was packed with familiar faces, alive with conversation and laughter, and the sound of Sinatra oldies blaring from the stereo. The boys joined the other kids.

Albert was the first to greet her. "Alright, darlin'? You scrub up well," he said in his thick Cockney accent.

"Why, thank you, Albert," She replied warmly, giving him a peck on the cheek. Peggy spotted them on the other side of the room and immediately made a beeline for them. Annie's scathing remarks about Albert's desire to be with her during their argument resonated deeply with her. "Oi you, stop chatting her up and fetch her a drink." Peggy laughed.

"Yes, dear," Albert remarked, "What would you like?"

"Tonic water, please."

"Are you sure you don't want anything stronger?"

"No thanks, tonic water is fine."

As Albert went off to fetch her drink, Peggy approached Annie and looked her up and down. "Blimey, look at you. You look amazing. Nice to see you back to being yourself. You, my love, are going to let your hair down and have a wonderful time tonight, you hear me?"

As Albert was pouring her drink, Eric walked towards him. "Is that for Mum?"

"It is, indeed," Albert replied.

"Here, I'll take it to her."

Albert handed him the drink; he took a sniff to make sure it was tonic water and not something stronger.

An hour or so had passed. Several people had showered Annie with compliments, and she was well aware of her stunning appearance. Although she gave off the impression of being confident and self-assured, this was all a facade for how she was truly feeling.

By now, the drinks were flowing, everyone was slightly intoxicated, and they were having a wonderful time. Several people had offered to top Annie's glass up with something stronger, but she had politely declined their offer. However, the temptation proved too much. Throughout the course of the evening, as people arrived and left, she had discreetly been scooping up other people's drinks and knocking them down when nobody was looking.

By 11.30 pm it was time to go home. She rounded the boys up and said her goodbyes to each and every person. Peggy reluctantly showed them to the front door and insisted that they stay for a little while longer because the night was still young in her eyes. At least for one night, she wanted them to stay, dance, and forget about the world.

However, Annie wanted to get home and get the boys settled. Peggy leaned in and whispered in her ear. "Just stay; you're having a good time and you're not hurting anyone, are ya? You're only across the road."

She resisted the temptation for a moment, she wanted to be on her own. "I can't, Peg; I must get home." Peggy broke free from their embrace and gave her a knowing grin before scruffing the boys' hair.

"Go on, get yourselves home, and I'll see you tomorrow. And make sure you two look after your mother, okay?"

They walked through their front door and removed their shoes. "Come on, you two; time for bed."

"Can't we stay up a bit longer?" John sighed.

"It's late, love, and it's been a busy day."

"C'mon John, Mum's right, let's go to bed." Eric sighed, ushering him towards the stairs.

The boys said goodnight and disappeared upstairs. Annie followed a few minutes later and walked into their room. It was freezing cold; condensation ran down the inside of the window, and she could see her warm breath in the icy air. The boys were in bed and settled under several layers of blankets. She sat down on John's bed and brushed the hair out of his eyes before planting a kiss on his forehead. "Love you."

She walked over to Eric, placed her hands on his cold cheeks, and kissed him. "I love you; get some sleep now. Goodnight and God bless." She turned the light off, closed the door, and headed to her room. She sat on the stool at the dressing table and checked herself in the mirror before reaching down to the bottom drawer. She grabbed the bottle of vodka and sat staring at it for a moment. Her thoughts turned to how this drink had helped her cope with all the heartaches and disappointments she had gone through. A few glasses would numb the pain and help to try and put things into perspective. A bottle would make her forget about everything and help her sleep.

This, however, was no elixir. Alcohol could be your best friend and your worst enemy, and the insufferable headaches, the vomiting, and the hangovers were a vivid reminder of what she had endured. She cradled the bottle in her arms and headed back downstairs.

She grabbed a glass from the kitchen cupboard and poured herself a large one, walked into the living room, flicked a side lamp on, and slumped on the sofa before lighting a cigarette. Her thoughts turned to Joe. He was due back in the next day or so, the anxiety and anticipation of not knowing when he would turn up lingered in the air.

Just as she was about to go to bed, she heard the back door open. She knew who it was; he was back, but this time she didn't care. She'd had one too many and felt now was the time to stand up for herself. He walked in to find her standing in front of the fireplace, all dolled up. He yelled at her. "Who the fuck is he?" he said aggressively.

Silence.

"I said, who the fuck is he?"

"What? What are you on about?"

"Who have you tarted yourself up for, ya fucking slag. While I was away in the nick, who were ya playing happy families with?"

She exhaled, raising her glass to her lips she muttered, "No such luck!"

"What did you just say?"

She erupted. "You come back here every now and again 'cause you're so paranoid that people are after you and all you do is cause disruption and chaos in our lives. By God, I wished I did have somebody else... I would've left you years ago!"

His vacant eyes turned dark as the red mist descended on him. Flying across the room in a rage, he swiped the glass from her hand and grabbed hold of her, dragging her to the floor in front of the fireplace. He pinned her down with all his weight and wiped her mouth with the back of his hand, leaving a huge red smudge over her face.

"Let go of me, you're hurting me, what are you doing?" She screamed in panic.

"You're not all gobby now, are ya?" He spat.

The confidence and 'fuck-you' attitude vanished instantaneously, returning her to the terrified, controlled, and humiliated woman she once was. "Listen to me very carefully, you bitch," he hissed as he straddled her. "I said, who... is... he?" His face was close to hers, his eyes penetrating into her soul. She tried to turn her face, but he gripped hold of her cheeks and pressed his lips onto hers. She couldn't fight him off, so the only thing she could do was bite him. She closed her eyes tightly and sank her teeth hard into his lip.

He attempted to pull back, but her teeth held his bottom lip in a vice-like grip. He tightened his hand, raised his arm, and hit her across the head with full force. Her mouth opened as she yelled in anguish, releasing his lip. He rained punches on her, and she curled into a foetal position, desperately trying to protect herself. He roared in her ear, the blood dripping from his mouth. "If I ever find out you've had a man in my house or even my bed, I'll fucking kill ya."

She screamed in agony, scrambling along the floor, desperately trying to escape from his ceaseless attack.

The boys were woken up from the commotion coming from downstairs; John was hesitant to see what was going on but knew Eric would go down, so he had to follow. They couldn't ignore the shouting and screaming coming from the lounge. John's words of warning from months back rang around his ears: one day he would kill her. And maybe today was that day.

"Leave her alone, you bastard!"

Eric stood a few feet away with a look of sheer shock on his face, the Army knife in his hand pointing towards his father. Behind him stood John, horrified at the sheer brutality he was witnessing. "Get your hands off her or I'll cut ya, I swear I will."

She sobbed hysterically as Joe stood up and faced Eric. He laughed in his face. "You think you're gonna cut me? I don't fucking think so."

He took a step towards him, but Eric stood his ground; his hand was shaking with fear as the adrenaline coursed through his veins. "I mean it. Leave her the fuck alone, or I'll stick it in ya."

"You what? You ain't got the guts!" Joe smirked as he walked toward him. Eric readied himself, his arm outstretched with the knife pointing at him.

Annie pleaded with him. "Leave him alone, please; he's your son."

Eric continued jabbing the knife out in front of him, but Joe showed no fear. "Come on then, boy, you think you're fucking hard?"

John was screaming hysterically. "Please, stop it, will you? Eric put it down."

Joe's eyes widened. "I'd listen to him if I were you." In one swift motion, he lunged at Eric, disarming him with terrifying ease; the knife clattered to the floor. He grabbed Eric's wrist, twisting it around until his knees buckled, and he dropped to the floor. Joe grabbed his face, pulled him back to his feet, and pushed his nose into his. The pungent smell of booze and fags wafted up his nostrils as Joe's dark, bloodshot eyes stared deeply into his. Eric felt spots of saliva land on his face as his dad shouted at him.

"You ain't so fucking tough now, are ya, ya little bastard." Joe drew back his head and delivered a forceful blow to the bridge of his nose. He fell to the floor in agony with blood gushing out. John rushed over to help him up, but as he got near, Joe pushed him backward, sending him flying across the room. She was terrified screaming, upset that she couldn't do anything to help.

Joe picked the knife up and pointed it at Eric. "You've got some balls, I'll give you that. You do anything like that to me ever again, and I will slit your fucking throat from ear to ear, you hear me? And that goes for all three of ya?" Eric lay on the floor. "Do you hear me?"

"Yeah." He held his swollen nose, trying to stem the blood.

Having been launched across the room, John leaned against the wall to catch his breath. Joe made his way upstairs to collect his clean clothes, leaving the carnage behind him. Annie crawled over to the boys, all three of them huddled together, as the clock ticked on in the background.

It was just before 4 am when Annie and the boys eventually peeled themselves off the sofa and wearily made their way to bed. She had dedicated hours to comforting them, tending to their wounds, and contemplating numerous ways to put an end to their suffering. In the darkness of the early hours, when everything was peaceful and quiet—or as peaceful as it could be, given the circumstances—her thoughts shifted to how her life had led her to become such a failure: how she was failing her sons as a mother, unable to protect and keep them safe from harm.

She knew she had to leave him, somehow or some way, but fear was the only thing stopping her.

THIRTY-SEVEN

John woke up with a headache. He hadn't slept much after what had happened a few nights back; he felt groggy and a bit befuddled. The impact of being thrown across the room caused his body to ache. He groaned as he hauled himself out of bed. Walking over to the mirror, he lifted his pyjama top and turned to the side, where the dark blue and black bruises from the attack were evident. He sighed and gingerly climbed back into bed, pulling the blankets up over his head and closing his eyes, hoping he would fall back to sleep. The door opened, and he buried his head further under the covers, praying it wasn't his dad.

"John?" Annie whispered quietly through the gap in the door, just in case he was asleep. "Are you okay, my darling?" He pulled the covers back and sat up in bed when he realised it was his mum. She walked over and sat on the end of his bed, giving him a half-hearted smile. However, he struggled to look at her; the bruising on her face was truly awful. He focused on the far corner of the room instead.

She sighed, knowing full well he couldn't look at her. "Look, John, your dad... he—"

"He's going to kill you one day," he interrupted.

Annie screwed up her face. "What? Don't be ridiculous! He wouldn't ever do that. I know he gets angry from time to time, but he'd never go that far."

Heavy footsteps suddenly approached his bedroom. As Annie turned to face the door, it flung open, and standing in the doorway was an enraged Joe. He had heard everything that had been said. "Yeah, he's right!" He grabbed Annie by the hair and pulled her head back, exposing her neck. Without hesitation, he pressed the blade of Eric's knife underneath Annie's left ear and ran it across her throat. Her neck gaped open, and a waterfall of dark red blood began spurting all over the room.

Annie brought her hands up to her throat, trying desperately to stem the flow. A horrifying gurgling sound echoed around the room as she gasped for breath. She fell to the floor; a crimson sea of blood gushed onto the floorboards, soaking Joe's boots as he stood over her without a flicker of emotion.

John sat in bed and watched on in horror. He tightened the blankets around his face, revealing only his eyes as he took in the entire scene. Joe waved the knife around in the air. "You're next, you little bastard."

"Please, Dad, please don't. I'm begging you." His heart was racing, and his breathing became more shallow and erratic. An arm pressed down on his body, pinning him to the bed; he screamed in horror and yelled out at the top of his voice. "No! Please don't kill me."

"Wake up, John. It's me, Eric."

He sat up straight in bed with Eric on the edge and his hand on his shoulder. He gasped for air, his eyes darting around the room, his body soaked with sweat. "It's me... it's me... you okay?" Eric rubbed his shoulder to try and calm him down. "You must've had a nightmare." John nodded as he came to his senses. Eric continued. "Listen, I'm going out with my mates; come with us if ya like? Mum's gone round to Peggy's, then she's going shopping, and... *he's* not in, so it's up to you. You'll be on your own otherwise."

John rubbed his eyes and looked at the floor, remembering his dream. Eric pressed him for an answer. "So, are you coming or not?"

"I'm gonna stay here. I'm tired." He lay back down and pulled the blankets over his head, afraid to close his eyes because he didn't want to go back to the dream. Eric left the bedroom, closing the door behind him. He heard John whisper to himself in a quiet and concerned voice. *"What are we gonna do?"*

Eric stood at the top of the stairs and thought to himself. *'Fucking hell, you're not wrong. What are we gonna do?'*

*

Mush, Norman, Spencer and another mate, Trev, sat on the bottom stairs of the shared entrance of a block of flats and passed a cigarette around. The place was dark and depressing —an echoey chasm of grey concrete, a cold, colourless box that reeked of piss and offered no such thing as a warm welcome whatsoever. Eric confidently stepped through the door. "Alright boys?"

"We've been waiting ages for ya; where have you been?" Spencer asked. All eyes suddenly fixed on Eric's face. With a cut on the bridge of his nose and two shiny black eyes, it was hard not to notice.

"Jesus, what the fuck happened to you?" Norman said, his mouth gaping.

Mush joined in. "Bloody hell Eric, who did that to ya?"

Spencer took a step back; he knew who had done it from the way Eric was behaving and because he had been through exactly the same thing with his dad. "It was your dad, wasn't it? A tough bastard like you wouldn't end up like that from anyone else."

Eric didn't answer; he looked towards him and gave him a half-hearted nod. He pulled up his jumper and reached into the band of his trousers and pulled out a small, black handgun. He waved it in the air and pointed at the boys, who cowered in fear and covered their faces with their arms. "What are you doing, you crazy bastard? Put it away, will you?" Norman shouted.

The boys' eyes widened with excitement as Eric grinned, enjoying their reactions. "Whoa, Eric, give us a look," Mush exclaimed, his voice tinged with excitement while internally shitting himself.

Eric revelled in the power it gave him—power he lacked when he was at home.

"Bloody hell, I can't believe your dad keeps that in the house?" Spencer said.

"This ain't a real one; this is a BB gun. Dad's got a real one at home, and one day I might use it on him; ya never know."

"Especially if he does that to you again." Spencer said, pointing to his injuries. "I can hold him down while you shoot him straight between the eyes."

The lads crowded round Eric to take a closer look. "I told ya I'd get a shooter one day, but you didn't believe me, did ya?"

Mush took the gun from Eric. "It's a beauty, innit?" he said, handing it back, "So what are you gonna do with it?"

He looked at it closely in his hand. "We're gonna have a bit of fun; that's what we're gonna do."

"C'mon, let's go." Said Spencer.

It was late morning, and the gang headed through the park. It was a bright but blustery, chilly day, and the first flutters of snow had started to gently tumble from the sky like icy confetti and settle on the ground. Not too long ago, the leaves on the trees began to transform into a kaleidoscope of colours, a final display of reds, purples, yellows, and oranges, before they succumbed to the colder days, as summer reluctantly gave way to an eager autumn.

The heavy traffic snaked its way through the busy main road as people went about their business. Eric and Spencer sat on top of a metal bus shelter with their legs dangling over the side.

Norman passed the ciggy to Mush, both leaning up against the bus shelter. Trev sat shivering on a small bench in front of a small row of shops across the road. In the distance, he spotted a red double-decker bus. "Here's one," he shouted across the road. The gun gleamed in the sunlight as Eric held it and extended his arm to aim. Spencer looked at him, "Now's your time. Go on, I dare you," he said.

As the bus approached within thirty feet, he prepared himself, closed one eye, and pulled the trigger.

With a flick of his finger, he fired a pellet. It hit the side of the bus with a tiny ping, barely discernible over the din of the bustling street. Eric wasn't pleased with his effort. He aimed higher, this time at the window.

The pellet struck the glass, causing a louder sound. A few bus passengers turned their heads; some cowered in their seats, startled by what had just hit the bus. Eric's friends burst into laughter, their breath misting in the biting cold air.

"Watch this," he said, firing another shot into the bus as it slowed down.

They all failed to grasp the gravity of this situation. It was all one big joke, and the consequences of his actions hadn't even crossed their minds. When he fired the gun in the farmer's field, there was nobody around other than John, the scarecrow, and the farmer. But here, in the middle of town with loads of people and traffic, this was very dangerous. He could have injured or even killed someone, but he didn't care. As long as he got a laugh from his mates, that's all that mattered.

"Bloody hell, what a shot!" Spencer joked, impressed by Eric's sharpshooting. The laughter continued before it stopped abruptly when the bus ground to a halt several feet in front of the bus stop. The driver jumped out of his cabin at the front, and the ticket inspector hopped off the back. If that wasn't bad enough, Norman saw two uniformed policemen across the street heading towards them.

"Fuck me, it's the rozzers! Run, run!"

Eric and Spencer jumped off the roof and dropped to the ground; the others ran off in different directions. "Oi, police! Stop!" Eric and Spencer took off along the high street, laughing as they swerved and ducked their way through the busy place with the police running after them. The boys turned off the main drag into a street with a row of terraced houses. They cut down the cobbled back alleys, carefully avoiding the ubiquitous dog turds and potholes.

As they ran through the lines of washing strung across the alley, they looked back to see the coppers gaining ground. Shit!

Several kids were playing in the alley. They took no notice as they raced past. It seemed it was a common sight around these parts. The coppers gained ground, and the boys split up; Spencer made a dogleg turn down a small passageway whilst Eric continued forward. The coppers split up and continued their individual chases.

Spencer began to tire. He looked back to see where his pursuer was. He saw him hunched over with his hands on his knees, gasping for breath, so he slowed down to a jog, a cocky grin on his face. He shouted to him. "You'll never catch me, you old bastard." He turned the corner to be faced with the copper that was meant to be chasing Eric; he barged into him, knocking him flying. In a moment of panic, he ran as fast as his legs could carry him.

Eric's run started to turn into a gentle jog; the adrenaline was still coursing through his body when he slowed down even further and started to walk, catching his breath. He heard a siren in the distance, and as he looked around, he began to feel increasingly paranoid, convinced that someone was following him.

He cautiously navigated through the narrow alleyways, down the back streets, and into the cobbled lanes, constantly monitoring his surroundings until he came to the realisation that the alarm was false and he was safe. He headed home, the gun under his jumper, tucked into his trousers.

THIRTY-EIGHT

It was a horrible, grim, ghastly day: the kind of day where you just wanted to stay at home and sit in front of the fire. On a day when you wanted the school to close, it never did. Regardless of the circumstances, it would always remain open.

Eric and John trudged slowly through the snow as the icy wind whipped mercilessly around them. Flurries of snow swirled aggressively in the breeze, sending shivers down the back of their necks and soaking them to the bone.

Through the gloom, the school appeared in the distance like a ghostly apparition looming on the horizon, a nondescript concrete and glass building standing strong and resilient against the elements.

Eric felt something hit him in the shoulder. The white puff of powder upon impact was obviously a snowball, but the question was who had thrown it? Eric saw two boys nearby and approached them with John in tow.

"Shit, is that you, Eric?" Kev said, his teeth chattering and voice trembling due to the cold. "Sorry, pal, I didn't mean to hit ya; it wasn't meant for you."

"Who the fuck was it meant for then?" Eric shouted as he looked around, "Because there's no one else around other than me and John. So who were ya aiming at, our John?"

Kev's mate Pete interrupted, "No, of course not; we were only messin' about, throwing a few snowballs. We never meant to hit anyone; it just happened to hit you by mistake."

Of all the people at school that snowball could have hit, Eric ended up on the receiving end. Both of them were all too familiar with Eric's reputation and certainly knew he was not someone to mess with. While they stared at each other, they realised they were in deep trouble.

Eric looked at them both, his eyes dark, almost evil. Taking them both by surprise, he smiled as he started to walk towards the school gates. Glancing back over his shoulder, he uttered the words. "Don't worry about it; accidents happen." Both of them widened their eyes, as if acknowledging their good fortune. *That was lucky.*

But before they could relax, Eric abruptly turned around and sprinted back towards Kev, delivering a forceful rugby tackle that sent him to the ground with a sickening thud. Eric straddled Kev, pinning him down, and punching him, mirroring his father's attack on his mum.

Kev was screaming in pain. He tried to cover his face with his arms as he kicked his legs in desperation while trying to fight Eric off. Pete watched helplessly as Eric continued hitting him.

John was screaming at him to stop. "Get off him; you're gonna kill him!"

Eric ignored everyone and carried on.

Pete and John tried to pull Eric off Kev, but they were no match for him, the red mist giving him almost superhuman strength. They both bounced off him and fell to the ground. "That's enough, Eric!" John shouted, almost pleading with him to stop.

Eric paid attention to what John had to say and crawled off him. The normally white snow was now crimson, covered in Kev's blood as he lay unconscious on the ground. John sat on the ground, trying to make sense of what had just happened. He was staring at his brother, but the person he was looking at wasn't someone he recognised; it was as if his father's soul had taken over him.

Eric was just sitting beside Kev at this point, catching his breath with his head in his hands. John crawled over to see if Kev was okay. His eyes were half open and his pupils dilated as he lay still on the ground. John gave him a little shake. "Y'alright, Kev?"

Kev didn't respond.

"Kev, come on, let's get you up off the snow." He shook him a little firmer, but again, there was no response.

"You've fucking killed him!" screamed Pete. "He's dead; he's fucking dead!"

John began to panic. "Come on, talk to me, please?" His voice started to break as he began to shake him vigorously.

Kev let out a deep, low groan and blinked a few times before opening his eyes. John exhaled a breath of relief, grasped his arm, and assisted Kev in sitting up. Pete hurried over to check he was okay.

Eric watched his brother help Kev to his feet. He could see everything going on around him, but he couldn't hear anything. It was like it was all a daze for him.

He headed into school like nothing had happened, leaving all three of them there, walking away, leaving the carnage behind him like his dad always did.

Eric went to the toilets and stood at the sink, washing the blood off his hands and staring vacantly in the mirror. He slapped his face and leant into the sink, splashing it with water. Upon entering the classroom, all eyes immediately turned and followed him as he walked slowly, deliberately, towards his desk. He was clearly late and had disrupted the class; the sound of whispers and giggles filled the room. The form tutor, Mr. Gallagher wasn't impressed. "Quiet, everybody." He yelled loudly, "I said quiet!" The class fell into silence as Eric pulled his

ADVERSITY

chair out, making a deafening screeching sound across the floor. "Maxwell, you're late again. We've completed the register and marked you as absent."

Eric didn't care. "Thank you, sir. Does this mean I can go home?"

He smiled as the whole class giggled. Mr. Gallagher wasn't impressed. "Always the clown, aren't you, Maxwell? You never take anything seriously, do you?"

"Sir, there was a problem outside school. A kid had fallen over, so I stopped to help him and__"

Before he could finish, the teacher interrupted. "I don't want to know. You've always got an excuse, you do. Now sit down and be quiet. I don't care what happened outside the school; I'm still marking you as late."

"Well, that's better than being absent, innit?" Eric being Eric, always seemed to want the last word. The class burst into laughter, yet Mr. Gallagher failed to recognise the humour. He glanced at the clock on the wall and licked his back teeth.

"It's only ten past nine, and I've had enough of you already. I don't want any more of your lip for the rest of this lesson, do you hear me?"

Eric loved being the centre of attention and making the class laugh.

There was a knock on the door, and a head popped around. "Mr. Gallagher, have you got a minute?"

"Yeah, sure."

"Outside?" Miss Irving gestured with her head. Mr. Gallagher addressed the class.

"Right everyone, open your books at page forty-seven and start reading. I'll be back in a minute." He headed outside, and the second the door closed, the pupils put their books down and started chatting to one another and throwing paper missiles in their teacher's absence. The nosy students at the front struggled to hear the conversation, but all they heard was indecipherable mumbling from behind the door.

After a few moments, Mr. Gallagher stood in the doorway as it flung open with such force that it nearly fell off its hinges. With a furious look on his face, he pointed over in the direction that Eric was sitting. "You boy, stand up!" The pupils looked at each other, not sure who he was addressing.

"You, Maxwell, stand up now!"

Eric's shoulders sagged as he got to his feet.

"It appears that the real reason you were late this morning wasn't because you were helping someone. Oh no, you are not capable of performing such a noble act, are you? You were late because you beat up a boy, didn't you?" Everyone in the class gasped. Eric remained nonplussed. Mr. Gallagher continued, raising his voice, almost shouting. "The headmaster is waiting for you, so you best get down there right now!"

Eric pushed his chair out from behind him; it scraped across the floor once more. "See ya later, everyone," he sneered. The class erupted with laughter as Eric made his way towards the door. Mr. Gallagher stood aside, allowing Eric to pass. He snapped back at him.

"You never learn, do you, Maxwell? Class, quiet!"

He slammed the door behind him and moved slowly up the corridor towards the head's office. He wasn't worried about the headmaster's reaction; he was more concerned about what his father would do to him should he ever find out. He loitered outside the office for a while, trying to muster the courage to knock. He rapped on the door with his knuckles, and a loud voice boomed out. "Come in."

The head peered at Eric over his round spectacles and sighed as he sat back in his leather chair. "You again, eh? You know why you were sent to see me, Maxwell?"

"No, sir," he said shrugging his shoulders and glancing out the window disrespectfully, "but I dare say you're gonna tell me."

The head leaned forward in his chair, his face a mix of astonishment and anger. "What did you say?"

He could feel his eyes burning into him. The head immediately exploded into action, leaping from his chair and slapping his hand down hard on his desk. "Don't play games with me, young man," he shouted furiously. "You know exactly why you are here, don't you?"

He remained calm, protesting his innocence. "I don't, sir!"

The head emerged from his desk and stood right in his face. "Well, just to refresh your memory, I'm going to tell you. It's come to my attention that somebody—who shall remain nameless—notified one of my staff that you attacked Kevin Cartwright outside the school gates this morning. Is this true?"

If this was an attempt to intimidate, it had clearly failed. "Attacked, sir? Nah, I never did that. When I arrived, he was already lying on the floor. I swear. All I did was try to help him. You can ask our John; he was with me."

The head smirked. "Ask John? He's your brother, so he's bound to cover for you."

"Sir, I was outside the school, and I saw him lying there. So I went over and helped him because he looked in a bad way." The head looked at him in astonishment, as he knew what Eric was like and could smell his bullshit a mile away. Eric continued. "You see, if I'd have walked past him and not done anything to help, I'd have been in trouble. But I did stop, I did help, and I'm here anyway."

"Is that so?" The head replied, his eyes darting around, gauging his reaction.

"Sir, whoever said it was me, well, they are lying. They probably don't like me or are trying to get me into trouble or something. Ask Kev; he will tell you it wasn't me."

"Oh, I intend to, don't you worry, Maxwell. You've got a bit of a reputation around here, haven't you? And it's a rather unsavoury one as well."

Eric looked to the floor and didn't reply. The head had had enough. He interpreted this as a disrespectful gesture, assuming that he was disregarding him or didn't care about his point of view. "You, my lad, are skating on very thin ice," he said through gritted teeth. "You attacked Cartwright and beat him up, didn't you? Just admit it."

"I didn't, so what else do you want me to say?" he protested.

Unbeknownst to Eric, Miss Irving had escorted Cartwright to see the head immediately upon his arrival at school, informing him that he had slipped and fallen on some ice outside. The head didn't believe a word he had said, but as he didn't have any evidence that such a ferocious, frenetic, and downright dangerous attack had taken place, he couldn't do anything about it because it was his word against his.

"I'm giving you a week's detention, Maxwell."

"But why, sir? I didn't do anything, and Kev'll tell you that, 'n' all."

The head clenched his jaw. "I don't care. I'm giving you a week's detention, and it starts tomorrow, you hear me?" He walked around his desk back to his chair. "Don't think this is the end of the matter, Maxwell. There must have been witnesses to what happened, and I intend to delve deeper and make further enquiries. Rest assured, I will uncover the truth."

"Yes, sir, thank you, sir," he said, pretending to care. "Can I go now?"

"There's no point in contacting your parents on this occasion, but if you darken this door again, I will have no choice. Do you understand? You can go."

The head waved his hand like he was swatting a fly and mumbled to himself under his breath as Eric walked out of the room.

THIRTY-NINE

After an uneventful evening of dinner and watching television, the boys were in their beds. John's conversation turned to Kev. He had been thinking about it for the past few weeks, and the situation had calmed down. He thought this was the time to chat about it. "You scared me."

"When? What are you on about?" he said, puzzled.

"What happened to Kev? I thought you were gonna kill him, y'know, he was lifeless on the floor, and his face was covered in blood."

Eric scoffed, "There was nothing wrong with him; I hardly touched him."

"Why is everything a joke to you?"

"It's not. And well, if he hadn't thrown that snowball at me, then that wouldn't have fucking happened."

"He said it was an accident; he didn't mean to do it. You scared me, Eric; it was like it wasn't you attacking him for no reason. You reminded me of *him*."

"Who, Dad?"

John lowered his eyes and nodded. Eric snapped back. "Don't you ever say that. I'm nothing like that bastard."

"You battered him. You could have killed him, then what would have happened? You'd have ended up in prison or worse if Dad had found out; he probably would have killed you himself," John whispered.

Eric snorted under his breath. "Give over, will ya? I'm too young for that. I'd have ended up in borstal, which to be fair, would be better than living here with Dad, so it probably wouldn't be any worse." He laughed. "And here I am listening to you whinge on about something that happened weeks ago. And anyway, he was alright, wasn't he? He only suffered a few cuts and bruises. You know what, though, John? He didn't squeal; he never told a soul what happened, so actually, talking about it has made me realise I should thank him."

John glanced at him, rolling his eyes. "You seemed to enjoy it."

Eric slipped his hand underneath his pyjama bottoms and started to fondle himself. "What do you mean— enjoy it? No, I didn't."

John pressed on, concerned. "You were sitting on top of him, punching him—blood everywhere—and you didn't stop. You've changed, you have, and I don't know why. And you always seem to be flashing money around. Where did you get that from?"

Eric let out a heavy sigh. "I told ya, I'm working. It's late, now shut up, and go to sleep."

John huffed and turned his back to Eric. Eric climbed out of bed. "Where are you going?"

"I'm going to the toilet," he snapped back. "You wanna come and hold it for me?"

Downstairs, Eric locked the toilet door and sat down, pulled his penis out of his pyjamas, and started to masturbate. John was right—he had enjoyed every minute of what he had done to Kev.

*

The boys toilets at school were a cesspit of filth. One side had a large metal trough running the entire length of the wall where the boys stood and urinated. There were never any deodorising urinal blocks available, and the whole room smelt of acrid ammonia. Some boys would aim their piss at various discarded items that found their way into the trough: little crumpled balls of paper, cigarette butts (a common favourite), and even the odd feather or leaf that had been blown in through the open window would be swept down the yellow river in a race to the finish line. If only such imagination could have been applied in lessons.

Not everyone could manage to aim straight, however, and it was common for boys to end up with wet shoes, a wet leg, or stepping in a large puddle of piss on the floor. Some miscreants could even manage to hit the dizzy heights of the ceiling, achieving cult-like status among their peers as the ceiling rained its tropical waterfall down on the heads of the uninitiated who failed to look up.

It was disgusting.

Opposite this unpleasant farmyard contraption were three cubicles; most, if not all, of them were covered in scribbles, messages, or drawings. Public Service Announcements such as 'Sharon is a slag,' 'Fuck ya Mum,' or messages purporting to question the sexuality of the teachers with 'Mr Gallagher is a queer' would sit alongside the obligatory artwork depicting a penis with three pubic hairs sticking out of its balls and three drops of whatever coming out the end of it. A scribbly pair of tits would accompany such masterpieces.

Eric strode confidently down the corridor and entered the toilets. The room seemed empty upon first inspection, but something caught Eric's eye. A white plume of smoke emanated from the only occupied cubicle. He walked quietly over to the sinks and waited patiently for the door to open. He didn't have to wait long. The toilet flushed, and the door opened.

"Bloody hell, Eric, you scared the shit out of me there." Kev said, clutching his chest. "The other toilets are free, y'know."

Kev walked past him and hunched over the sink, running his fingertips under the tap, then running them through his hair.

ADVERSITY

After checking himself out in the cracked mirror on the wall, he turned to leave only to find Eric standing right behind him. "Alright, Kev?" he asked, chewing some gum. "How are you feeling now? Are you okay?"

"Yeah, I'm fine," he replied nervously. He'd managed to avoid Eric since that day, but he knew one day he'd have to face him, and today was clearly that day. "What are you doing here? School's finished, mate."

"I needed a piss, so I popped in here, and here you are."

Bumping into Kev was no coincidence. For some time, Eric had been following him closely, observing his every action, patiently waiting for the opportunity to confront him when no one else was present. "Actually, I've been wanting to talk to you, but I think you've been avoiding me."

Kev gulped. "No, I haven't. We just haven't crossed paths. It's a big school, and I've been busy. I've not been avoiding you."

"I never knew you'd signed up for extra lessons." Eric stated, completely changing the subject. Kev was surprised. He hadn't said a word to anybody that he had started extra tuition classes. How did he know?

"Nor did I, to be honest," he said, "It was my mum who made me do it."

"Well, Mums know best, don't they?" Eric had a cocky swagger about him.

"Mum wants me to do well now that my sister Jeannie's left home."

Eric jumped in, always the joker. "Jeannie? Your mum can't rub her lamp and make everything okay, can she, especially now your dad's in the nick?" Kev laughed with a sense of uneasiness, not knowing where this conversation was heading. The thought crossed his mind that Eric might shake his hand, or he might

234

batter him. Who was to know?

"It'll be up to me to get a good job and look after Mum. And I just want to make her proud."

Eric looked him in the eyes. "Proud? I'm sure she will be, 'cause I am. I'm proud of you for not grassing me up to the headmaster the other week. Why didn't you?"

"Because you're my mate."

Eric gave a reassuring nod and then looked at him menacingly. "Mate? But I don't even know you."

Kev started to feel nervous. "Well, that's true, but my dad always taught me not to be a grass."

Eric nodded, impressed by what he'd said. "Your dad taught you well." He brushed past him, entered the cubicle, and sat down on the toilet seat. He unzipped his trousers, reached into his underwear, and pulled his penis out. Kev looked on in shock. "What the fuck are ya doing?"

"I'm gonna show you how proud I am of you," Eric said menacingly. "So get over here 'cause it ain't gonna suck itself."

Kev sniggered, not in fun or amusement, but in total astonishment and fear. "You're fucking about, aren't you? This is a joke, isn't it?" Eric continued to stare at him with unblinking eyes. "You tried to kill me a few weeks ago, and now you're telling me to do this. Why?"

"Because I can, and you will." Eric replied calmly, in a sinister voice. Kev quickly realised the seriousness of the situation by looking in his eyes. Eric beckoned him over and said, "Give my Genie a rub and then suck it 'til my wishes come in ya mouth."

Kev nervously glanced at the door, unsure whether to make a run for it. "And don't think about scarpering," Eric called out, "otherwise I'll do a proper job on ya next time."

A sense of hopelessness and dread washed over him. He found

himself in a dire situation with no way out. He checked that nobody was coming in, and he shuffled towards the cubicle, knowing he had no choice. He knelt down in front of him and started to rub his erect penis. "Open ya mouth," he demanded.

Kev closed his eyes and shuddered as he took it in his mouth. Eric moaned with pleasure as his mouth went up and down his shaft. He grabbed his head with both hands and pushed it down onto him, holding him in position as he gagged on his throbbing cock.

Eric pushed him away once he'd finished. "You dirty little cunt, are you a poofter or something?" Kev got up from the floor, disgusted by what had happened and astonished at what he had said. He walked over to the sink, splashing water into his mouth and spitting it out, trying not to be sick. Eric wiped his cock with tissue paper, then stood and zipped his trousers up.

He stood in the cubicle doorway. "Chuck us a fag, will ya?" Kev's upper lip curled in disdain. He looked at him in utter bewilderment, not knowing what else to do, so he reached into his pocket, grabbed a cigarette, and chucked it over to him. Eric caught it and then carried on. "Oh, and don't even fucking think about telling anyone about this. Then again, I know you won't as you're not a grass, are ya?" He smirked. "Now sort yourself out, and off you go." Kev picked up his bag from the floor, wiped his mouth with his shirt sleeve, and ran.

FORTY

Eric's behaviour had changed; he began to distance himself from his friends. After leaving school, he began working for Ronnie, earning good money, and receiving guidance from Roy. His aspirations for bigger and better things made him feel that his friends were no longer in his league. His arrogance and confidence grew. He felt he was untouchable; he still had this anger towards his dad, which in turn fuelled his actions. He had to prove himself to Ronnie to make him believe he was nothing like his dad.

Under Roy's guidance, he performed small tasks, such as delivering and collecting packages. He still had no idea what was in them; he was just simply the courier, delivering them to undesirable places. He wasn't stupid; he knew exactly what he was doing was illegal, but he didn't care. He loved the thrill, and aside from that, the money was good.

He loved and respected his mum, but he had now become argumentative, rebellious, and problematic. She wanted to know what he was up to all the time, and not for one minute did she believe that he was working in the fishing tackle shop. She seemed to have lost total control of him; her once sweet little boy had turned into a younger version of his father.

She sat at the kitchen table and sighed. Pouring another large drink, she took a sip. It was eerily quiet with only the faint rumble of noise permeating from outside. She looked around the room, her eyes darting all around it, in deep contemplation. Here she was, on her own and feeling lonely in this empty, soulless house. She reminisced about the good times she had experienced when she and Joe had first moved in, a flood of mixed emotions filling her mind.

Back then they were young and in love, just two carefree people who had recently married and dreamed of an exciting future ahead of them. Like any couple, they experienced their share of ups and downs. Things really changed when Eric was born. Joe didn't want children—let alone two—and he didn't even want to get married, but it was illegal to be the person he really wanted to be, and, of course, she wasn't aware of any of his deep, dark secrets.

As the tears welled in her eyes, she could see the ghostly silhouettes of all the people who had shared their lives flicker and then fade from view as they swept through the room. Every friend, neighbour, and colleague who had attended parties—both sets of parents that had visited at Christmas, and family and friends who had celebrated the boys' christenings—were now firm fixtures of the past and remained bittersweet memories in her mind. This place was never somewhere she could really call home. It lacked love, but not from her. She had always lived in fear, and yes, Peggy had always been right when she said that he wasn't the right man for her. She hoped things would get better over time, but they never did.

She stood up from the table and took a swig out of the glass in front of her before heading to her bedroom. She dragged the stool from underneath her dressing table over to the wardrobe and climbed on it, steadying herself. She grabbed the leather suitcase from the top of the wardrobe, hopped down, and walked over to the bed. She laid it down and unbuckled it, and then, opening her drawers, she grabbed her clothes and stuffed as much as she could fit inside.

The tears were now streaming down her cheeks. She kept clutching her chest; the pain she felt was as if her heart was actually breaking. After grabbing a few belongings, she picked up a photo frame from her dressing table. Her two boys, standing side by side on a beach with the sun on their backs and a carefree attitude, were smiling back at her. The two most precious things in her life made her hark back to happier times. Closing her eyes, she placed the photo over her heart, taking a deep breath.

She gently placed the frame on top of her clothes and closed her case before grabbing it from the bed and lugging it down the stairs. She headed to the kitchen, placing the case by the backdoor. She grabbed a pen, paper, and envelopes and sat down at the table. Unscrewing the lid off the bottle, she filled her glass to the brim, lit a cigarette, and took a swig. She hated the smell and taste, but this numbed some of her pain and helped her get through every day. Joe had pushed her to the limits; his constant attacks, his bullying, and the relentless barrage of abuse had taken its toll on her; he had finally forced her into submission as she started to write.

She wasn't just standing on the cliff edge anymore, looking down as the waves crashed against the rocks below. She was staring into the abyss. For the next couple of hours, she sat at the kitchen table writing down all the thoughts that swirled inside her mind. At first she struggled, screwing several pieces of paper up into little balls and throwing them on the floor beside her.

The more she drank, the easier it became, and soon her emotions started to flood onto the pages. Her eyes fixed and dilated on what she was writing, she became lost in her emotional words, every syllable and sentence effortlessly pouring out.

She put the letter for her boys into an envelope, alongside a gold crucifix chain and her wedding ring, which had both been given to her by her late mother. The other letter was for Peggy. She left them propped up on the table.

Her plan was to flee as far as possible; she considered either taking the train to the coast or boarding a coach to a tranquil, rural village where she could live without the constant shadow of Joe hanging over her. After settling down and waiting for the dust to settle, she would contact Peggy to have her most prized possessions sent to her: her boys.

For years, she had set aside a little bit of her allowance each week, knowing that it would be necessary when she finally found the courage to leave him. But the more she drank, the more she realised there was no escape; no matter where she ended up, he would always find her. If she stayed, the boys would end up resenting her for being with their dad. She felt trapped, desperate, and unable to see a way out. Swigging the last of her drink down and wiping her mouth with the back of her hand, she stumbled through the house and ascended the stairs to the bedroom, removing her drab clothes as she opened the wardrobe.

She pulled out the dress she wore the night she met Joe and slipped it on. Even after all those years, it still fitted her perfectly. She carried the stool over to the dressing table and sat down, running the brush through her hair as she stared vacantly into the mirror. She applied her bright red lipstick, then brushed her eyelashes with mascara, the tears kept streaming down her cheeks. These were tears of a clown thanks to Edward. She had spent so long looking after everybody else that she had forgotten who she was.

She stood up and stepped into her high-heeled shoes, closing her eyes and inhaled deeply as if to reassure herself that this was the right thing to do. A white, fluffy dressing gown hung on a hook on the back of the door. She removed the belt and whispered to herself, "It's time."

Dragging the stool chair across the bedroom floor and onto the landing, she placed it at the top of the stairs and stood on top of it. She fashioned a noose, looped the end of the belt over the beam above her head, and secured it tightly before slipping the other end around her slim neck. She swallowed hard; her body started to tremble as her thoughts immediately turned to her boys.

The magnitude of the situation began to resonate, and the doubt began to grow.

What the hell was she thinking? How could she be so stupid, so selfish? This was the easy way out, the coward's way out. How would the boys cope without her? They needed her, and she needed them. This had gone too far. This was a mistake —a stupid, drunken, crying-for-help mistake. She couldn't go through with this. She had to stop now but realised she couldn't; it had gone too far.

With both hands, she started to fumble with the knot, trying to release it from her neck. The chair wobbled, but she regained her balance, digging her fingers underneath the belt to loosen it. The knot was tight and wouldn't budge as she began to grow increasingly frustrated. Despite her efforts, it was futile, and after several attempts to free herself, panic began to overwhelm her, causing the knot to tighten even further.

The stool wobbled again as she frantically began clawing at her neck, desperately trying to loosen it, but her despairing efforts made her feet slip off the stool. She began to choke, frantically kicking her legs trying to feel for the stool as she fought for breath. But in her attempt to find her footing, she inadvertently kicked it over. Her eyes widened, the veins in her neck bulged, and her mouth began to foam, her mind raced as she knew the game was over it was too late.

Within moments her body began to twitch, her arms and legs eventually went limp, and as she drew her last breath, life drained out of her, and the house fell silent.

FORTY-ONE

John was first in as usual, kicking his shoes off at the bottom of the stairs. "Mum, we're home," he called out, placing his jacket on the bannister. Eric followed. They were about to head to the kitchen when something caught Eric's eye. He raised his head and saw two feet dangling from the top of the stairs."Mum! No, Mum, no!" he wailed, his voice cracking as he screamed.

"What's the matter? What's happening?" John yelled, confused. Eric bolted up the stairs, two at a time; John's eyes followed, then he spotted two feet dangling in the air—one shoe on, one off—and panic set in. He froze, then started wailing hysterically; Eric's voice boomed back at him. "Get a knife!"

He ran to the kitchen in a state of desperation, searching for any knife he could find. Eric shouted as loud as he'd ever done before. "Hurry up, will you!"

He found one, sprinted up the stairs, and gave it to Eric. He picked up the stool and stood on it. He lifted her limp body up by her waist in a vain attempt to release the tension around her neck. "Help me grab her legs; don't just stand there and fucking look at me," he shouted. John handed him the knife, grabbed his mum's legs, and tried his hardest to lift her, but she was too heavy. Eric started to cut through the belt, the blade flashing back and forth in a sawing action. "Lift her higher, will ya?"

"I'm trying to... but she's heavy." John grunted as he closed his eyes with a realisation that this was his mum he was holding on to. They were not sure how long she had been hanging there, but they knew their efforts were futile. Her skin had taken on a blue/grey hue, and her body felt cold to the touch. He eventually managed to cut her loose; her dead weight landed on John's shoulders, sending them all tumbling to the floor with a sickening thud.

Eric rocked back on his heels, clasped his head in his hands, and began to cry out in excruciating pain. John couldn't cry; he just lay next to her, stroking her hair to comfort her. Eric lay down next to them both, and for the next hour or so, they remained there with Eric repeatedly muttering to his mum. "I'm sorry. I'm so sorry I couldn't save you, but I've been too selfish to even realise the pain you were in."

The house was in total darkness. For hours the boys just lay next to their mum, each with their own thoughts and emotions. It was incomprehensible that she wouldn't be here anymore. They could understand why she had done it, but it didn't make it any easier for them. The heartbreaking, distressing pain and devastation they were feeling morphed into guilt and remorse before turning to outrage, fury, and hatred.

Eric asked John to go and get a sheet from the airing cupboard. Looking down at his mum's face, he brushed the hair away from her once-piercing green eyes, which were now bloodshot and vacant, and gently wiped away his tears that had fallen onto her face. He placed his hand tenderly over her eyes and closed them. "I'm so sorry I couldn't save you from that bastard," he said again, "but I promise you one thing: I will always love you. You have my word and my honour that I will love and protect John at all costs, no matter what."

John put his hand on his shoulder and handed the sheet to him. He kissed his mum on the forehead and then turned to John, who held his hands out and pulled Eric off the floor. "Say bye, John, and kiss Mum goodnight."

He knelt down beside her, put his hands on either side of her face, and kissed her. Through his sobs he whispered gently in her ear, "I love you so much," before clambering to his feet. Eric unfolded the sheet and shook it loosely before placing it over her body. After everything these boys had been through, they had shown courage and dignity beyond their tender ages.

They walked downstairs. Eric put his arm around John's shoulder and pulled him in close. "At least she is at peace now and doesn't have to put up with his shit anymore. She's with Grandma and Grandad now, and they will look after her, won't they?"

John nodded and looked up the stairs, his lips quivering as he continued to quietly weep to himself. Eric grabbed his hand and smiled reassuringly, giving it a gentle squeeze before leading him through the living room and into the kitchen. Turning on the light, they noticed a suitcase by the back door. Eric shook his head, and his heart sank as he realised she didn't intend to take her life; she was going to leave.

He wished she had.

They both spotted envelopes propped up against a bottle on the table. Eric picked up the letters and saw one addressed to the boys and one addressed to Aunt Peggy. "I can smell her," Eric said, putting the envelopes to his nose and taking a deep breath through it. "Here, have a smell." He waved it under John's nose. He could smell the faintest whiff of her perfume. They sat down at the table. He opened the envelope addressed to them both, and he read the letter aloud.

To my boys,

I'm sorry for what I've become, and I'm sorry for leaving like this, but I don't have a choice anymore. You will never know how much I love you both, but I can no longer take this. I feel so desperately unhappy, but I thought if I wasn't here, you wouldn't have to see what you've seen over the years.

My first plan was for us all to leave, but I was let down again. Then I was saving money but had to use it when he went to prison, realising if we left, he would find us, and we would never live in peace.

So I'm afraid this was my only option. Please, please don't be mad. You may think going through with this is a sign of weakness, that I took the coward's way out, and I am selfish for doing so, but that is truly not the case. I have thought about this long and hard for ages, and in time I hope you will understand. Please don't hate me.

Eric, I have left my necklace for you, as you have always loved it. My wedding ring is for John, and I want you both to wear these forever, knowing I am always with you.

Love you.

Always and forever, Mum X

John leaned over the table, rested his head on his folded arms, and started to sob. Eric sat back in his chair and buried his head in his hands, both of them in floods of tears. Not only had they found their mum hanging, but now they had to process the reasons behind her actions. Eric was brokenhearted. He whispered to himself. "I wish I could have saved you." A wave of guilt crashed around him, engulfing him in a sea of moral emotion and dragging him to the depths where turmoil lay waiting.

Eric picked up the gold crucifix chain and kissed it, putting it around his neck and tucking it under his shirt and jumper so he could feel it against his skin. He picked up Aunt Peggy's letter, stood up, and put it in his trouser's back pocket in case their dad came back. The boys sat in silence, alone with their thoughts and together in their grief. They were exhausted and felt numb.

John whispered softly. "Should we go over and tell Aunt Peggy?"

"No, John, we can't, I don't want to go over there, not yet."

"But Mum's left her a letter as well. I think we should take it over; we need to tell her." He pleaded. Eric shook his head.

"No, not now. Don't bring up the letters anymore, I don't want to talk about it."

John lowered his head. He put her ring on his finger and gazed at it vacantly.

"Never take that off, John, you understand?" Wiping his tears with the back of his hand, he nodded as he twiddled the ring around his finger.

FORTY-TWO

Joe staggered along the narrow corridor of the rundown boarding house, breathing in the stench of stale smoke and mould clinging to the peeling walls. Since getting out of prison, he hadn't been able to pull himself together. The world outside had moved on, but he hadn't.

The whiskey in the bottle was his only company these days, and it was almost empty. He stumbled on his feet, opened the door to his little, dingy room and dropped into the lumpy bed. The springs creaked beneath him, but he didn't care; he was a drunken mess, and he knew it.

He had not always been like this. People once feared him, but they also admired him. He had connections, power, and a life built on control. He knew he had to get away, not just leave town, but leave the country completely. He would never be able to show his face around here again. Ronnie was after him, and he knew when he eventually found him, he would show no mercy.

He drank from the bottle, and wished the voices in his head would disappear, but they didn't. He groaned as he threw it across the room. Smashing against the wall, shards of glass flying everywhere. Nothing really mattered anymore. He was spiralling out of control.

He forced himself to his feet and staggered into the bathroom, his hands shaking as he grasped the sink's edge, gazing at himself in the cracked mirror. He had sunken cheeks, bloodshot eyes, and his face sported a thick, rough growth of stubble. Who was this man staring back at him?

He slammed his fist against the sink in frustration. He knew he was out of his depth now, and all the ghosts from his past were coming back to haunt him. He collapsed to the floor and let out a sinister laugh. He was a coward, escaping a life he couldn't change, hiding in a boarding house, and drowning in alcohol. With the drink dulling his senses and the darkness creeping in, he realised there was no escape. There was nothing left to protect him from himself; he had burnt all his bridges and was no longer in charge of anything. He was finished, and he knew it.

It was late at night when Joe entered the house through the backdoor, paranoid and pissed as usual. He was still in hiding, only coming home to get a change of clothes and to check who had been looking for him. "Annie?" he shouted.

Nothing.

"Annie, did you fucking hear me?"

Silence.

"Has anyone been looking for me?"

Still no response.

"Where are you?" he growled, angry and inpatient.

He heard quiet voices coming from the living room. "Are you fucking ignoring me?" he slurred. The boy's heard him stumbling about in the kitchen and wrestling to take his coat off without much success. "What the fuck is going on?" he yelled as he entered the living room and turned on the light.

The boys blinked and turned their heads towards him, rubbing their eyes, trying to adjust to the bright light. Sitting next to each other on the sofa, Eric held the letter from their mum tightly in his hand. They sat dazed without acknowledging him.

Joe staggered over to them. "Why are you both ignoring me? And don't say you didn't hear me, 'cause I know you did. And why were you sitting in the dark?"

John looked at the floor and didn't say a word. Eric glared at his dad's empty eyes, a reflection of his own. "I'm talking to you both, didn't you fucking hear me? Don't just sit there looking at me gormlessly. Where's your mum?"

Eric raised his hand and pointed at the ceiling. "She's upstairs."

"What's she doing up there? Is she packing me clean clothes?" His gaze shifted to the ceiling. "Annie, get down here now; I can't hang around; you dunno who's watching."

Eric got up from the sofa and stood tall. "You won't be getting any more clean clothes. As a matter of fact, you won't be getting anything from her anymore."

"What did you just say?" Fixing him with a stare as he swayed on the spot.

"She's dead!" John interrupted, "She's killed herself. And it's all because of you!"

Joe looked at John in astonishment, scratching the back of his neck. "So, she finally decided to do it then," he said nonchalantly, without one iota of sorrow or remorse. "Upstairs, is she?" He headed upstairs with the boys slowly following behind. He drunkenly walked up each step, steadying himself while leaning against the wall. Reaching the top, he saw two feet peeking from underneath a sheet.

He grabbed the bannister to steady himself and stepped over her lifeless body. Stooping over to pull back the sheet, he almost fell on top of her before Eric grabbed hold and steadied him. He peeled the sheet from her face and looked at her for a few moments, shaking his head and tutting before turning his attention to the boys.

"See, she's always been fucking selfish. She's a useless mother and wife... she's actually better off dead."

He looked back down at her and inhaled deeply, gathering the snot and sputum from the back of his throat with a disgusting snorting, hacking sound before pursing his lips and gobbing in her face.

Eric was absolutely flabbergasted. His dad had done some despicable things in his life—and he knew he was an evil bastard—but he couldn't believe it; this was the lowest of the low. He couldn't contain his emotions any longer and exploded with rage. He lunged at Joe, tackling him with the ferocity of a prop forward and knocking him off his unsteady feet and onto the floor. Both of them crashed onto the landing next to Annie's body, John screamed at them to stop. With the wind knocked out of Joe, Eric managed to climb on top of him, placing his hands firmly on his cheeks and turning his head to face his mum.

"Look at her, you bastard! Look at her!" He growled. "You spit in her face? Who do you think you are? You're not a man; you're a fucking coward!"

Joe hit the roof. "Who do you think you're speaking to?"

John stood behind Eric; he grabbed the back of his jumper and tried to pull him off their dad, but Joe wasn't a man to lie down for long. He grabbed Eric by his collar and tried to push him off, but he hung on for dear life, enraged at the whole injustice of it all and determined to finally assert himself. The three of them tussled and wrestled each other, pushing and pulling backwards and forwards. Eric had both hands on his dad's throat, pressing down on his windpipe with every bit of strength he had, squeezing it tighter and tighter as his face turned scarlet, his eyes bulging out of their sockets, struggling to fight him off.

John was screaming. "You're gonna kill him! You're gonna kill him!" But Eric didn't care. He finally had his dad where he wanted him, and he wasn't about to relent. He was gaining immense pleasure in seeing him struggle and receive some of his own retribution for a change, but as Joe fought for breath, fatigue set in.

Eric released his grip on his neck, exhausted and breathing

heavily from all that exertion. Joe started coughing and spluttering on the floor, gasping for air, his face dripping in sweat. Eric slowly rose to his feet and looked down at him menacingly. John was still holding onto the back of Eric's jumper, too afraid to let go.

Just as Eric was about to deliver a blow, Joe lifted his legs and forcefully kicked him in the chest, causing him to stagger back towards the stairs. Eric spread his arms out, making a grab for the bannister to break his fall, but John wasn't so fortunate. The force of the kick made him lose his grip on Eric's jumper, and he fell backwards down the stairs. He fell head over heels, crashing and bouncing off the wall with a sickening thud, and ended up in a heap at the bottom of the stairs.

Eric bounded down the stairs after him. "Oh my God, are you okay? John! John, answer me!"

John lay on his back, winded and disorientated. Eric knelt down beside him and checked he was alright when Joe's deep, angry voice thundered down the stairs. "If you think you're gonna get away with this, think again. I'll make you regret this, you little bastard. I promise you that."

Standing at the top of the stairs, his legs straddling Annie's body, he peered down at the boys and made a threatening gesture to them with his fists. "You'll keep, son; mark my words, you'll keep." He grunted, stepping over her body before adding, "Oh, and sort your fucking mum out, will ya? She's in the way lying here; maybe get that nosy bitch over the road to help you."

Grabbing a bag full of clothes from the bedroom, he stepped over Annie, padded down the stairs, and disappeared out the front door. The boys had taken refuge in the living room, turning off the lights and fervently hoping they would never see him again.

FORTY-THREE

It had been a long and emotional day, and a sleepless night followed. The boys had barricaded themselves in their bedroom overnight, blocking the door with their chest of drawers in anticipation of Joe returning and killing them in their sleep. Eric was the night watchman with his knife in hand while John lay beside him; they both tried their hardest to stay awake, but they soon succumbed to fatigue and were fast asleep in no time.

The first light of the day twinkled through the curtains, accompanied by the sound of birdsong chirping their happy melodies on the roof outside the bedroom window. Everything seemed serene and peaceful. Eric started to stir from his sleep. He slowly blinked his eyes as the light of day illuminated his face, blanketing him in a soothing warmth; it felt like the embrace he used to get from his mum.

He lay there for a moment, lost in his thoughts, until the sound of John's snoring brought him back to the harsh reality: his mum was lying on the landing floor outside their bedroom, and today was the day they had to sort everything out.

He crept out of bed, making sure not to wake his brother, and gazed towards the blocked door. He pushed the chest of drawers back, grasped the door handle, and opened it. His throat tightened, praying that what happened yesterday was only a bad dream. But this wasn't a dream; it was a nightmare that actually came true.

John started to stir; he opened his eyes to see Eric standing in the doorway. "Alright? What are ya doing?" He asked, rubbing sleep from his eyes.

"C'mon, we've got stuff to do." Reluctant to face their responsibilities, they got dressed, knowing they needed to tell Peggy.

Eric checked his back pocket to make sure her letter was there. He placed his hands on John's shoulders. "Look, Mum's still on the floor; we have to go over to Peggy's and get her to help us, okay?"

As they stood on the doorstep, poised to knock, Eric caught a glimpse of Peggy walking down the street, carrying a shopping bag.

"Hello boys," she said cheerfully, not noticing their vacant, sad faces, "what's your mum sent you over for now?"

The boys didn't say anything.

"I've just been up the shop to get some cake for our catch-up later—you know how she loves her sponge—she says only a little bit, but she ends up eating half of it," she smiled, before realising something was wrong. Terribly wrong. John started to cry; Eric's face crumpled in agonising pain.

"Whatever's the matter? What happened?"

"She's dead," Eric wailed.

"Who?" Peggy said.

"Mum she's dead."

Peggy's face dropped as the news hit her like a ton of weight. The bags slipped out of her hands and went tumbling to the floor, spilling the contents all over the pavement. For a few seconds, she stood motionless, trying to comprehend what had been said as the boys began to cry uncontrollably next to her.

"What...? How...? Why...?"

She screamed and ran across the road; the boys followed. She burst in through the door. "Where is she?" she yelled in despair. "Where's ya mum?"

Eric pointed up the stairs. She saw two feet under a sheet, ran up the stairs and saw the outline of her body.

Her legs buckled underneath her, she collapsed into a sobbing heap with her head in her hands. The boys stood behind her on the stairs. She pulled the sheet off her face and stroked her hair gently. She gasped, not knowing what had actually happened and, more importantly, who had done this to her. Her immediate thoughts turned to Joe. Had he strangled her in a fit of rage? Looking at the bruises and the crimson line across her throat, she realised she had taken her life.

Peggy was heartbroken. It was such a sad, lonely, and violent end to such a beautiful soul.

"No, Annie, no!" She lamented, "Why didn't you talk to me... why?"

The boys were distraught. They had never seen her like this. She was their Aunt Peggy, a strong, kind woman who wouldn't take any shit from anybody—not the broken, traumatised woman before them.

She eventually gathered her composure and covered her face back over with the sheet. She pulled a tissue out from under her sleeve, wiped her tears, and blew her nose. She stood up and looked at both of them. "Right, my darlin's, let's sort this all out, shall we?"

She sat them down on the sofa and asked if they had seen their dad lately. Eric explained everything to her in great detail, and Peggy's shock soon turned from disbelief to anger. She gathered the boys in her arms, reassuring them that everything would be okay, and she would sort it out.

"Mum left us letters," John said as he was being consoled by her; she blinked away a few tears, knowing exactly what these 'letters' were, and offered some words of comfort.

"That's good to know. She loved you both so much, you know."

Eric reached into his back pocket and pulled it out. "She left one for you, too," handing it to her, his hand trembling. She sat down and opened the letter. She composed herself, and, taking a deep breath, began to read.

My dearest best friend Peggy,

I am so sorry that you're reading this letter under the most extreme circumstances, but here goes.

I can't take it any longer. I've tried so hard to get by; God knows I have. I know you know this, but he has made my life unbearable. It's not fair for the boys to put up with this life, and I am genuinely scared he will eventually kill me one day. I don't want to give him the satisfaction so I have decided to do it myself. Every day I live in fear of this man, and I've tolerated it for too long. I've reached a breaking point where I can no longer bear it. I'm broken, and this is my only way out. I have no other option. I have thought about leaving so many times, but I know he will find me. Of course you will be upset and angry at me, but time heals.

You have been and will always be my most dearest friend, and I will miss our chats. But promise me one thing: please look out for my boys, whom I love with all my heart. I know you won't let me down.

Well, time to say goodbye.

Thanks for everything, all my love.

Your friend/sister.

Annie x

Tears dripped onto the letter as Peggy pored over every word. She glanced at the boys, folded it up, and placed it into the envelope. "Right, let's get your beautiful mother sorted."

Peggy was no procrastinator. She made them have some breakfast, called the school explaining why they wouldn't be in for a couple of days, then spent the rest of the morning notifying the relevant authorities.

The police arrived within an hour of receiving her call, and after being briefed on the circumstances surrounding her death, they arranged to have someone come and collect her.

Peggy held the boy's hands as their mum's body was brought down the stairs by two gentlemen in black suits. Her body was loaded into the back of a private ambulance. A few neighbours stood on their doorsteps; those that knew her well watched on, curious as to what had happened, while those on less-familiar terms gossiped among each other with strained necks.

The ambulance drove off. Peggy went back inside and started to tidy up. Upstairs, she moved the stool from the landing and put it back in Annie's bedroom before sitting on the edge of the bed, trying to feel the desperation she would have felt. She had displayed great strength in front of the boys, but in this quiet moment, alone with her thoughts, her lips started to quiver, she broke down in floods of tears.

Even a few days after her death, the house felt strangely silent. The boys had not said much, simply going through the motions, trying to make sense of it all. Eric spent more time with Roy, avoiding the house whenever possible, whereas John kept to himself and mooched around the house. Peggy had done her best to care for them, keeping the house clean and tidy, cooking dinner every evening, and just being there to guide them through their grief.

"Why don't you come and stay with me?"

Peggy asked the same question every night for the past few nights, and Eric had replied with the same answer. He was adamant he was old enough to stay at home and look after John, and if they needed her, she was only across the road. "Right, I'll be off then. There's a fresh pot of tea on top of the stove, don't forget to lock the doors, and don't be too late going to bed. I will pop over tomorrow."

She kissed them both on the forehead and headed to the hallway. John remained engrossed in the war film on TV, oblivious to her attention. "Bye," Eric said. She put her coat on and grabbed her brolly. She opened the front door and was about to leave, when she heard the back door open and slam shut. Pausing for a second, she turned around, and walked back into the living room. She put her finger towards her lips, gesturing to the boys to be quiet, and listened. She obviously knew who it was; who else would come into the house via the back door?

The sight of Peggy standing in front of him clutching her brolly caught Joe off guard as he opened the door and froze. "What are you doing here?" she asked firmly.

"What the bloody hell do you think I'm doing here? I live here," he slurred, his eyes a watery red.

Peggy pulled a face. "You've got a bloody nerve you have. You think you can just waltz in here, after walking out on these boys, leaving them to deal with what's happened?"

Joe, looking scruffy and dishevelled, like he hadn't slept in days, placed his hand against the door frame to steady himself and leaned in towards Peggy. "Quite frankly, you nosy old cunt, it's got fuck all to do with you," he said through gritted teeth, "so why don't you just fuck off home?"

He made a grab for her arm. Eric leaped off the sofa, getting prepared to rush over and help her out of fear that he might hit her. However, Peggy stepped aside and watched Joe stumble forward and collapse to the floor. She wasted no time, launching herself into a barrage of strikes to the head with her brolly and repeatedly kicking him while yelling at him.

"You bastard... you killed her! This is all your fault... I wish she never met you; you're nothing but a low-life piece of shit. You won't get away with this, you hear me? I know he's after you, and mark my words, he will fucking kill you. I won't let you get away with this! Get up, get the shit you came for, and leave." The boys sat open-mouthed, not used to seeing their dad lying on the floor being beaten, especially by a woman.

FORTY-FOUR

The boys sat in the living room, not saying a word, staring blankly out of the window, waiting for the cars to arrive. Peggy and Albert sat on either side of them like two bodyguards in full protective mode, reassuringly stroking their hands and offering words of encouragement and comfort. Annie lay in rest in her coffin in the middle of the room. Ronnie sat opposite with a drink in his hand. He checked the time on his watch. "I knew he wouldn't turn up."

Peggy twisted her face and pursed her lips. "What did you expect him to do, just roll up all grief-stricken and bury his wife? He doesn't give a flying fuck about her. He's the one who's put her in that coffin. And he knew you would be here; that's why he's not." She didn't like Ronnie—they had history between them—and the last place she wanted to be was in his company. But today, of all days, she had to stay composed and tolerate him.

Everybody sat with their thoughts for a moment until Albert offered to get everyone another drink. "Boys, go and help ya Uncle." They did as she said, leaving Peggy and Ronnie alone.

"Makes you wonder, doesn't it?" He said.

"What?"

"I've known you for years. If I didn't have Virginia on my arm that night, things would've been different." He smiled arrogantly.

"Erm, I don't think so. I was with Albert that night, and in case you hadn't noticed, we're still together." She raised her left hand and showed him her wedding ring. "Loyalty is a concept you may not be familiar with," she said sarcastically.

"What do you mean? I helped you out for years."

"Yeah, you did! That was the least you could have done. But as soon as I told you, you shut me down and went straight back to her. And where is she now? She's buggered off like they all do."

He sank the remainder of his drink and lit a cigarette. "Does Albert know?"

She frowned."Erm, no, it's not something we ever discussed, funny enough."

"How are they both doing?"

"You've got a fucking nerve. You've never bothered to ask about them before. All you could do was throw money at me, and now all of a sudden you're interested in them? They're in the army, if you must know. Albert's their dad—not you—and nobody knows any different. I didn't even tell her," she pointed at the coffin and made the sign of the cross, "God bless her soul."

Albert and the boys walked back into the room with the drinks.

"You boys are looking so smart today." Peggy said, "I love your suits." She leaned in and rubbed the material on Eric's jacket. "Lovely material. They feel expensive."

"They were!" Ronnie announced, "But nothing's too expensive for my boys."

Peggy glared at him, her eyes widened, and through gritted teeth muttered, "I think you're forgetting; they're not your boys."

"Well, where the fuck is their father?" Ronnie barked. "Excuse my language, boys."

Peggy sat up in her chair and leaned forward. "Since when have you been worried about your language?"

As John hovered near the curtains, Eric sat in silence, listening to every word. "The cars are here," he mumbled.

A gleaming black Austin Princess hearse, followed by a Rolls-Royce Phantom V limousine, parked up outside. Albert stood up and walked towards the front door to let the funeral staff in.

A large crowd of children had gathered around the hearse, fascinated that such beautiful cars were parked in the street. Neighbours gathered near the house; some stood in doorways and on doorsteps, eager to pay their respects while keeping a respectful distance. The boys stood outside, looking overwhelmed.

The coffin was carried out through the front door and was instantly bathed in glorious warm sunshine. She was being carried out for the final time, a sobering and difficult moment for them to witness. They bowed their heads and gathered their thoughts as it was placed into the hearse.

An elderly gentleman with a white moustache and red face climbed out of the roller. He was immaculately dressed in a black suit jacket and grey pinstripe trousers with a tall top hat on his head, looking more like a punter on a day at the races than at a funeral. He opened the back door and Ronnie told the boys to get in the back of the car. They climbed in and shuffled along the seats; he sat next to them. Peggy and Albert got in the black taxi, parked directly across from the hearse.

The boys stared through the front window, with their eyes fixated on the hearse in front of them. They'd never been to a funeral before and were unsure how to behave or what to say—or not to say—and if that wasn't difficult enough, they had to deal with the fact it was their mum's funeral.

The procession started to move. Peggy watched on as her beloved friend's coffin started to move, followed by the car the boys were in with Ronnie. She looked at them and could see the pain on their faces matched hers. Her eyes left their faces as the car drove past, and she made eye contact with Ronnie. For a brief moment they looked at each other before she turned and kissed

Albert on the cheek, a defiant sign of the loyalty she had for him.

A sparse crowd of mourners gathered around the graveside—just the immediate family and a few neighbours and friends who had wanted to pay their respects. The boys wept silently with their heads bowed and hands crossed as the priest read out his final prayers. Ronnie placed his hands on their shoulders. They dried their eyes and watched their mum being lowered into the ground. They threw a red rose on top of the coffin; their tears dripped from the ends of their noses onto the ground beneath their feet. Eventually everybody slowly filtered off.

"Are you okay, boys?" Peggy asked. They nodded; she gestured towards them. "Come on, let's go."

"You go; we will be up in a minute," Eric said. "We just want to stand here a while longer."

Albert clasped her hand. "Come on, love, leave them with their mum."

"We'll see you back at the club," Eric replied as Albert led her towards their awaiting cab. "It will be okay, y'know. As long as we've got each other and well Uncle Ronnie, that's all that matters."

"What about Aunt Peggy?" John asked.

"Yeah, and her. Of course," he said nonchalantly.

They stood gazing at the coffin for a short while, when Ronnie approached. "Come on, lads, let's get you to the car; it's cold out here."

John walked off without acknowledging him. Eric looked up at Ronnie. "Thanks for everything; we both appreciate it, and sorry about him walking off; it's just… it's been a tough day."

"I know it's been hard, but you'll get over it. This will toughen you up, make a man of you." Eric was shocked at what he was saying but knew he couldn't show any emotion.

A large, local working men's club at the end of a busy main street hosted the wake. The room was a huge, expansive place adorned with brown wood panelling and red/gold Fleur-De-Lis wallpaper. The chairs and tables were laid out in rows on top of a thick red carpet that felt sticky underfoot. At one end of the room stood a stage with a drum kit and a huge brown Hammond organ in front of a glitzy, shiny curtain. Two crusty old bar stewards, as old as the place itself, manned the bar opposite the stage.

The room seemed to engulf the small group of mourners. The drinks flowed as people picked their way through the buffet on a table in the corner of the room; a couple of neighbours who had known Annie for years chatted with the boys and reminisced about days gone by. They listened intently and smiled at some of the funny stories, bringing them a welcome relief from the gloom that had hung over them.

It was getting late, and the afternoon slowly turned into early evening. They talked to people and listened to their stories all day, enjoying their company and being grateful for their presence.

Peggy and Albert were ready to go home. Albert gathered their coats from the back of their chairs as she turned to the boys. "C'mon, it's been a long day, we'll take you back to ours. I don't want you at home on your own, not tonight."

"We're not ready to go yet, are we?" Eric said, shoving him in the shoulder.

"Well, actually I'm tired."

Eric glared. "No, you're not, we will go home in a bit and stay at ours."

"Erm, okay, we'll stay a little longer here and stay at ours tonight."

"Well, I think you should come home with us," she snapped as she pointed at Ronnie, "He doesn't look like he is going anywhere soon, and frankly, I don't want to leave you here with him."

Peggy's words were audible to Ronnie. He raised his hand, and Roy bowed down and leaned in close. "Go over to Peggy and tell her I want a quick word with her."

Roy walked towards Peggy and tapped her on her shoulder. She turned around expecting to be greeted by one of the other mourners, but instead it was a familiar face standing right in front of her. Her smile suddenly faded. "Yeah?" She could see Ronnie peering over towards her.

"Ronnie would like a quick word with you."

"Oh, would he now? What does he want?"

"I don't know; he just said he wants a word."

"Well, we best go and find out." She turned to the boys and Albert. "Wait here; I won't be a minute." She breezed past Roy, and headed over towards him. As she approached, he stood up—ever the gentleman.

"Roy said you wanted a word, so cut the crap and tell me what you want."

"I overheard you say you were leaving and wanted to take them home. I don't think they're ready to go," he said, taking a drag on his cigar.

"Well, Eric may not be, but John, on the other hand, is tired, so they are coming with me." Peggy snapped.

"If they are not ready to go, I will get Cyril to drop them home later."

"I don't think so! Did you not hear what I said? John's tired, so we are leaving. They are coming with me, and that's final!" She folded her arms and stared at him.

Eric overheard them bickering and made his way towards them. Peggy smiled and held her arm out to him, but he walked straight past her and stood next to Ronnie. "Look Aunt Peggy, we'd like to stay a bit longer, and if Uncle Ronnie is happy to drop us home, then we will leave with him later."

She wasn't sure what she was more annoyed at: the fact Eric had walked past her and stood next to him or the fact he had just called him Uncle. With her authority undermined and her nose firmly put out of joint, she thought in her mind Ronnie wasn't interested in his own kids, and now he is trying to make up for his mistakes by looking after somebody else's.

She had no choice but to relent. She looked at Eric; her voice softened; she unfolded her arms because at that moment she knew she was losing him to Ronnie. "So is that what you want to do, then?"

"Well, I did say we weren't ready to go yet," he said, quite matter-of-factly.

She raised her eyebrows. "Okay, well I will pop over and see you in the morning." She leaned in and gave him a kiss on his forehead; she walked over to where Albert and John were standing, grabbing her coat from his arm. "Right, come on, Albert, we are leaving. John, you're staying with your brother," she said rather sharply. John rolled his eyes; he didn't want to stay, and he certainly didn't want to stay with Ronnie, but he knew he had no choice.

The last few stragglers started to leave. Ronnie waited outside with the boys as Cyril fetched the car to take them home. "I'll see you both tomorrow," he said as they climbed into the back. He closed the door, and they drove off.

The boys walked into their bedroom and started to undress quickly. The room was cold, and a damp chill hung in the air. Pyjamas on, John jumped into bed and tucked himself beneath the bedclothes. Eric turned the light off and got into bed, taking stock of the emotional day. His mind wandered to the conversation he had with Ronnie and how he was going to look after them both, and before long, he finally closed his eyes and drifted off to sleep.

It was early morning when he began to wake up; he opened his eyes, yawned, and glanced across the room, where John remained soundly asleep. The first rays of sunshine flickered through the curtains, a fanfare of light announcing another glorious sunny day was on its way.

Eric's thoughts turned to all the terrible moments in his life: the heinous and despicable things his dad had done to him over the years, the beatings they had all suffered, and his mum taking her own life. He decided to disregard the past and focus solely on the present, realising that he would never be the same person again or experience the same emotions.

FORTY-FIVE

Eric came in through the back door of the kitchen; he had been to the shop to get some things for breakfast. "John, are you awake?" he called out at the bottom of the stairs.

"I am now!"

It had been a few days since they had buried their mum. Apart from the daily visit by Peggy to bring their dinner over and make sure everything was okay, they had hunkered down at home. John hadn't been to school since she had died, and Eric hadn't heard from Ronnie for a few days.

The house was empty; they found themselves rattling around in it. The days of dancing and singing along to the radio while Annie baked cakes when they were very young, the gangs of kids that used to hang around their backyard or play made-up games on the front doorstep, were distant memories.

On the plus side, the negative aspects of the past, such as arguments, fights, and violence, had now faded.

Eric went upstairs and opened the bedroom door to see John sitting and staring out the window. "I'm making eggs on toast; do you want some?"

"Not bothered, whatever."

Eric knew he was in pain and hurting more than he was letting on. Despite his quiet demeanour, he recently became even more introverted and reserved.

John stared at the pigeons sitting on the rooftops through the window. "What are we gonna do, Eric?"

"What d'ya mean?"

"Without Mum. What are we gonna do? She's gone, and she ain't ever coming back. Dad's not around anymore, and when he is, he treats us like shit. Aunt Peggy pops in to see if we are okay and brings us dinner over like we're some prisoners in jail and you're working with... well, you know who."

"I'm working for him because it's good money and to be fair it's none of your business. Look, I understand that things are difficult right now; they truly are, but everything will work out in the end."

"That's all you ever say; everything will be okay. Well, everything's not okay." John's throat started to tighten, and his eyes began to well. "Where are we gonna go, 'cause we can't stay here?"

"Why not?"

"Because we're kids. We can't stay here on our own; we don't know the first thing about running a house." He shook his head in frustration.

"Uncle Ronnie's sorted everything, he owns the house anyway. He said if we need anything, we only need to call, and he will sort it."

Just as John was about to let out a moan, something caught his attention out the window. "Dad's here."

"What?" Eric rushed over to the window and looked down into the yard. Indeed, their father was there, looking unkempt, with a cigarette dangling from the corner of his mouth. "Fuck! Right, hide! We don't want him to know we are here. Get under the bed!"

"Why?"

"Shush, will ya? Just do as I say; we don't want him to find us."

They dropped to the floor and scrambled underneath Eric's

bed, pressing themselves up against the wall. Despite the tight space, they managed to squeeze in as they heard heavy footsteps approaching their room. John closed his eyes tightly.

The door opened slightly, and a deep, gruff voice called out. "Is anyone here?" They both held their breath and lay still, refusing to make a sound. Joe closed the door; they could hear him opening and closing the drawers in his bedroom, frantically bashing and slamming about and mumbling to himself. "Where the fuck has she put it?" Then finally they heard him walking down the stairs.

Eric crawled out from under the bed; John remained. "Where are you going?"

"I won't be long; I just wanna see what he's up to. You stay here," he replied, his voice barely above a whisper.

He stood at the top of the stairs; he could now hear drawers and cupboards being pulled open and the contents being thrown onto the floor. Joe seemed to be getting increasingly annoyed, almost desperate, as he ransacked the house, clearly looking for something important. Eventually, Eric heard him mutter to himself, "Yes, yes!" He must have found whatever he was looking for. He made his way down the rest of the stairs and peered around the corner of the door to see him waving his passport around. He grabbed his bags and rushed out the back door.

Eric waited a few moments before setting off to follow him. Joe was in a hurry, but he managed to keep a safe distance as he tracked him through the back streets of town before realising where he was headed—his allotment.

Joe entered through the gates to the allotment. Eric headed to a nearby telephone box. He pulled the card out of his pocket—which Ronnie had given him—and dialled the number.

"Hello?"

"Can I speak to Ronnie, please?"

"Who is it?"

"It's Eric."

"Eric who?"

"Eric Maxwell, tell him it's urgent."

He could hear mumbling in the background and waited for Ronnie to come to the phone. It seemed like ages, but it was only a few seconds.

"What's the problem?"

He started to speak quickly. "You said to call if I saw my dad; well, I have."

Ronnie sighed. "Speak clearly; I can't understand a word you're saying. Now, slow down and say it all again."

"It's Dad; he's been home."

"Is he still there?"

"No, he left about twenty minutes ago."

"Well, what'd he say?"

"Well, he didn't know I was there. He grabbed his passport and some bags; he's at the allotment now. I know there is cash there, so that's why he has come here. I think he is gonna leave."

"I see. I'll send Roy up to you. He'll be there in ten minutes."

Eric hung up the receiver and took a deep breath. He felt nervous as he walked down the street and stood outside the gates. He waited patiently; he was anxious, looking up and down the street waiting for Roy to appear, but also hoped his dad would not come out the gates.

Roy sat in silence in the back seat of the car as Cyril drove to the allotment. The car snaked its way through the streets and soon headed down a ramshackle road filled with rows and rows of Nissen huts masquerading as houses.

The car took a right at the end of the road; Cyril looked at Roy in the rearview mirror. "There he is."

"Pull over behind this car, will you?"

A nervous-looking Eric stood in front of a 6 foot chain link fence with the gate to the entrance slightly open. Beyond that was an oasis of green: row upon row of fruit and vegetable plots and sheds; it was a big area stretching for a good few acres.

Roy opened the back door and climbed out. He looked at Eric. "Are you sure he's here?"

"Yeah," he nodded as he pointed, "There's his car. He didn't drive to the house because he didn't want anyone to see him. And he'll need that to get to the airport, won't he?"

"Come on, lead me to him." He knew this wasn't going to end well, but his dad deserved everything that was coming to him. They walked through the gates and up the path.

Eric had never felt comfortable being at the allotment, but with Roy by his side, he knew that his dad couldn't hurt him anymore. He lengthened his stride; Roy's presence gave him a sense of purpose and an inner confidence. It was early morning and a weekday, so naturally the place was empty, only the sound of the birds and a dog barking in the distance.

Perfect.

Roy didn't care if the place was filled with people; he had no fear of anyone or anything.

"Ronnie's told me that you've got to prove yourself; are you up for it?"

"Yeah, what do you want me to do?"

"Let's make sure he's here first, then I'll tell you."

They headed over to the far end of the allotment and approached Joe's shed. The door was closed, but they could hear someone inside. "That's him; he's in there," Eric whispered.

Roy glanced at him and spoke quietly. "I want you to pick that shovel up and show us what you're made of."

"What do ya mean?"

"Open that door and hit him."

Eric stuttered. "I... I thought—"

"You thought wrong, didn't you?"

He looked at Roy, and without any hesitation, he grabbed the shovel, his mind racing with all the heinous things his dad had done to him over the years. His temper started to rise. There was no turning back now.

Roy stood to the side of the shed as he flung the door open with such force and anger. Joe had his back to him, stuffing money into the bags. The door opening startled him, making him jump. Eric stood behind him with a determined look on his face and holding a shovel in the air.

The surprised look on Joe's face soon disappeared when he realised it was only Eric. He was no threat to him even with the shovel in his hand. "What the fucking hell are you doing up here?" he tutted as he stepped towards him.

"Don't come any closer, otherwise I'll hit ya." He started waving the shovel in the air.

Joe cackled, "Really? I don't fucking think so." He stepped forward, and Eric stepped backward until they were both outside. Joe could see a shadow out of the corner of his eye. As he turned to see who it was, Eric suddenly raised the shovel and crashed it down onto Joe's head. He slumped to his knees, his blood splattering all over the place.

Joe moaned deeply as he raised the shovel over his shoulder and hit him again. Roy stood aside and watched on. Eric loomed over him, staring at him on the ground in a pool of blood, not moving. Instead of being horrified about what he had just done, he actually felt exhilarated, closing his eyes to savour a natural rush that no drug could replicate. For the first time in his life, he felt in control and alive.

Eric tossed the shovel to one side and looked Roy in the eyes. "Have I proved myself?" he said, wiping the splattered blood from his face.

Roy nodded.

"He finally got what he fucking deserved, the bastard." He sniffed and snorted, gathering as much phlegm as he possibly could in his mouth and spat on his lifeless, bloodied body. "That's from Mum."

Roy tapped his shoulder. "Right, let's go."

They walked down the path to the car, leaving him behind. "What happens now?" Eric asked.

"Cyril will drop you off at home; clean yourself up, and I will contact you."

"I mean about Dad?"

"I'm gonna sort it out; don't worry about him."

Cyril was leaning against the car, enjoying a cigarette, when they arrived. "Sorted?"

"Yeah, he did good; we'll drop him home, then come back with Carlton, and we'll get rid of him."

"Whereabouts, the usual place?"

"Yeah, he won't be lonely down there."

*

Eric looked down, examining his blood-stained shirt. He was worried John would see him and start to ask questions. He opened the front door and shouted up the stairs. "I'm home."

No answer.

He took his shirt off and hurried through to the kitchen. He bundled it into the bottom of the bin before turning the tap on, washing his hands, and splashing his face. As the bloodied water ran down the plughole, the sight of his dad etched in his mind.

He heard the front door open. "Eric, are you home?" John shouted from the hallway.

"Yeah, I'm in the kitchen. Where have you been?" He called out.

John walked through to see him standing at the sink, dripping wet. "I've been over Aunt Peggy's." Before Eric could speak, he jumped in again. "Where have you been? Where's ya top, and why are you so wet?"

"Fucking hell, John, one question at a time! I followed him for ages but lost him when he got to the car." Eric said, avoiding all questions. "He came here for his passport, so that means he's gotta be leaving the country, which means he won't be coming back here again."

Eric dried himself with a tea towel and went into the living room, paranoid and uncomfortable with John quizzing him. John followed him. Eric clasped his hands and stared at the clock on the mantelpiece, watching the second hand tick by, wondering if Carlton had gone up the allotment to get rid of the body.

"You okay?" John asked. He didn't answer, his mind whirling around in circles trying to comprehend what he had just done. John asked again.

"What?" Eric finally snapped into focus. "Yeah, yeah, I'm good, just a bit tired, that's all."

A few hours had passed, and Roy hadn't called. He was hoping no news was good news.

Nigel pulled up at the allotment on his bicycle and made his way through the gate. He wheeled it up the pathway towards his plot when he saw a body lying on the ground in front of Joe's shed. Dropping his bike to the ground, he ran over; he could see he was in a bad way. He dropped to his knees to try to help before realising it was Joe Maxwell.

"Bloody hell!" He placed his hand on his back. "Joe, Joe, can you hear me? It's Nigel."

Nothing.

"Joe? Joe!" His voice quivered as he tried to shake him awake. He stood up and looked around to see if anybody was about. The place was empty. As he went to leave to get help, he heard a deep, gurgled groan.

"Jesus Christ, you're alive!"

Eric busied himself. He still hadn't heard anything, and now he was starting to worry. He put his hand in his trouser pocket and pulled out Ronnie's card. He began pacing up and down the backyard, lighting cigarette after cigarette, not sure whether to call to see what was happening.

Suddenly, there was a rasping knock on the door. Eric shouted, "Get the door, will ya?" He exhaled with a sense of relief. *That'll be him; he's come to tell me it's sorted.*

John rolled his eyes as he got up and opened the door. In front of him stood two policemen holding their helmets under their arms and wearing a concerned look on their faces. "Eric Maxwell?" one of the coppers asked.

"No, I'm John." he replied nervously.

"May we come in for a moment?"

He nodded, stepped to one side, and shouted. "Eric, you best come quick."

Eric walked through the kitchen, and the smile on his face instantly turned to shock. He thought it would be Roy standing in front of him, but it wasn't. His heart sank into his stomach.

"Would you both like to sit down, as we need to discuss your father, Joe Maxwell," the older officer said quietly.

Eric felt nervous. Surely if they were coming to arrest him they wouldn't be this calm. They would cuff you without asking any questions. However, the extreme politeness of these two officers set him on edge.

"We found him at an allotment a few miles from here with severe head injuries. Seems somebody has attacked him."

John gasped in shock. Eric widened his eyes. "Oh, no!" he said disingenuously.

The second copper continued. "I know this news has come as a bit of a shock to you both, given the look on your faces, but he is currently in the hospital receiving treatment."

"Treatment? You mean he's alive?" Eric said breathlessly.

"Yeah, he's alive, but only just. They've sedated him just so they can monitor him and do some tests to see if he's suffered any brain damage. And I know it's early days, but they're hopeful he should pull through eventually, so that's positive news, isn't it?"

They looked at each other open-mouthed.

"So, when you're ready, we'll take you down to see him."

Eric stared at the floor. *'Fuck! Fuck! What am I gonna do? Right, keep calm, compose yourself, and stay focused. I can't let anyone know what I've done.'*

He looked at John. "Right, get ya shoes on. We need to go and see him."

E.J. ECCLES

ACKNOWLEDGEMENT

We would like to acknowledge and give our warmest thanks to the following.

Harry Holmes and Lily-Mai Eccles for their input ideas and support throughout the process.

Reece Mackay-Smith and Alfie Mackay-Smith for their ongoing support.

Carmel Gee for her advice and critique.

Sheryl Perkins (Gifted Guidance and Gems) for her guidance and life coaching.

ABOUT THE AUTHOR

E J Eccles & R J Smith

Emma and Roy, joint authors and partners for a decade, started the creative journey of writing their first novel four years ago. It was challenging at times but it has also brought them joy along the way. They look forward to a long and exciting career together as they truly are "Partners in Crime."

Printed in Great Britain
by Amazon